OTHER NOVELS BY J. L. REICHMAN

Now available at Amazon.com

The Dying Season

Under the Roses

Coming soon

Baker's Dozen
Fractured

To Joyce — Aren't we lucky to have a friend like Marilyn. Enjoy the read. Merry Christmas. Joyce Reichman

SUMMER OF FIRE

J. L. REICHMAN

Lakeside Press
Lake Lotawana, MO

ISBN 13-978-1530915057
19L 153981558

ACKNOWLEDGEMENTS

Thanks to my writers' group. Each of them made suggestions and helped improve this work. Several of them are mentioned in this story.

A tip of the hat to Marilyn True who edited and encouraged me, and thanks to Penny Gilliland for her advice.

Applause to Stan Gilliland (no relationship to Penny) for the information about businesses around the square and the series of fires in our class reunion's booklet, information obtained at the Pittsburg-Crawford County Genealogy Museum.

All the characters in this work are purely fictional and are not based on any person now dead or alive.

You can reach me at 2016reichman34@gmail.com.

ONE

Looking back, I vividly remember the summer the fires began. Though decades have passed, the summer of '53 left an indelible imprint on me. That summer my brother Dan abandoned me. He spent hours at Smithton's garage with his head under some jalopy's hood and dreamed of owning his own hotrod. My mother fretted about Glen Smithton being a bad influence, but Luke said he wasn't a bad sort, only a bit wild and bored in our small town. That's my dad, Luke, and Dan and I called him by his first name except to his face. He was the Glendale police chief, so everybody in town knew him and me and Dan, too.

Four years older than me, Dan would start high school in the fall and was under the impression that he was all grown up, too old to have a ten-year-old brother tagalong like me. So when he told me I wasn't invited to Smithton's garage, I told him right back that I had no interest in Glen Smithton, his dad's garage or his stupid cars which was right and true. Being separated from Dan made it harder for me to get to the truth, to an understanding of what I saw and heard. With understanding now, I can look back and realize that if I'd been with Dan, I wouldn't have seen and heard all that I did.

Glen Smithton was two years older than Dan but no taller. Dan shot up so fast during that last school year that he was always wearing high-waders, and Mom bought him new jeans three times. He bragged he'd soon be as tall as Luke who was six foot, but he looked about four inches short of his goal to me.

Though no taller than Dan, Glen had filled out with broad shoulders, a barrel chest and muscular arms. He wore his brown hair in a flat top and rolled up his T-shirt sleeves to hold a pack of cigarettes—a style James Dean made famous a couple of years later.

Still slim and lanky, Dan began to imitate this fashion to Mom's consternation, and he pestered her to buy him a pair of what he called motorcycle boots. I avoided this tug-of-war by leaving the house whenever I could.

I could usually leave the house whenever I wished if I'd finished my chores, practiced the piano and told Mom where I was going—the swimming pool, the library, the square, the park to play ball. Sometimes she sent me on errands, but wherever I went, I loitered along the way, watching people and listening to their conversations. We lived on Pawnee Street in the middle of the block in a two-story house with a large porch facing east. It was nothing fancy like the houses in the north end of Glendale, but it was comfortable and safe.

I still can't figure out the start of it, so I'm probably telling this wrong, but one place to begin is the night of the first fire on a Saturday night in mid-April of '53. A boom rattled our bedroom windows and about knocked me from my bed. My first thought was that lightning struck nearby, but when I sat up and looked out the window, no rain was falling. Duke, who'd been sleeping by my bed, jumped up into my arms, wagging his tail and licking my face.

"Good God Almighty," I said. "What was that?"

Dan threw off his covers. "An explosion, maybe?"

I heard Luke's feet hit the floor, and the phone downstairs began to shrill. Dan shucked off his pajamas and pulled on a pair of jeans. I reassured my dog Duke that everything was okay and followed suit as I heard Luke thunder down the stairs.

Then the town whistle began to blow, a sure sign of disaster as it only shrieked at eight, noon and five on a normal day. I just pulled a shirt over my head when Dan opened the bedroom door. Mom stood at the top of the stairs looking down.

"What is it?" Dan said.

Mom, dressed only in her nightgown, shrugged. "Hush." She brushed her curly hair back from her forehead and concentrated on the phone conversation below.

I stood in the bedroom doorway with Duke beside me as Luke dashed up the stairs wearing only his khaki pants.

"It's the mill," Luke said. "I've got to go." In his bedroom, he pulled on a shirt and his boots. "Some kind of explosion. Big fire."

"Can we go?" Dan said.

"It's after two o'clock," Mom said.

"But, Mom, everybody in town will be there," Dan said.

"I think it'll be okay," Luke said. "But you keep back. Let the firemen do their job." He kissed Mom's cheek and rushed down the stairs.

"Hurry, Mom." Dan sat on his bed to put on his shoes.

"Have you seen Matilda?" Mom's tabby, an excellent hunter, disappeared at the first sign of visitors and hid during times of panic.

"She's probably under your bed." I pulled my shoes from under mine.

"You boys go to the bathroom first." Mom shut her bedroom door.

Duke ran around the bedroom, yipping in excitement. I fumbled trying to tie my shoes, my fingers in such a hurry they wouldn't cooperate. I heard Luke's siren fade away into the distance and wondered what he'd be doing at the fire. He wasn't a fireman. I hurried to the bathroom and met Dan coming out.

"Why would the mill explode?" I said.

"Don't know." Dan zipped up his pants. "Don't take forever like you usually do."

A flash of anger whipped through me at that remark, and I briefly considered taking my leisurely time. Only the fear of being left behind spurred me to make haste and follow Dan down the stairs. Duke jumped around the two of us.

"Come on, Mom," Dan called up the stairs.

Mom appeared in a pair of slacks and an old blouse she usually wore to work in the garden. "I'll be there in a minute." She went into the bathroom.

"Women," Dan fumed. "Always last to be ready. It ain't the time to put on lipstick and such."

"You're not supposed to say ain't," I pointed out.

"Shut up, Twirp." Dan smacked the back of my head just as Mom came down the stairs.

"That was uncalled for." Mom pinned her hair back and took the car keys from the hook next to the back door.

"Can I drive?" Dan said.

"Not tonight, Danny."

I laughed inside. Dan, who'd recently got his learner's permit, hated to be called Danny, a little kid's name, and he often called me 'Mikey' to emphasize what he considered my infantile state.

Mom turned on the backyard light so we could see our way to the detached garage housing our '49 Chevy. "Put Duke out. It's warm enough he should be outside earning his keep."

I gave Duke one last pet and opened the gate into the fenced part of the back yard. "We'll be right back, boy."

"What's wrong, Joan?" I recognized the querulous voice of old Mrs. Gensill, our neighbor.

"Valetti's mill exploded," Mom said. "We're off to see the fire. Want to come?"

"No, dear. Don't believe I could stand that long."

Well, I was glad of that. Mrs. Gensill was a nice old lady who let me watch *The Lone Ranger* on her television, but I'd hate to be saddled with holding her hand all night. I was also pleased that Mom was driving. Dan had yet to master the stick shift, and as a result, riding with him was as close to riding a bucking bronco as I wished to get.

"Shotgun!" Dan ran to the car and claimed the passenger's seat.

I climbed into the back seat. "Aw. You got shotgun last time."

"Well, ain't that a bite?"

"I'll not tolerate you using ain't like some uneducated illiterate." Mom started the car. "Now behave or you can stay home."

"Okay. Okay." Dan huffed as though he was put upon.

I sat on the edge of the seat, put my arms across the back of the front seat and leaned my chin on my hands to look out the windshield. Lights were on all along our street with people standing in front yards, and as we passed, several cars pulled out to follow us.

"They're following us 'cause we know where to go," Dan said.

Except for our little caravan of cars which grew with each block we traversed, we met no traffic until the corner of Bennett's Laundry where we joined the steady stream of vehicles heading east toward the Co-op grain elevator and the railroad tracks. An orange glow filled the sky lighting up the rising smoke. Soon we came upon Harvey Lake, one of Luke's patrolmen, who directed us to park along the street.

"Can't get any closer," Harvey said. "It's walking from here, Mrs. Martin."

"Is Luke directing traffic, too?" Mom asked.

"He's keeping Ozark Street open for emergency vehicles," Harvey said. "We're expecting the department from Pattonburg to show up any time."

We joined the flow of townspeople, everyone talking excitedly about how loud the explosion was and how their dogs howled and barked at the whistle going off and such. After a couple of blocks, we cut to the left up the elevator's drive to join the crowd watching the fire and the men trying to contain it.

"There's Dean." Dan pointed to a friend of his. "Okay if I join him?"

"As long as you stay back and out of the way," Mom said. "You know where the car is. We'll meet you there when they put this out."

An old stone building, Valetti's Mill stood about thirty yards from the grain elevator. The side of the mill toward the elevator was gone, and the Co-op's office windows lay shattered upon the scales. Flames towered into the night sky driven by a southwest breeze toward the Co-op office. Volunteer firemen, unrecognizable in their gear, directed a feeble stream from the pumper truck onto the Co-op roof while another team hooked up a long hose to the nearest fire hydrant beside the elevator.

Soon it was like our whole town was there. I saw the mayor, our minister, several of our neighbors and kids I knew from school. We kids acknowledged each other with a nod but instinctively knew this was no time for play. Mom and I joined a group of our neighbors. Mostly silent, we stared at the spectacle, transfixed by the flames and the small dark figures of the firemen outlined against the orange background.

"I hate to see the old mill go." The fire lit Mrs. Gladding's face.

I heard a siren wailing in the distance and drawing closer. The firemen turned on the hose from the grain elevator and aimed it at the base of the flames while the pumper truck maintained its withering stream onto the Co-op roof. Another firetruck pulled up behind the mill.

"Looks like the boys from Harrington," Mr. Gladding said.

After consultation, the Harrington truck circled the mill and set up on the west side.

"Look," Mr. Parkinson said. "There's a propane tank on that side of the mill."

"My God," Mrs. Parkinson said, "we could all be in danger if that thing blows."

The Harrington volunteers unreeled a hose and carried it to the back of the mill.

"Must be another hydrant on that side," Mr. Kennedy said.

"Over on Ozark Street, I suppose." Mom rested her hands on my shoulders.

"The mill's been here for as long as I can remember," old man Heuer said.

I figured if he could remember it for that long, it must be a hundred years. At long last, the Harrington crew aimed water at the fire, and a sigh of relief swept the crowd.

"This is a real loss to the town," Mr. Gladding said.

Mrs. Kennedy nodded. "Every farmer in the county has his flour milled here."

"And Valetti's flour is a hot seller at Roman's Market," Mrs. Parkinson said.

"I always buy it," Mom said. "Bob makes a fine product."

"Don't know what I'll do without it," Mrs. Gladding complained.

"Hey, Mike," Pete Parkinson said. "Far out, huh?"

I shrugged. "I guess so."

Pete, a classmate of mine, often copied my math homework. He sidled up to me and leaned close. "Can I come over tomorrow for, you know?"

"You'll have to do it in my room." Ever since I'd given him my homework and he'd not returned it, I didn't let my papers out of my sight.

I heard another siren in the distance drawing closer. Now the mill's roof sagged toward the missing wall sending sparks skyward, and the tenor of the fire changed to a deep roar. Suddenly, the whole roof gave way, plunging down into the flames. The stone front of the mill collapsed outward.

The crowd gasped and moaned and shouted "Watch out!" More black figures could be seen silhouetted against the fire.

"Pattonburg's shown up." Gene Gladding wiped his balding head with a handkerchief. A bus driver during the school year, Mr. Gladding owned an auto repair business rivaling Glen Smithton's dad.

"About time." The conflagration reflected from George Parkinson's glasses making it look as though his eyes were on fire.

I watched the Pattonburg Fire Department quickly get another hose going and attack the fire from a different angle. I thought they made our volunteer force look slow and bumbling, but Pattonburg was over four times as large as Glendale and could afford a trained permanent fire department. Out of water, the pumper truck pulled back. Now the Glendale crew focused on saving the Co-op office while Pattonburg fighters poured water onto the mill.

"Oh, Joan. Isn't it awful?" Thelma Horlacher, Mom's friend from high school, joined the crowd, looking as though she'd not stopped to comb her hair.

"Why I didn't expect you here," Mom said. "Don't tell me you could hear the explosion way out there."

The Horlachers lived a mile east of town. Ed and Thelma were close friends of my parents and their son Bruce was my best friend.

"Hear it?" Thelma said. "Why the boom reverberated off the hills and set Old Blue to carrying on, and then the whistle shrieked. We couldn't see anything for the trees, so Ed walked to the road. Came back and said a fire lit up the horizon, so we hurried on in. Had to park on the other side of the tracks there was such a crowd."

"Luke here?" Ed said.

"Directing traffic." Mom brushed her hair back from her forehead.

I looked around for Bruce and spotted him with his older brother Rob and younger sister Madge. All three seemed mesmerized by the fire, so I waited until he'd had his fill before approaching him. Kids at school learned early to pronounce Bruce's last name correctly as Horlocker as Bruce pummeled anyone who said whore lacker.

"I don't understand this explosion," Ed said.

"Grain dust, I suppose." George Parkinson wiped his glasses on his shirt tail.

"I know all about the danger of grain dust," Ed said. "Bob ran a clean operation. Had modern equipment. He ran a clean mill, and safety was his first concern."

"Grain dust was there," Mr. Parkinson said. "You might not see it, but the mill's over sixty years old. Dust sinks into the cracks and you can't get it all. A spark and boom."

"Electrical, then," Gene Gladding suggested. "An old building like that."

"Still seems suspicious to me," Ed said.

Bruce finally drew his attention away from the fire which was giving up under the onslaught of the Pattonburg contingency. "Hey, Mike. Been here long?"

I told him all about what went on, about the pumper truck, the roof collapsing after the Harrington volunteers came and finally the Pattonburg Department showing up. We watched the last of the flames die away, and the Pattonburg crew poured streams of water onto the charred, sodden pile of machinery and wood.

"Wish I'd been here from the beginning," Bruce said. "Our old wreck of a car wouldn't start. Pop had to shove it down the hill for Momma to pop the clutch and get it running."

"But how'll you get home?" I said.

"Pop left it running. Nobody in his right mind would steal it."

"Guess the show's over." Mrs. Murphy uttered her first words of the evening. Her husband Lester, a deputy sheriff, had left her with their daughter Donna to go help direct traffic.

"Sure feel sorry for Bob Valetti," Mom said.

"He was riding high Friday night after hitting that homerun to win the game," Thelma said.

"Hope he had good insurance." Mrs. Gladding reached for her daughter's hand. "Joy, you've seen plenty. Let's go."

"Bob better rebuild. We need the mill," Ed said.

"Come, Mike," Mom said. "Time to go home."

Dan caught up with us on the walk to our car. "Did you see that roof collapse? What a blast! Never seen anything like it."

I didn't argue about riding shotgun but climbed into the back seat, lay down and fell asleep to the hum and rocking of the car.

TWO

Growing up in the '50's, I thought Glendale perfect. About twenty-five hundred people lived there and Luke said speeding was the biggest crime with most of the speeders people passing through. Designated the county seat, Glendale sat in the middle of Courdry County in southeast Kansas. Huge oaks and a lush lawn surrounded the three-story limestone courthouse with its marble floors and staircase. Around the courthouse square, businesses thrived. Cafes, groceries, five and dimes, barber and beauty shops shared the square with the bank, a hardware, an appliance store, drug stores and a department store. The town had a hotel and a movie theater. Apartments and offices occupied space above the retail stores. The town hummed with activity, and I had the run of it.

The Methodist Church buzzed with speculation Sunday morning after the fire. Relegated to my Sunday school class, I received little information from my classmates—all fourth, fifth and sixth graders. The class was a mix of northend kids who went to Hawthorne Elementary and southend kids like me and Bruce who went to Melville Elementary. We knew the Melville kids well but not the others.

"My dad says the fire was set," Judy James said. "He's on the fire department, you know, so he got a good look."

"How'd he get a good look?" Bobbi Bennett said. "All our fire department did was hose down the Co-op."

"It was important to save it," Judy said.

"Our fire department is a joke," David Miller said.

"Well, they ain't paid like real firefighters," Janice Zordani said.

"And your dad don't know nothin'," Harry Adams said. "It was an electric spark set off the grain dust. My dad works for the electric company and he knows."

"What does working for the electric company have to do with it?" Clark Davenport said.

"Hey, Mike, what's your dad think?" Bobbi said.

"He'll wait for the results of the investigation," I said.

Miss Walker halted this scintillating non-informative debate, so Bruce and I took our seats to learn about Moses and the Bulrushers as Huck Finn said. At last, we escaped from the tedium of Moses and his problems to enjoy a fifteen-minute respite before church service.

"Gonna listen to the Cards game this afternoon?" The season had begun, and as a rabid Cardinals fan, I listened to every game I could, and baseball dominated my mind and conversation.

"Why would I?" Bruce said. "They aren't any good."

"They are, too. Stan Musial's hitting well." I sprawled on the grass under a tree next to the Reynolds Community Home across the street from the church.

"So? They'll never beat the Dodgers." Bruce sat down beside me.

"But they'll have a good season." I stretched out with my arms behind my head.

"I hear Musial's getting fifty-seven thousand this year."

"Wow! That's a lot of money." I wondered how much Luke earned as police chief.

"Poppa doesn't like me to listen to the Cards games. Too many beer commercials."

"That's 'cause Anheuser-Busch bought the team."

Bruce leaned back on his elbows. "Besides, the Cards are losers."

I wanted to wrestle him for that remark but I knew I'd lose. Bruce excelled as a wrestler, besides I knew what Mom would do if I got grass stains on my clothes. "We don't get Dodgers games on the radio," I said.

"Wish Kansas City had a team."

"They'll get one, just you see." I'd heard some rumors about it on the radio.

"You hear Mickey Mantle hit a five-hundred-sixty-five foot homerun?"

"Yeah. Bet your dad could do that."

"Say." Bruce suddenly sat up. "Is that Dan?" He pointed down the street.

I sat up to see where he was pointing. "Sure is. What's he doing?"

"Looks like he's cutting out."

I stumbled to my feet and took off after him. He was walking fast and had a head start, so I had to run my fastest to catch up. "Hey! Hey, Dan!" He turned to wait for me. "Where you going?"

"None of your business." He turned to walk away and I followed.

"You skipping church?"

"What's it look like?"

"You'll get in trouble."

"Why don't you just go and tattle on me, you little turd."

I stopped as though I'd hit a brick wall. This was over the top, entirely against the rules of decorum our parents enforced. What was wrong with him? I watched him walk away until he turned the corner and was gone.

As both Bruce's parents and mine sang in the church choir, I sat with the Horlacher kids for church. I usually enjoyed Mrs. DeCarlo's organ playing (she often played a Bach prelude while everyone took their seats), but my mind was busy replaying the short conversation with Dan and puzzling over his bizarre behavior.

I foresaw trouble and wished for the church service to never end, but it was over entirely too soon. I headed next door to Tony's Market for an ice cream bar, my weekly reward for good church behavior, but my heart wasn't in it.

Through the screen, I saw Mr. DeCarlo with his back to me, putting cans onto a shelf. Another man stood a bit behind and to one side of him. I slowly opened the screen door and closed it gently behind me. I scooted to the other side of the shelving next to the freezer containing the ice cream bars.

"You're the only goddamned place open on Sunday," the man said. "Whole square's shut up tight. You against religion?"

"Not really. My wife's the religious one," Tony said. "She plays the organ next door at the Methodist Church."

"But you ain't religious? You an atheist?" I couldn't recognize the man's voice.

"No, I'm not." I heard Tony rise to his feet and move down the aisle. "An agnoosetic, maybe."

"What the hell is that?" The man's raspy voice seemed smoke roughed.

"Just call me a fallen-away Catholic if you must call me something." Tony sounded irritated.

"Well, those communists MacArthur's talkin' about are atheists to the core. Don't hold with God at all."

"I believe you mean McCarthy." I could tell that Tony had moved behind the check-out counter.

"What 'cha mean?"

"You said MacArthur. He's the general that Truman fired. Senator McCarthy is the one after communists in the government."

"Makes no difference. MacArthur. McCarthy. You know what I'm talkin' about."

Tony sighed. "Not sure that I do."

"We got one of them right here." The man had lowered his voice to almost a whisper.

"What? A communist?" Tony chuckled.

"It's that publisher. The one with the big press over on Hamilton. The *Little Red Books*, you know."

"Emile Hrabosky? He's no communist. He's a socialist."

"Same difference. He's a furiner. Comes from a communist country. Hungary, I think. Prints lies about America. What can you expect from a Jew?"

"We have freedom of speech and press here."

"His damned place should be burned to the ground with him in it."

"Emile Hrabosky is a good man. He can say and print whatever he wishes." Mr. DeCarlo sounded angry.

"Then how come the FBI was after him?"

"I guess J. Edgar didn't appreciate what Emile wrote about him."

Just then, I dropped the lid of the chest freezer containing the ice cream bars.

"Who's there?" Tony said.

"Just me, Mr. DeCarlo." I walked around the shelving to the check-out counter. "Getting my usual ice cream bar."

"You been sneakin' around, boy?"

I looked up into a face I'd seen before. Someone who worked for the city, I thought, but I couldn't place a name.

"No, sir." I tried to look as innocent as possible. "I just came from church." I handed my dime to Tony. "Thanks, Mr. DeCarlo."

As the screen door slammed behind me, I heard the man say, "Ain't that Luke's boy?"

I paused to hear what he said. "Sure is," Tony said. "He's a real nice kid."

"Don't like him listenin' to my damn conversations," the man said.

I headed back to the church in a hurry to tell Luke and find out what the men had been talking about. Atheist. Agnoosetic. I'd never heard those words. Communist I knew as I'd seen that word in the newspaper. Socialist? Must be some kind of society bigwig. A foreigner from Hungary. A Jew. The FBI. Who was J. Edgar? It was all a puzzle to me. Luke, Mom and Grandma Jenkins stood in the shade talking to the Jameses. Luke, in his gray suit, fanned himself with his hat.

"Don't drip that onto your tie," Mom said. She wore a flowered dress with her yellow wide-brimmed hat and looked cool even on this warm April day.

"I'll be careful." I took another bite of my quickly melting ice cream bar. "Hi, Grandma. You walk up to church today?"

"Perfect morning for it."

Standing next to Grandma Jenkins, I realized I was taller than she was and wondered if I could beat her at arm wrestling now. She wore her short silver hair in tightly permed curls topped by her usual round black hat with its fake berry trim. Her belted gray dress hung on her slender frame to mid-calf. My mother's mother, Grandma Jenkins lived two blocks from the Methodist Church down Antelope Street. Luke's tone of voice drew me to his conversation with Mr. James.

“They’re Catholic,” Mr. James said. “Their church will help them out.”

“You’re one of our team coaches,” Luke said. “You know Bob Valetti’s one of our sponsors and his son Vinny is on the team. They’ll have a tough time with the mill gone.”

“I know all that.”

“I thought you were all for cooperation between the churches.”

“Protestant churches,” Mr. James said. “Leave the Catholics out of it.”

“But Bob’s our friend. It doesn’t matter what church he belongs to.”

“It does to me.”

“I hate to hear you talk this way.”

“We’ve too many Catholics in this country. They multiply like rats—Irish and Italians, especially. They bring organized crime.”

“Most of them are honest, hard-working people.”

“They’re getting the upper hand. Mark my words, we’ll have one for president soon and the Pope will be running the country.”

“I had no idea you felt this way.”

“You can propose your idea to the board, but I’ll oppose it.” Mr. James turned on his heel and stalked away.

“Well.” Luke fanned himself with his hat. “Guess I got put in my place.”

“It’s a good idea,” Mom said. “You talk to the other board members. Surely they don’t all feel like Clyde James.”

Luke turned to me. “Where’s your brother?”

I shrugged. “Don’t know.” Luke could lay down a minefield of questions with the best of them, so I had to be careful and answer as truthfully as possible without giving anything away.

“I didn’t see him in church. Was he there?”

Well, I couldn’t answer that truthfully, so I shrugged and said, “I didn’t see him, either.”

Luke looked at me and seemed to evaluate that comment. “You were awfully quiet during service. Something wrong?”

“Nothing I know of.” I focused my attention on my ice cream bar.

Luke turned to Mom. "I'll drive you home and then look for him."

I finished my ice cream bar in one huge bite which gave me an ice cream headache. No one spoke on the drive home. We walked into the house to the heavenly smell of roast beef. My stomach growled in anticipation.

"Momma, if you'll mash the potatoes," Mom said, "I'll make gravy and get the beans on. Mike, you get out of your Sunday clothes and set the table."

I shuffled up the stairs to my room and discovered Dan's Sunday clothes tossed across his bed. He'd been home, changed into his jeans and left. I decided to keep my mouth shut.

Sundays we ate in the dining room rather than at the table in the kitchen. Mom used the dining room table for her sewing and crafts during the week, so I first removed her sewing machine and carefully gathered her materials to lay on the sideboard. I spread the tablecloth, distributed five of her best plates, and put out the company silverware. I could hear Mom and Grandma Jenkins talk in the kitchen.

"Evan came by Wednesday," Grandma said.

That was Mom's older brother who farmed about seven miles north up by Harrington. Uncle Evan's son Ricky was my age, but he went to the elementary in Harrington, a drive-through village of some twenty houses with a church, a post office, and a service station. Our town team played the Harrington team, a tough group of farm men and boys.

"Here's more cream for those potatoes," Mom said. "Evan never comes by to see me. What did he want?"

"Oh, only to visit."

"Hmm." Mom sounded doubtful about that. "The gravy's ready. Green beans are done. Hope Luke gets back soon."

"I have deliveries to make Tuesday." Grandma Jenkins sold Avon products, taking orders by phone, but as she didn't own a car, Mom drove her around to make deliveries.

"That's fine," Mom said. "We can shop for groceries afterward."

"Where do you suppose that boy's gone?"

"He's never done this before."

I heard the car come up the drive. Doors slammed. Dan hurried through the kitchen and up the stairs without a word.

Luke closed the back door. “I found him in the park on a swing.”

“What’s wrong with him?” Mom said.

“All I got was a jumbled story about George Buckner at Friday night’s game.” Luke washed his hands. “I’ve sent him to his room for the afternoon. Let’s eat.”

“The boy has to eat,” Grandma said.

“I’ll fix him a plate later,” Mom said.

Somehow, that wonderful meal might as well have been cardboard. It went down my throat and settled into a concrete mass. Luke left to check into his office and Mom took a plate up to Dan, so Grandma and I cleaned up.

I dried the dinner plate she handed to me. “Grandma, what’s an atheist?”

“Why, wherever did you hear that word?” Grandma scrubbed the next plate as though it had mud on it.

“Some guy talking to Mr. DeCarlo in the market. He asked him if he was one.”

Grandma dipped the plate into the hot rinse water and handed it to me. “What guy?”

“Don’t know his name.” I put the dry plate onto the stack. “Works for the city, I think. Burly guy with a mustache.”

“Sounds like that Kelvin Rogers.” She scrubbed the silverware and dropped it into the rinse water. “He always did have some funny ideas.”

“But what’s an atheist?”

“Someone who denies the existence of God.”

“No.” I jerked a handful of silverware from the hot water. “No one can do that.”

Mom returned with Dan’s empty plate. “You go on, Mike. I’ll help Momma finish up.”

I remembered about Pete coming over to copy my homework, but it wouldn’t work with Dan in our bedroom. I decided I’d take it over to his house, and I climbed the stairs to get it. I tapped at the closed door.

“It’s open,” Dan said.

I peeked around the door to see if he would fling a shoe at me.

"It's safe." Dan was lying on his bed. "I'm not mad at you."

"I just need to get my math homework," I said.

"Pete going to copy it again?" Dan put aside the book he'd been reading.

"You know about that?" I pulled my math book from the pile on the shelf beside my bed.

"I think everyone does." Dan put his feet onto the floor. "Say, Squirt, I'm real sorry I called you a bad name. I wasn't mad at you."

"Who were you mad at?"

"Doesn't matter. I'm sorry I took it out on you."

"It's okay."

"Sometimes it's awfully hard being Luke's son."

It'd never been hard for me. "What do you mean?"

"You'll find out some day."

First thing I did was write down all the words I'd heard at the market. Someday I hoped to get an explanation. I rescued Duke from the back yard, and we set off for Pete's house.

THREE

I didn't have the advantage of being anonymous in Glendale. Friends, relatives, neighbors—even people I didn't know like Mr. Rogers—all knew I was Luke's son. One day I happened to hang around Hale's Pool Hall, curious about what went on inside. Through the open door, I heard the clacking of balls. Loud voices, laughter, and cigarette smoke drifted to the sidewalk, and I peeked inside only to be told to move along. By the time I got home, several people had called Mom to inform her. Three of Mom's aunts and uncles lived in town, Grandma Jenkins's brothers and their wives, so Mom had a bevy of first cousins who produced second cousins about my age. Years passed before I could keep all these relationships straight. Luckily, Luke grew up in Pattonburg where his parents and a brother still lived. Luke's sister Liz and her family were Wichita residents, so I didn't have Luke's side of the family scrutinizing my every move.

The week settled into what my classmates termed tedious boredom. I liked school, but I quickly learned that verbalizing my appreciation would earn me only scorn. As a result, I complained along with my classmates although I often had trouble thinking up something to complain about. Of the twenty-four kids in my fourth grade class, exactly half were from town while the other half were country kids like Bruce who rode the bus. Girls outnumbered the boys, but I mostly ignored them. The one girl I wanted on my team was Bobbi Bennett who was vicious at dodgeball and could outplay everyone but Bruce, Charlie and me at baseball.

The school year was grinding to a halt, and our teacher Mrs. Gaston seemed content to let us drift. After mastering the multiplication tables last year, she threw math word problems at us.

We wrote so many book reports that I ran out of interesting baseball stories and first read *Riders of the Purple Sage* by Zane Grey and then *The Adventures of Huckleberry Finn* by Mr. Mark Twain. Huckleberry gave me some trouble and I didn't understand all of it, but I liked the friendship between Huck and Jim.

We conjugated verbs out to the future perfect tense, studied the colonies and the Revolutionary War, investigated plants, rocks and insects, and toured South America, Africa, Asia and Europe. Mrs. Gaston required our papers in cursive writing which caused me some difficulty, and she forbid me from reporting on baseball as a current event, emphasizing the need to inform the class on events of national and international import. No amount of persuasion changed her mind. In more positive affairs, I won the fourth grade spelling bee against Hawthorne Elementary which earned me some notoriety as my picture was printed in the *Glendale Courier*.

Next year, Mrs. Herrick would be my teacher. Her husband played on the town team so I saw her every Friday night during the season.

After fifth grade, I'd go to the junior high which comprised sixth, seventh and eighth grades. While Hawthorne and Melville both had only one class each of kindergarten through fifth, the junior high classes were larger. Both elementries fed into the junior high with the addition of students bussing in from outlying elementary schools like Harrington. So my little fourth grade class of twenty-four where I was a star pupil would balloon to seventy or so in sixth grade, and competition would increase.

Dan had done well in junior high and would receive the American Legion award at his eighth grade graduation ceremony. I could see more pressure being applied in junior high as the teachers would expect the same from me. It was hard being Dan's brother. I vowed to enjoy the fifth grade—my last year in stress-free elementary.

Attention focused on Dan. Luke and Mom discussed what he should wear at graduation for a week before deciding to buy his first full suit with the pants a couple of inches too long and the jacket a size too big so he'd grow into it. Mom would hem the pants to let out as needed and alter the jacket with removable stitches.

A trip to Pattonburg followed, and no fifteen-mile journey to that great city was complete without visiting Grandma and Grandpa Martin and Luke's brother Uncle Matthew. Shopping came first. I had endeavored to avoid this excursion, but when my efforts failed, I accompanied the rest of the family into Pattonburg's best men's clothing store in the hope that someone would notice the shabby state of my attire, take pity on me, and buy me some new shoes to play ball that summer. Instead, I was subjected to the tiresome performance of Dan's trying on "The Suit."

A slender, short man with several long strands of hair attempting to cover his bald head volunteered to help us. He led us to an area with chairs and three mirrors, whipped out a tape and measured Dan from head to foot. Mom explained what she had in mind. He shook his head and took off on a long lecture denigrating her plans. Not to be deterred, Mom assured him that she was an excellent seamstress and hinted that we could take our business down the street. The man disappeared into the back and returned with a dark blue suit with a narrow stripe. Mom fingered the material, examined the suit's construction and sent Dan with the salesman to try it on. When he returned, she checked the waist, turned up the pants legs and sleeves, checked the fit over the shoulders and directed Dan to walk around while she studied it. She rejected the suit.

The salesman brought out a brown affair which Mom sent back immediately saying that such a color would make Dan with his light brown hair and blue-green eyes seem washed out. Next came a light gray suit and the routine was repeated. Dark gray followed. Mom rejected black out of hand, so a light blue was tried. Each outfit seemed so staid and that I began hoping for one in green or red or yellow. Finally, Mom asked to see the dark blue again. After a thorough examination during which Dan expressed his impatience, Mom decided it would do.

At last we left the store behind us and headed toward the car. I paused to investigate the display of shoes in a store down the block, hoping someone would get the hint, but they walked on without me. I hurried to catch up.

"I believe Mike needs new shoes." Luke winked at me.

Ah, someone noticed. I looked down at my old Keds.

Mom stopped in her tracks. "Why, so he does. I'd forgotten completely."

We turned around and entered the shoe store.

"Good morning, Ma'am. How can I help you?" The salesman instinctively recognized who was in charge.

"Some shoes for my youngest," Mom said.

"Have a seat and let's get a measure."

I took a chair and the salesman brought over his slanted contraption for me to rest my foot upon. He removed my sneaker, put my foot onto the metal rule and moved the slides for width and length. I was happy I'd worn clean socks.

"We'll allow a bit for growth," he said.

"A dress shoe, in brown, I think," Mom said.

Oh, no! Not that. Couldn't she see how worn my sneakers were?

The salesman returned with a pair of Buster Browns, fitted them onto my feet and suggested I walk around in them.

"How do they feel?" Mom asked.

"A bit stiff."

"Well, they would," Mom said. "They're new. I think they'll be just fine."

She took an hour to select Dan's suit and five minutes to buy a pair of shoes I didn't even want.

"Ma'am, I don't mean to presume, but I noticed the shoes the young man is wearing." The salesman picked up my old sneaker. "See the wear here? His toe will soon be jutting through, and the tread is worn off the sole."

"So it is. I never noticed. I guess he needs some new sneakers, too."

I left the store with a smile on my face and a box containing red sneakers under my arm.

"I need thread to match Dan's new suit," Mom said. "I can pick it up at the Singer shop."

Grandma Ada clerked at the Singer shop and waved at us when we walked in. Mom lay the suit over the thread counter and searched for a matching spool while Grandma finished up with her customer.

"Dan's new suit?" Years of heavy smoking coarsened Grandma Ada's voice.

"Just bought it today," Mom said. "I need to make some alterations."

"Put it on, Danny," Grandma said. "We'll see what needs to be done."

So Dan had to put on "The Suit" again, and Mom and Grandma fussed over it and discussed what alterations needed to be made.

"Luke, your father will be here in a few minutes. Matthew and Esther will close the insurance agency and meet us for lunch over at Kresge's." Grandpa John worked as an accountant for Allied Coal, so he had Saturdays off.

I had no interest in visiting with Uncle Matthew or Aunt Esther and hoped my cousins stayed home. We'd seen the whole clan over Easter, and it hadn't gone well. Cousin Jim's superior attitude about the Brooklyn Dodgers rankled me. Then he said Stan the Man didn't deserve the moniker as he was a sissy wimp who ought to play in the nigger leagues. Even though he was bigger than me, I charged and tackled him. We rolled around in the grass for a while, and somehow Jim got a fat lip and a torn shirt. Uncle Matthew turned me over his knee and whipped me like I was a child. Luke said I was in the wrong and made me apologize which I did, but I hadn't forgiven Jim or Uncle Matthew.

On the way home that day, Luke said I needed to control my temper and use my head. He pointed out that Musial had a better batting average than any of the Dodger players, and if I'd quoted facts to Jim, I could've won the argument and avoided the fight. In addition, Jackie Robinson, a black man, played for the Dodgers, and they were to be commended for that. Many players in the Negro Leagues were just as good as any major league player, Luke said. Luckily I didn't have to deal with Uncle Matthew as the adults crowded into a big circular booth, and Dan and I ate at the lunch counter where I consumed two grilled cheese sandwiches.

The following week was all about “The Suit.” First, Dan stood still in his dress pants while Mom with a mouthful of straight pins turned up his cuffs. The next evening, he put them on again for Mom to check her work. Then she pressed the trousers and hung them in the closet.

The third evening, Mom worked on the jacket with Dan in it while we listened to Lamont Cranston solve another mystery on *The Shadow*. Another fitting was necessary the following evening as Mom fussed over her work and decided to move the buttons over. By the weekend, “The Suit” hung in Dan’s closet awaiting the grand graduation ceremony.

The final day of school arrived. In the morning, we bussed to the high school football field for a track meet with our rivals from Hawthorne Elementary. I took second in the fifty-yard dash and our relay team won first. Following the meet, busses took all of us to the city park for a picnic then back to the school to clean out our desks. After all the goodbyes, my feet dragged on the walk home.

The big night was upon us. Decked out in “The Suit,” Dan preened in front of the bathroom mirror for so long that little time was left for the rest of us. We picked up Grandma Jenkins and arrived at the high school auditorium with no time to spare. Music swelled and Dan’s class marched in, the girls in colorful dresses and the boys in slacks, shirts and ties. Only a few boys wore suits. The superintendent spoke. The principal droned on. Awards were handed out and pictures taken. Finally, the principal called names as students walked across the stage to receive their certificates.

The payoff came when we got home. Relatives from both sides of the family crowded the living and dining rooms stacking gifts and cards onto the table. Mom's aunts and uncles each gave Dan a card with a five dollar bill in it. Grandma Jenkins contributed a small record player. Uncle Evan and Aunt Sarah presented Dan with a new ball glove. Grandpa and Grandma Martin gave him a radio. Uncle Matthew and Aunt Esther handed over a tie and ten dollars, and Aunt Liz sent a card from Wichita along with a check. Luke escorted Dan to the back patio where a basketball backboard decorated with a Jayhawk leaned against the house. Luke's beloved KU won the NCAA championship decisively over St. John's the previous year, but when the Jayhawks lost to Indiana by one point in March, Luke moped for days.

Next came cake, coffee and iced tea. Dan and I joined our cousins Ricky, Jim, Shirley and Sharon at the kitchen table. Mom's relatives sedately ate cake in the living and dining rooms. Luke's family occupied the front porch where they smoked and drank beer.

"Hey, Ricky," I said, "is Uncle Evan playing for the Harrington team this year?"

"Nah." Ricky finished the last of his cake and looked around for more. As he was as thin as I was, I figured he could use another piece or two.

"Why not?" I said.

"Dad says he'll do better as the third base coach. We got lots of good young guys on the team."

Uncle Evan injured his knee a couple of years ago, and I assumed he couldn't get around the bases any more.

"We'll see how good they are Friday night," Dan said.

"You'll be in high school next year," Sharon said. "How many kids in your class?"

"Seventy-three right now."

Sharon sniffed. "That's frightfully small. There's over three hundred in mine."

Sharon attended Pattonburg High where she'd be a junior.

"Dad says we're in for trouble with a no-nothing as president." A mouthful of cake muffled Jim's words.

"Eisenhower's not a no-nothing," Dan protested, "and we're lucky to have a good Kansas man in the White House."

"He's never held any elective office, Dad says, so he won't know what to do. Say, what'd you get that award for?" Jim said.

Dan frowned at him. "You heard what they said."

"I wasn't listening. I thought the whole thing was Nowheresville."

"It was for being an all-around good student," I said. "You know, sports and leadership. School activities and good grades."

"You some kinda nerd?"

Dan leaned across the table. "A nerd doesn't play basketball and baseball. A nerd isn't a class officer. And making good grades doesn't make me a nerd. You're just all around bad news, fat boy."

Jim got to his feet, knocking over his chair. "You take that back!"

Dan leaned back in his chair. "Make me."

Mom walked into the kitchen. "What's all the noise in here?"

Jim busied himself righting the chair.

"It was nothing, Mom," Dan said. "Jim had a bit of trouble getting out of his chair."

I began stacking the cake plates. "I'll clean up in here, Mom."

"Come here, Shirley Belle," Mom said. "Let's wash your hands. And look, you've got chocolate on your dress."

It's strange that Mom and Luke married as their families were so different. Luke's family tended to be tall, overweight, flabby and pale. They worked in offices and stores, drank, smoked, cussed and voted Democrat. Mom's relatives farmed and worked outside in fields and gardens. They were slender, tanned muscular people who never smoked, drank or used coarse language. They, of course, were die-hard Republicans.

FOUR

I woke to rain on the windowpane. Dan's bed lay empty but unmade, his new possessions on the top shelf beside his bed. I longed to try on the ball glove, but feared Dan might return at any minute. I hurried to dress as it felt late.

Downstairs, Mom washed dishes. "Oh, good. You're up." She sat a box of Wheaties onto the table. "Eat your breakfast and finish the dishes. I'm stripping the beds and going to the laundromat." She dried her hands and left me standing in the doorway.

I considered this a poor start to summer vacation. I studied the baseball standings in the *Pattonburg Sun* while I ate. In third place, the Cardinals were having a winning season, and Enos Slaughter hit another homerun. Still, the Dodgers seemed unbeatable with Roy Campanella, Duke Snyder and Jackie Robinson all hitting above three hundred.

When she returned, Mom carried a full laundry basket on her hip. "After you've done the dishes, clean your room."

"Aw, Mom."

"You've nothing else to do with the rain." She pulled on her raincoat and flipped up the hood.

"Where's Dan?"

"Luke's dropping him at Dean's to organize for church camp. It's your turn to clean the room."

Alone with only Duke for company and drudgery ahead. An even worse start to summer break. Finished with the dishes, I found a mop and bucket, a dust cloth and polish, crept up the stairs and surveyed our room. My eyes lit on Dan's new glove and my spirits rose. Forgetting my assignment, I abandoned the cleaning provisions and picked up the glove. It felt perfect, a bit rigid, but flexibility came with use, and the glove would improve my game.

I examined the small record player for forty-fives. Maybe I could buy some with my allowance. The radio. I turned it on to static. I searched for the Springfield station that carried the Cardinal's games. It first came in only faintly until I located and raised the antenna. This would be a vast improvement over the heavy cabinet radio I used now. But none of this was mine, and getting the use of any of the three gifts would take diplomacy.

I tuned the radio to Kansas City's WHB and toiled happily for an hour while pop tunes played. Rosemary Clooney belted out *Come on a My House*. Jo Stafford crooned *You Belong to Me*. I hummed, dusted, swept and mopped. The floors shined and the scent of furniture polish perfumed the air.

I stacked our school books. Mom would return them to the store that handled the school district's texts for a refund. My notebook fell open to the words I'd heard at Tony's Market. That guy Mc something-or-other was after bad people he called communists, and if we had one here in Glendale, Luke needed to know.

Downstairs, I pulled the dictionary from the shelf, opened it on the table and looked up atheist. Grandma Jenkins was right. The dictionary said an atheist denies the existence of God. But Tony said he might be an agnoosetic, and I couldn't find it in the dictionary. Thinking I might have misspelled it, I looked through the words beginning with ag and there it was. Agnostic: one who believes it impossible to know if God exists or not.

I copied down the definition word for word and did the same for communist and socialist though I couldn't tell the difference between those two. I decided the dictionary wasn't a good source of information for me. Maybe an encyclopedia contained better facts, but that required a trip to the library. Frustrated, I practiced the piano.

The rain lessened to a drizzle by the time I heard a car door slam. I scrambled to open the door for Mom.

"Oh, thank you." She sat the laundry basket onto the countertop and removed her raincoat. "Finish your room?"

"Sure. And I practiced, too."

Duke padded into the kitchen to satisfy his curiosity.

"He needs to go out." Mom opened the back door.

"He'll get wet."

"Time you gave him a bath." She picked up the laundry basket. "You can do that when the sun comes out. Right now, I want you to help me make the beds."

Aw, gee whiz. When does my summer vacation begin? I glumly climbed the stairs after her.

Mom sniffed. "Why, your room smells wonderful. And the floor shines like an ice rink." She ruffled my hair. "You really do a good job when you set your mind to it."

Sunlight flooded the room.

"Can I go over to Pete's after lunch?"

"After Duke's bath." Mom flipped a sheet over Dan's bed. "Now fold the corners tight."

I pulled the sheet taut, tucked it in and followed her instructions. "Mom, what's a communist?"

"Why do you want to know?"

I shrugged. "I see it in the newspaper and hear it on the radio. It's bad, I guess."

Mom fanned the top sheet. "Tuck in the bottom on your side."

"But what is it?"

"Why, I'm not sure I can explain it." She moved to my bed and spread the bottom sheet. "It's a way of government where the government owns all the farms and factories, I guess."

I folded the sheet's corner tight. "So the government makes all the money?"

Mom frowned. "I think the profit is supposed to be spread around to the citizens, but it doesn't seem to work that way in the Soviet Union."

The top sheet went on. "Why is it bad?"

"It's very repressive."

"What's that mean?"

"We're finished here. Now our bed." She hefted the laundry basket and left the room.

"What's repressive?"

"Boy, you are full of questions today." She fanned a sheet over the bed. "Repressive means you have no freedom. Where you live, where you work, what you do, the government controls it all."

I thought about what she'd said as we finished making the bed. "Bruce's dad owns a farm. Would the communists take it away from him?"

Mom chuckled. "It won't happen here. Don't you worry."

"But it did happen?"

Mom guided me ahead of her out of the bedroom. "Years ago when the communists took over in Russia and Stalin came to power."

"What happened to the farmers?"

"Many of them starved." Mom turned me around and looked me in the eye. "Now Stalin's dead. Why are you asking all these questions?"

"Well." I studied my new red sneakers to think. "That guy, the one in the government after communists."

"You mean McCarthy?"

"Yeah. He says there are communists everywhere."

Mom patted my shoulder. "He's been claiming that for years and he's never proved anything. Now you get that plastic wading pool hanging in the garage. Fill it on the patio to warm in the sun for Duke's bath. I'll make lunch."

"Duke's wet." My friend Pete looked out at us through the screen door.

"Just gave him a bath. He'll dry in the sun."

Pete slammed out of the house. "Let's climb the pear tree out back."

We trotted around the house with Duke loping along with us, his tongue hanging out.

"Isn't this the Gladding's tree?"

Pete reached up for a branch, stepped into the crotch formed in the trunk and pulled himself up. "They don't mind. I do it all the time."

I followed Pete's example and soon we sat on branches high in the tree. I could hear a loud voice coming from the Gladding house.

"Joy's mother," Pete said. "She's always yelling at her."

Mrs. Gladding never seemed glad about anything. Joy, only a year behind us in school, still wore her hair in the pigtails her mother insisted upon. The kids teased her which made her withdraw, and Mrs. Gladding criticized her for being shy.

"Boy, you can see a long way from here," I said.

"Yeah. This is a great place to spy on the neighborhood."

"Spy." I almost let go of the branch in my excitement. "Say, I know someone who needs to be spied on."

"Who's that?"

"The publisher guy. Emile something."

"Mr. Hrabosky? Why spy on him?"

"He's a communist, that's why." I told him about the conversation between Mr. Rogers and Mr. DeCarlo in Tony's Market. "Mr. DeCarlo said he wasn't. That he was a socialist but Mr. Rogers said same difference. And I looked them up in the dictionary, and they are almost exactly the same."

"My mother says Mr. Hrabosky is a nice guy. He eats lunch at Esther's Café every day." Pete's mother waitressed at the café.

"Nice guy or not, he's a communist. That's why he prints those *Little Red Books.* Communists are called reds, you know."

"How'll we spy on him?"

"Why follow him around, of course. See where he goes, what he does, who he talks to. There may be a whole ring of communists around here."

"We'll keep a log of his activities."

I could feel Pete's enthusiasm rise. "Mr. Rogers said the FBI was after Mr. Hrabosky."

"The FBI? What'd they want him for?"

"Mr. DeCarlo said he printed something bad about J. Edgar."

"J. Edgar Hoover? The head of the FBI?"

Well, I was glad to find out who J. Edgar was. "That's what he said."

Pete looked off into the distance for a bit then turned to me with sparkling eyes. "We'll be helping out the FBI. We'll be heroes."

"We can get Gary and Sonny to spy, too."

Pete shook his head. "Gary can't keep a secret."

Gary Kennedy, the mayor's son, found it impossible to keep his mouth shut. His mother wanted him to be the head of everything and raised heck when he wasn't made captain of the baseball team.

"We can't tell Sonny, then. He's Gary's best friend and he'd tell Gary for sure. Just you and me then," I said.

Pete nodded. "And our secret."

"When do we start?"

"You doing swim lessons?"

"Yeah. Monday and Wednesday mornings, and I have piano on Tuesday morning."

"And baseball on Thursday." Pete loved the sport, too.

"But everything is in the mornings, so we have the afternoons."

"You boys get out of that tree." Hands on her ample hips, Mrs. Gladding glared up at us. "Pete Parkinson, I've told you time and time again not to climb this tree. And Mike Martin, you should know better."

We scrambled down as Mrs. Gladding continued her harangue. "You'll damage my tree. Break the limbs. Fall out and hurt yourself and turn around and sue me, no doubt. Now get on home and take that mangy mutt with you."

We slunk away with her words following us. "I'm calling your parents. They'll know about this. You do it again, I'll see you get whipped."

We reached the front of Pete's house before her threats faded.

"Wow. She really gets worked up," I said.

Pete grinned. "She calls my parents all the time. They just laugh at her behind her back."

"Can you go tomorrow? To spy, I mean."

"Sure." Pete bit his lip. "I'll ask Momma tonight what time he eats at the café, and we can follow him from there."

"Mrs. Gladding called."

I looked up from my dinner plate and studied Mom's face.

"What'd she want?" Luke asked.

"She was upset about Mike being up her pear tree." Mom winked at me.

"She's always upset about something." Luke cut into his pork chop.

"I assured her that Mike had no idea she'd forbidden climbing the tree, and if he'd known, he wouldn't have. I'm sure it won't happen again."

"Thanks, Mom." I dug into my mashed potatoes.

"It's always a wise policy to ask first, Mike," Luke said.

"Sure." This was contrary to my experience. If I asked, I usually got no for an answer, so it was wiser to just do what I wished. I could always apologize later.

"Did you make your plans for church camp?" Mom said.

Dan wrinkled his nose. "I don't see why I have to go again this year."

"Why, you've always enjoyed it," Mom said. "You'll be a cabin leader this summer."

"But a whole week with a bunch of little kids," Dan protested. "It'll be a nightmare."

"Well, it's too late to back out," Luke said. "You made the commitment and you'll stick to it."

"All right." Dan's face brightened. "Say, on the way home, I walked by Smithton's garage and Glen waved me over. Showed me this old Ford he's going to make into a hotrod."

"Isn't he the one with the car that roars down the street?" Mom said.

"That's his older brother," Dan said. "Glen says I can help him."

"I don't know," Mom said. "From what I've heard of him, I don't consider him a good influence."

"Now that the boy has his permit, he needs to learn about cars," Luke said. "A garage is a good place to get experience."

"But Glen Smithton is—"

"Boisterous, loud, full of undirected energy," Luke said. "I'm sure he and his friends put that outhouse on the school steps last Halloween. He's full of mischief but he's not a bad kid."

Mom's mouth turned down. "I don't want Dan putting an outhouse on the school steps."

"Dan's old enough to make his decisions. We've either raised him to make good ones or we haven't. He knows what we expect of him."

And so I was on my own for the summer.

FIVE

Friday morning, I thought I'd never be able to meet Pete as Mom insisted that we first practice. With Dan upstairs blowing his trumpet and me in the front room pounding on the piano, the resulting racket drove Mom from the house to tend her flower garden. Then she reminded Dan that he needed to mow and handed me a hoe with the dictate to destroy all the weeds in her garden.

Mom raised no vegetables but planted row upon row of marigolds, zinnias, larkspur, snapdragons, petunias, cosmos and sunflowers. The tulips, daffodils and narcissus were passed flowering and gathering strength to put on a show next spring. The other perennials like gladiolas, lilies, asters, daisies and coneflowers would blossom in their season. Heavy with bloom, the peonies anticipated Memorial Day's cemetery visit. Mom supplied bouquets for Sunday church service and entered her flower arrangements in the county fair where she usually took the grand championship.

Finally, I told Mom about the plan to meet Pete and ride to the square. I mentioned that Mr. Parkinson worked in the auto parts store there hoping she'd assume that was our destination. Mom was busy ironing and listening to her soap on the radio, so she asked no questions. I fixed a peanut butter sandwich and Duke and I set out for Pete's house.

Pete frowned. "You brought Duke?"

"He's cover. Everybody loves a dog."

Pete said we had plenty of time, so we carefully biked across the highway that bisected the town north to south and dropped by the park to see who was there. We watched some kids play ball for a while. Then Pete noticed he had a low tire, so we went to Simmons's Hardware on the square to buy a tire pump.

Pete put down his kick stand. "I'll put it on my dad's tab."

Duke and I followed him into the store where I recognized the man in overalls who mopped the floor.

"Hi, Malcolm." I stopped in front of him.

A wide grin split Malcolm's round face. "Hi, yourself. You brought Duke." He knelt and fondled Duke's ears. "Know what I found?"

I shook my head. "No."

"I'll show you." Malcolm dropped the mop and searched his pocket. "It's in here." He pulled out a broken piece of pottery. "See."

I took the fragment from him. "That's very pretty."

"I think it's old." Malcolm's mouth twisted when he spoke making his words hard to understand. "My mother said it was valuable."

Though in his mid-twenties, Malcolm lived with his parents because of his disability.

"Better keep it safe, Malcolm." I returned his treasure.

Malcolm picked up his mop handle. "I'm working. Next I go to the Write place. I go early today 'cause of the holiday weekend."

"He means Write Publishing," Mr. Simmons said as he and Pete joined us. "Did he show you his new find?"

I nodded. "He's a lucky guy."

"Want to see?" Malcolm handed the broken pottery to Pete.

Pete turned it over. "Made in Japan."

"That's far away." Malcolm held out his hand. "That makes it worth lots of money." He pocketed his prize.

"I'll air up my tire." Pete slammed out of the store.

"Going to the game tonight, Malcolm?" I said.

"Sure."

"See you there." I joined Pete on the sidewalk where he pumped furiously. The frown on his face told me something was wrong.

"What happened?" I said.

"That piece is nothing but trash."

"He doesn't know that."

Pete unfastened the pump and capped the stem. "People shouldn't mislead him just because he's retarded. He should be told the truth."

I shrugged. "It's harmless. It makes him happy."

"I feel sorry for him." Pete put the pump in my bike's basket.

"Mom said something happened when he was born. Didn't get enough oxygen or something."

"Let's go."

Everyone in Glendale knew Malcolm Carroll who cleaned several stores on the square. Malcolm's child-like innocence and cheerful disposition made him welcome around town. We parked our bikes at the café's front, told Duke to stay and entered. Noontime customers crowded the cafe, so we waited for seats to open up at the counter.

"That's him." Pete nodded toward a booth. "Third booth back facing us."

I recognized the face. "I've seen him before. Mom stopped on the street and talked to him."

"Quit staring at him," Pete whispered. "Spies have to be sneaky. Act normal."

"Malcolm cleans Write Publishing. Is that Mr. Hrabosky's place?"

"Yeah. It's that three-story brick building on Hamilton Street next to the tracks."

"There's a couple of seats."

We quickly occupied the two empty stools.

"Who's that with him in the booth?" Pete said.

I looked over my shoulder. "Mr. Paternik from the music store." Mr. Paternik's bushy hair gave him away. It reminded me of pictures I'd seen of Beethoven.

"Think he's one of them, too?"

I shrugged. "Don't know. We'll have to see if they meet often." I doubted that Mr. Paternik was a communist. After all, he helped sponsor the town team.

"Hi, Mike." Pete's mother removed the empty plates in front of us and wiped the counter. "I hope you boys are behaving yourselves."

"I needed a tire pump for my bike," Pete said, "so we rode up to get one and that made us thirsty."

"Cokes then?" Mrs. Parkinson said.

"Sure. And make them to go." Pete waited until his mother left. "Look. We can see him in the mirror."

My view was partially obscured by a stack of saucers. "I can see part of him."

"He's lighting a cigarette. He'll be leaving soon."

Mrs. Parkinson returned with our Cokes. "That'll be a nickel each."

"I'll buy." I put a dime into her hand. "Thank you, Mrs. Parkinson."

"Such good manners." She smiled at me. "I hope that rubs off on Pete."

Pete watched his mother ring up the sale at the end of the counter. "Come on. We can wait for him outside."

We moved our bikes down the sidewalk to the awning shelter at Ziggy's Jewelry.

Sipping my Coke, I looked at the vehicles parked nose in to the curb, mostly older cars and trucks. A large blue Buick with chrome strips down the side stood out from the rest.

"I'll bet that's his car." I pointed it out to Pete. I figured the blue whale would create turbulence like an eighteen-wheeler.

"We can't follow him if he goes too fast."

"Here he comes." I turned to the jewelry display. "See that watch? I'd like to buy it for Luke's birthday."

Pete's eyes slid left. "He's getting into the car."

"Don't turn around. Wait for him to back out." I heard the engine catch and rev.

"I see his reflection in the glass," Pete murmured. "He's backing out. Going east."

"Wait 'til he's down the block." I glanced over my shoulder. "Now."

We hopped onto our bikes in time to see the blue car turn north. Rounding the corner, I almost hit Duke and dropped my cup. I could hear Mom lecturing me about littering. We pedaled hard, trying to follow the blue behemoth a block ahead.

"He's turning onto Hamilton," Pete called.

"Slow down." Pete braked and I pulled up beside him. "We know where he's going."

"Yeah." Pete nodded. "Let's cruise by and make sure his car's there."

We pedaled leisurely down Hamilton to the plant which faced north. The blue car crouched in the parking lot to the right of the building along with many others. Across the street, I stepped from my bike under the shade of a hackberry tree. Panting, Duke flopped onto the ground.

Pete stopped beside me. “He may be in there for hours.”

“Yeah.”

Through the open third story windows, I could hear a humming and clacking clamor. “Must be the presses making all that uproar,” I said.

“Sure wouldn’t want to live across the street from that.”

I looked at the small bungalows along the street across from the plant. A sign next to the door of the house behind us announced that the Rogers lived there. My attention returned to the plant as a panel truck pulled up to the loading dock on the left. A man in blue coveralls emerged from the plant with several boxes on a dolly. He handed the boxes down to the truck driver who stowed them in the back of the truck and drove away.

“What do we do now?” Pete asked.

I thought back to the café. “We have only one clue.”

“What’s that?”

“Mr. Paternik. I know him. I buy my music at his store.”

Pete shrugged. “Huh. Doesn’t seem like a clue to me.”

“We’ll talk to him. Come on.”

We rode back to the square. Paternik Music sat on the west side down the block from Simmons Hardware.

“Let me do the talking.” I opened the door. “Hello, Mr. Paternik.”

“Mike, my boy. Need some more sheet music?” Mr. Paternik spoke with a slight accent so sheet sounded more like shit, and Pete snickered.

“Not today.” I moved down the aisle. “My brother got a record player for his graduation. I thought I might look at your forty-fives.”

“Oh, I have many. All the most popular. If you need something special, I can always order. Right over here.”

“Hank Williams has a new one out,” Pete said.

"Oh, yes." Mr. Paternik flipped through the forty-fives. "*Hey, Good Lookin'*." He chuckled. "I not call you good lookin'. That's the name of the song."

"How about *Your Cheatin' Heart*?" I said.

"Oh, yes. I got that one, too."

I noticed the price tag on the cover. "I get my allowance tomorrow, Mr. Paternik. I can buy it then."

"Tomorrow." Mr. Paternik put his index finger on his chin. "Saturday. Busy day. I let you have it today. You pay me next week." He shook his head. "Not Monday. That's Memorial Day."

"Really, Mr. Paternik? You trust me?"

"You a regular customer." He grinned. "Besides, I know your father."

"Thank you."

"I get you a bag." He took the record to the counter.

"You had lunch at the café," I said. "Who was in the booth with you?"

"Oh, that's Mr. Hrabosky."

"You know him well?"

"Oh, yes. Mrs. Paternik works for him. He's a fine fellow." He held out a bag. "I put the bill in the bag along with the record so you won't forget to pay."

"I won't forget, Mr. Paternik."

Out on the sidewalk, Pete laughed. "So you buy shit music here."

I joined in the laughter. "All the time."

"We didn't learn much."

"We've got to write everything down." I mounted up. "Never can tell what's important."

"You write it." Pete rode beside me. "You write better than me."

I expected this. Pete was smart enough to make good grades in school, but he avoided what he considered work.

"What now?" I said.

"Let's go to my house and listen to the Cardinals' game."

I braked to a stop. "Five and dime. I need a notebook to write in."

We backtracked to Wayfords. I considered a Big Chief tablet, checked my meager funds and looked for something smaller.

"Hey, Leonard." Two men burst into the store, one calling loudly for Mr. Wayford. The loudmouth's brushed-back hair shone with grease and dirt streaked his sleeveless T-shirt. I recognized the second man as Glen Smithton's older brother Everett who worked with his father in the garage.

"Leonard." The man shouted again. "Front and center."

Mrs. Hill, the store clerk approached. "I can help you, sir."

The man sneered. "We don't deal with the help, lady."

"Mr. Wayford is upstairs in the office."

"Well go get him." The man gestured to the back. "Hop to it."

Mrs. Hill hurried away.

"That's Alex Buckner," Pete whispered.

Luke spoke of him. Said he'd been booted out of the army and had picked up some bad habits. I pulled Pete to the other side of the display where hanging shirts hid us from view.

"This Podunk town is the pits." Alex's gruff voice was easy to recognize.

"Glendale's quiet, that's all." Everett's softer voice was distinctive.

I heard footsteps approach. "How can I help you gentlemen?"

"I got me a date tonight, Leonard." Alex lowered his voice slightly. "I need me some rubbers."

Mr. Wayford coughed. "I'm sorry, Buckner. I've told you before that we don't sell that product."

Everybody in town knew you couldn't buy shoes at the five and dime, and why would he need rubbers for a date? Was he going wading?

"Don't sell rubbers?" Alex sounded outraged. "I figured you had a request you'd get some in."

"I do not intend to stock them."

"Fine way to run a business. Hey, where you going?"

"To look at shirts," Everett said.

The shirt in front of me suddenly moved aside and I was staring into Everett Smithton's square face. His eyebrows rose. "Well, look what we got here."

Heavy boots clomped across the wooden floor. "What'd you find?"

"It's that Martin kid." Everett rounded the display counter. "Hiding over here behind the shirts."

Pete's face turned white. "We ain't hiding."

Alex towered above us. "Funny way to shop, all crouched over like that."

"What's your name, kid?" Everett pulled Pete to his feet.

"P . . . Pete Parkinson."

"Well, P . . . Pete. What you doing? Shoplifting?"

I stood. All I could see was a big chain hooked to a loop on Alex's jeans and running down to his pocket. I looked up into his narrow eyes. "We came in to buy a notebook."

"Ain't no notebooks in this aisle." Everett pointed to me. "This one's wimpy brother hangs around the garage with Glen."

"His old man's the cop?"

"Yeah."

Mr. Wayford stepped between the men. "I'd appreciate it if you didn't bother my customers."

I admired his bravery. A thin old man with gray hair, Mr. Wayford only reached Alex's shoulder.

Alex snickered. "You'd appreciate it, huh?"

"Come boys." Mr. Wayford herded us down the aisle.

"You ought to appreciate us finding the little thieves," Alex called after us.

"Don't mind them," Mr. Wayford said.

"Let's blow this joint," Everett said.

"Yeah. We get no appreciation here."

Mr. Wayford escorted us to the counter as the two men tramped to the door and disappeared. "I'm sorry about that," he said.

"We weren't stealing, Mr. Wayford," I said. "When those men came in, we thought it best to vanish."

Pete nodded. "They're scary."

Mr. Wayford sighed. "They're a couple of bullies. Best way to deal with them is to stand up to them."

"Or avoid them," I said.

"That's another way," Mr. Wayford said. "Now what can I do for you?"

"I wanted this notebook." I held it out to him.

He waved me away. "It's yours. On the house and I'm sorry for your trouble."

Conversation seemed unnecessary on the ride home. Poor Duke needed a drink and a rest, and I realized that if he was going to help us spy, I needed to carry water for him. We listened to the Cardinals lose as I recorded our adventures in my new notebook.

SIX

Luke folded back a page of his newspaper. "It says here that grain dust caused the Valetti mill fire."

"Took them long enough to decide that," Mom said.

"Must've done a thorough investigation."

"About the movie. I read that it's anti-American," Mom said. "Maybe the boys shouldn't see it."

"It's a western with Gary Cooper. Nothing anti-American about it." Luke sounded annoyed.

"But one of the writers is a communist. He got fired and blacklisted."

Luke rattled his newspaper. "More of that McCarthy crap."

"Luke!"

"Poor man's probably innocent. Loses his job and can't get another all because of that blowhard."

I looked back and forth between them as they decided my fate. Would I get to see *High Noon* or not?

"All my friends are going," Dan said.

Mom put her cereal bowl into the sink. "We'll not make decisions based on what everyone else does."

"Dean's going and his dad's our minister," Dan said. Rev. Norris's son Dean was Dan's best friend and forbidden to visit the Smithton's garage.

Luke looked at Dan. "Well, it's obvious you want to go. What about you, Mike? Want to see *High Noon*?"

"Yes, sir."

"If Rev. Norris approves of the movie," Luke said, "it'd be silly of us to disapprove."

"Okay, I guess." Mom cleared the breakfast table. "But don't you two make yourselves sick on candy."

"Maybe you and I can see the movie Sunday evening," Luke said.

With the town full to bursting on Saturday afternoon and evening, Luke kept busy walking the streets to prevent trouble.

"We'll see." Mom pulled the ice trays from the freezer and ran water over them to loosen the cubes. "I'm stocking up on ice for tomorrow's picnic, so go easy on using ice today."

Luke finished his coffee. "Dan, I'll run to the hardware store for brackets. You can help me mount that backboard this morning."

"Can I go and drive?" Dan said.

Mom refilled the ice trays. "You've got to practice."

"I'll do that afterward. Promise."

"If you don't, you'll be home this afternoon until you do." Mom put the ice trays back into the freezer. "Mike, you can practice while they're gone."

"Can I call Bruce first?"

"Well, don't stay on the phone too long. You know how their neighbors are."

The phone, located in the kitchen for Mom's convenience, had a long cord, so I sat on the bottom of the stairs to talk. Mrs. Horlacher answered and called Bruce to the phone.

"I can go," I said.

"Who's on this phone?" a loud female voice asked.

"It's only me, Mrs. Thornton," Bruce said.

"You kids are on the phone constantly. This is a party line, you know. You need to respect your neighbors."

"I'll only be a minute, Mrs. Thornton." Bruce waited until he heard the click of the receiver being replaced. "Nosy old biddy. She knew the ring wasn't for her. Just wanted to see who was calling."

"I can go," I repeated. "What about you?"

"We're all going," Bruce said.

"You coming to town this afternoon?"

"Yeah. Not sure what time."

"I'll be on the square walking clockwise."

"I'll find you."

Bruce and I had learned if one of us walked clockwise and the other counterclockwise, we'd be sure to meet.

I practiced until my fingers ached, then Mom sent me to the garden to deadhead her flowers while Luke and Dan installed the basketball goal.

Cars and trucks of all shapes, sizes and vintages filled the parking spaces on the square forcing latecomers to parallel park on adjacent streets. Doors jangled and buzzed announcing the arrival of customers. Farmers, clad in overalls, sat on truck tailgates to visit with friends and neighbors. Their wives put up impromptu markets offering vegetables, breads, desserts and crafts for sale. People lounged on blankets under the oaks surrounding the courthouse. A holiday atmosphere prevailed.

I first paid Mr. Paternik for the record which I'd given to Dan as a graduation present. In return, he said I could use the record player when he wasn't spinning his own platters. Diplomatic negotiations were underway and I'd reached one-third of my goal. Next, I longed for use of the ball glove. At the five and dime, I persuaded Mr. Wayford to take money for the notebook, insisting that I felt badly about not paying for it. I felt it important to keep in the good graces of the merchants around the square who were leaders in the community. Satisfied with myself, I bought a cherry Coke at the Rexall fountain and set out to meet Bruce.

"Hey, Mike!"

I turned to see Pete Parkinson and Gary Kennedy running to meet me.

"I saw Mr. Hrabosky," Pete said excitedly.

"Where?"

"Coming out of the Keyland Hotel with another man. Both of them in suits."

"What's so important about Mr. Hrabosky?" Gary said.

Pete's eyes shifted side to side as he realized his mistake. "Don't you know?" he said.

I looked around for help and remembered the conversation in Tony's Market. "I'll bet the FBI's in town again."

"Yes, that's it," Pete said.

Gary's eyes widened. "You think that guy with Mr. Hrabosky is FBI?"

"Who else would wear a suit in town on Saturday?" I said.

"My dad wears a suit all the time," Gary said.

I shrugged. “So? He’s the mayor.”

“Look.” Pete pointed to a big blue car cruising up the street.

As the car passed us, I noticed Mr. Hrabosky at the wheel. “Must not be the FBI. A G-man wouldn’t let Mr. Hrabosky drive his own car.”

Pete’s mouth fell. “Guess it was nothing after all.”

“You going to the two o’clock movie?” Gary asked.

“Nah.” I shook my head. “I’m meeting Bruce. The matinee’s just for little kids anyway. We’re going tonight.” An animated feature showed at two o’clock.

“Even some high school kids go to the matinee,” Gary protested, “and I can’t go tonight. We’re leaving for my aunt’s house in Chanute.”

Just then I spotted Bruce. “Here he comes.”

“Hey, guys.” Bruce wore frayed jeans cut off just below the knee and an old shirt with the sleeves hacked off. He looked as I imagined Huck Finn might appear, and I envied his carefree attire.

“We’re off to the movie,” Pete said. “You coming?”

“Nah. I’ll hang with Mike.”

“Okay. See you later, alligator.” Pete and Gary sauntered off.

“I can’t stay long,” Bruce said. “Momma’s buying groceries at Ray’s Market. I’m supposed to meet her there.”

Ray’s sat on the square’s west side while we were on the east, so we wound our way through the crowds on the sidewalk. The crowd thinned as we crossed the street to the south side.

“What time will you be in for *High Noon*?” I asked.

“We milk at five,” Bruce said. “By the time we eat and such, we’ll probably be late and miss the previews.”

“I’ll save you a seat on the back row before the balcony.” Near the next corner, I noticed a group of four men.

“Momma says I can play ball on Thursday.”

“All right! We’ll be the youngest on the team. No chance of being captain.”

Bruce chuckled. “Too bad for Gary.”

“Charlie and Pete will be on the team.”

As we drew closer to the group, I recognized the greased-back hair of Alex Buckner. I slowed and studied the group. Everett Smithton stood beside Alex, but I didn't recognize the other guy. The three surrounded Malcolm Carroll. My feet refused to go further.

"What is it?" Bruce said.

"Those guys." I pulled Bruce into the recessed doorway of Saulk's Department Store and told him about the incident at the five and dime. "Alex Buckner is bad news."

Bruce stuck his head around the corner to examine the group. "They're teasing Malcolm. He looks upset, like he could cry." He moved back beside me. "What'll we do?"

I peeked around the corner. Alex Buckner laughed and slapped Everett on the back. We could cross the street to the courthouse lawn and ignore the scene. We needed help. Luke would stop them, but I didn't know where he was. I searched for someone else, but all seemed oblivious to Malcolm's plight. Mr. Wayford said to confront bullies. I looked at the group and shivered. I stood back beside Bruce, hidden from the men.

"You got that French coin your aunt gave you?"

"Sure." Bruce pulled on a leather cord worn around his neck and the coin appeared from under his shirt, a large brown franc with a hole in its center.

"I've got an idea. Just follow my lead." I lurched from the doorway so terrified I doubted I could speak.

Bruce trotted to catch up. "What you going to do?"

"Act natural," I said. "Concentrate on Malcolm and ignore the others."

Up close, I recognized Junior Rogers as the third man. He held a wiggling puppy.

"Dog meat's a delicacy," I heard one of them say, but I was focused on Malcolm whose lower lip quivered.

I edged between two of the men and stood directly in front of Malcolm. "Hey, Malcolm."

Malcolm looked down. "Hey, yourself."

"I saw you at the ball game last night. You had an ice cream cone. What flavor was it?"

"Quit buttin' in, kid," someone said.

"Vanilla. My favorite," Malcolm said.

"Do you know my friend Bruce?" I tugged Bruce's arm to stand him beside me.

"Sure." Malcolm grinned. "From the ballpark."

"His dad hit a homerun last night," I said.

Malcolm nodded. "Mr. Horlacher."

"Horlacher," one man sneered. "Does he lack a whore?"

Bruce's arm stiffened under my hand. He'd heard this often enough, but it still stung.

I kept edging forward toward Malcolm so he would back away from the men. "You showed me the treasure you found," I said. "Bruce has a treasure, too."

"Want to see?" Bruce asked.

"Sure."

Bruce angled to Malcolm's side as he pulled on the coin's leather cord. "I don't want them to know what I got." He nodded toward the men and opened his hand.

"What is it?" Malcolm bent for a better look.

Bruce stepped back and Malcolm followed. "It's money from a country called France."

Malcolm turned his back to the men. "Is that far away?"

"It's very far away," I said as I led Malcolm to the corner. "It's across a huge ocean."

"It must be very valuable, then."

"Want to hold it?" Bruce drew the cord over his head.

"Sure." Malcolm fingered the coin and examined it. "It's got writing on it. What's it say?"

Bruce shrugged. "Don't know. It's in French."

By now, we'd reached the west side of the square, and Malcolm glanced back at his tormenters. "They're going to eat that puppy," he said.

"No, Malcolm," I said. "They were only teasing."

"Not funny." Malcolm sniffed and handed the coin back to Bruce. "You keep this safe. I got to see Mr. Simmons. I get paid today."

We watched him shuffle away.

Except for the gunfight, *High Noon* was a disappointment. The sheriff, played by Gary Cooper, could get no one to help him face the ruthless men who came in on the train. Minutes ticked away on the clock. Finally, after two boring hours, the sheriff's wife helped him defeat the outlaws. The sheriff flipped his star into the dust and rode away with his bride. I could see nothing anti-American about it. Maybe it was the implication that most people are cowards. The gunfight inspired a week's-long explosion of gunplay around the neighborhood.

Luke and Mom saw the movie Sunday night after the picnic at Harrington Lake and considered it one of the year's best movies worthy of an Academy Award. Mom's family gathered for the picnic, so Dan and I swam and fished with a bunch of second cousins and returned home sunburned and tired.

Mom kept us busy on Memorial Day. First, we attended the parade on the square. Crowds reminiscent of Saturday's lined the streets to watch veterans from the American Legion march along with the high school band. Tractors pulled decorated floats on flatbed wagons. Last year's homecoming queen waved to everyone.

Back at the house, Mom boxed up tall juice cans she'd saved for the occasion and filled glass gallon jugs with water while Dan and I cut peony blossoms. Then we visited the Harrington, Glendale and Pattonburg cemeteries to leave bouquets on the graves of dead relatives.

I considered this a waste of time and energy as these deceased kin couldn't see or smell the flowers, though I liked hearing stories about these people I'd never known and the cemeteries looked like fancy gardens with their colorful decorations and flags.

The week settled into a summer routine of swim lessons, piano and trumpet lessons, and baseball games interspersed with gunfights. Pete and I searched for Mr. Hrabosky and discovered he was out of town for the week. We assumed he was attending a communist convention somewhere, probably in Washington, D. C. or Hollywood as that's where Senator McCarthy seemed to believe Communists were concentrated. Without exaggerating too much, I told Pete about the confrontation with Everett Smithton, Junior Rogers and Alex Buckner on the square when they teased Malcolm about eating a puppy, and he was impressed with our bravery.

Before dawn one morning, Mom hustled Dan and me from bed and took us to the Horlacher farm to pick green beans. The Horlachers owned a huge orchard, grew a vegetable garden with produce for sale and had milk and beef cattle roaming a large pasture. Ed also raised wheat, soybeans, corn for silage and hay for his cattle.

Dew covered the ground and plants as the sun rose over the horizon. A slight breeze rustled the leaves and only birdsong disturbed the silence. I moved from plant to plant, stripping them of their largess and filling my basket. When our bushel was full, Mom called a halt. I asked Mrs. Horlacher about Bruce. She said he was milking the cows and I envied him his idyllic life.

I fell asleep on the way home and Mom sent me back to bed while Dan helped her prepare the beans for canning. When I next stumbled down the stairs, steam hung in the kitchen air as a pot filled with Mason jars bubbled on the stove. Mom's hair hung in limp strands and sweat shined her forehead. A strident voice boomed from the radio.

"What's that?"

Mom turned off the radio. "A reporter interviewing Senator McCarthy."

"He sounded really mad."

Mom rubbed her forehead with a kitchen towel. "He's a man of strong beliefs."

We didn't know those strong beliefs would have consequences in Glendale.

SEVEN

I elbowed Bruce. “There’s George Buckner.”

“He looks sober tonight,” Bruce said.

On the first base side, we occupied our usual seats in the bleacher’s highest row for the Friday night game between the Glendale Bombers and the Harrington Harvesters whose fans sat on the third base side.

“Sure wasn’t sober at the first game,” I said.

At that game, George Buckner stumbled into the Glendale dugout in a dirty uniform. A discussion followed between George and Gideon McKinley, the high school principal and the team captain. Wendell Markmann, called Windy and one of the team sponsors, joined the argument.

From our seats, Bruce and I could only interpret gestures. Gideon waved Luke in off the field and pointed to the parking lot. Luke escorted George to his truck, took his keys, and left him to sleep it off.

Later, Luke said the team voted to ban George from the game. He wasn’t much of a loss. An outfielder, he had a good arm but he was slow on the bases. Luke said the school board considered firing George from his custodial job for being a poor example to students.

Many town merchants sponsored the team making it a community project, and home games drew a large crowd. Some of the players were related to a sponsor. Bob Valetti’s son Vinny took George Buckner’s position in the outfield. Anton Paternik played center field. The banker’s son, Buddy Schiedler, held the catcher’s position, and third baseman Chevy Turnbow’s father owned a car dealership.

In my opinion, Ed Horlacher pitched a better game than either Zordani or Kirkpatrick. Although his fastball had lost some of its zip, he had a wicked slider, a great curveball and possessed consistent control. A potential fastball would fall away leaving the batter swinging at the air, and the outfielders could count on a dozen fly balls with Ed on the mound.

Raucous laughter drew my attention back to George Buckner, and I identified the man next to him as Kelvin Rogers. I wondered if they were talking about Emile Hrabosky being a Communist and remembered Bruce didn't know. I couldn't keep a secret from my best friend and knew he wouldn't tell a soul, so I told him about the conversation at Tony's Market and about spying on Mr. Hrabosky with Pete.

"Do you really think he's a commie?" Bruce said.

I shrugged. "I don't know but it's fun spying on people."

The crowd roared as Beach singled to drive in the first run for the Bombers, but the next batter flied out ending the first inning. Luke sat on the bench. He substituted as his job was likely to call him away during the game.

"Want to spy on Buckner and Rogers?" Bruce asked.

The two men stood at the end of the bleachers. "No cover," I said. "We can't just walk up behind them to hear what they say."

Horlacher struck out the first Harrington batter and the second flied out. Below us at the other end of the bleachers, a group of young men muscled into the first and second rows, making people move over to give them room. I recognized the greased-back locks of Alex Buckner.

I elbowed Bruce. "See what just blew in?"

"Those three who were teasing Malcolm."

The Harrington batter hit a single up the middle but I couldn't focus on the game.

Junior Rogers and Everett Smithton sat on either side of Buckner. Behind them, Glen Smithton and Aaron Farmer completed the gang. The five laughed and rough housed, and soon empty seats surrounded them as spectators moved away.

"I'd like to know what they're talking about," I said.

Bruce examined the group. "I'm not going down there."

"We could get under the bleachers."

Bruce's face lit up. "Come on."

We jumped to the ground, skirted the back of the bleachers, ducked in at the other end and crawled through discarded cups and cigarette butts to reach a prime position under the second row. Through the jeans-clad legs of Glen and Aaron, we could see the backs of Malcolm's three tormentors. The five talked over each other making it difficult to determine who was speaking.

". . . just watch him," someone said.

"Follow him, you mean?" I recognized Alex's voice. "My old man's on board."

"Pop's workin' on gettin' a crew together. What about your old man?"

"I'll talk to him." That sounded like Everett to the right of Alex, so Junior was on the left, but I wondered who they were watching.

"We set for tomorrow night?" Junior said.

"What time?"

"Nine," Alex said. "The Pattonburg place in the pits."

"Friggin' Hank runnin' his souped deuce?" Everett said.

"Takin' on all comers," Alex said.

"Galvin's bent eight really burns rubber," Junior said. "He might leave Hank in the dust."

Alex laughed. "Hell, I popped my rocket's friggin' clutch and left Galvin on the line. He ain't got a snowball's chance."

Glen chimed in. "Think you can take Hank?"

"My friggin' wheels are so hot, they'll leave the best patch."

A drag race somewhere in the strip pits. I knew Luke would be interested in this.

"Is the fix in?" Aaron said.

Alex chucked. "The heat ain't got a damned clue. We won't get rousted."

"Speaking of the man, there's that damned Martin kid been hangin' around the garage. Glen, you watch yourself around him. His keeper is heat."

"Yeah. He's damned square," Glen said.

"That brother of his and his pal. Interfered with our fun with Malcolm. Saw him up there a while ago but they ain't there now," Everett said.

"Those damned germs. I ain't finished with them," Alex said.

I looked at Bruce whose eyes widened. "He's talking about us," he whispered.

I nodded.

"There he is," Junior howled.

"Hey, Mal," Alex shouted. "Over here."

"He's so friggin' stupid, he's coming," Everett said.

"He's got smog in the noggin' for sure," Junior said.

"Say, Mal." Alex spoke soothingly as if he was talking to a three-year-old. "We wanted you to know the puppy was delicious."

"Yeah. We fried the mutt," Junior said.

"B . . . b . . . but Mike said you were teasing," Malcolm protested.

"That germ don't know nothin'," Everett said.

"I'll . . . I'll . . ." Malcolm stuttered.

"He's gonna go ape," Junior warned.

"Now don't get frosted, Mal," Alex said. "Mike was right. We're only funnin' ya."

"Not funny." Malcolm's voice quivered.

"Look, Mal." Alex stood and I was looking straight out at Malcolm. I ducked. "We want to be your friend, don't we guys?"

"Sure."

"We like you, Mal."

"Let me buy you a cone," Alex said. "Vanilla."

"Okay."

"We're tight, huh, Mal?" Alex put an arm over Malcolm's shoulders and led him away.

"What's he doing?" Everett said.

"No friggin' idea, but it'll give us a big tickle," Junior said.

"Slip me a weed," Arron said.

"Hey, Ev. Got any bread?" Glen said.

"Nah, I'm frail. Old man pays tomorrow."

"I got some nuggets," Junior said.

"I need to refuel. Slip me a thin one for a tube steak," Glen said. "Thanks, Junior."

With Glen's leaving, Bruce and I were becoming more and more exposed. We crawled back into the shadows.

"They talked about watching someone and getting a crew together," Bruce said. "Suppose they're planning to rob a bank?"

I hadn't thought of that. Kelvin Rogers, George Buckner, maybe Mr. Smithton plus those three bullies would make quite a gang. "Rob a bank? I don't know."

"Let's go rescue Malcolm."

"No. Alex won't do anything to him. Too many people around."

"What about the drag race?"

"Luke will be interested in that," I said.

Bruce pointed. "Alex is back. Let's see what happened."

We crawled back to our former positions.

"You what?" Everett said.

"Bought him a cone," Alex said.

"What for?" Junior said.

"We may need him later."

"That retard?" Everett said.

"He believes what he's told. We might be able to use him," Alex explained.

"Hey, baby," Everett said. "Let's play back seat bingo."

"Get lost," a girl's voice answered.

"That queen's a friggin' paper shaker. She's jacketed to that guy on first," Junior said.

"Don't friggin' care. She razzes my berries. I'm goin' over there."

"You're cruisin' for a brusin', buddy."

Everett left and we moved back a bit.

"I got me some damned rubbers," Alex said. "Gotta find me a friggin' date."

"What about that Delores you took to the movie last Saturday?" Junior said.

"She's got a classy chassis, but the movie was nowhere and I got shot down."

Bruce punched my arm and crawled back, his hand over his face. Wondering what was wrong, I followed. He ran to the end of the bleachers and sneezed twice.

"Sorry," he said. "I knew I couldn't hold it."

"I was getting bored, anyway."

"We've got to watch those guys. They'll get Malcolm in trouble."

"I know." I cleared my throat. "Say, Bruce. When Pete and I were in the five and dime, you know, Alex tried to buy rubbers for a date. I know they can't be wading boots, but what are they?"

"Rob explained them to me," Bruce said. "They're these coverings to put over your thing when you have sex so the girl doesn't get pregnant."

"Oh." I knew Bruce wouldn't laugh at my ignorance. "We haven't learned about sex, yet."

"I know all about sex. Watched the bull with a cow."

"What happened?"

Bruce learned close and lowered his voice. "Well, first he sniffed her. Her behind, you know. Then his thing . . . Rob says to call your thing a penis . . . it got real long. Almost dragged the ground."

"No kidding?" I didn't imagine Bruce would steer me wrong.

"Then he reared up and put his front hooves onto her back. His penis went inside her and he pumped a couple of times." Bruce chuckled. "It was kind of funny."

I couldn't picture it. "Sounds weird."

"Then his penis dripped stuff when he was finished."

"Is that what people do?"

Bruce nodded. "Something like that, I guess. But they do it in bed."

I knew Mom and Luke wouldn't do anything like that and I vowed I wouldn't either. I knew what girls looked like down there. Joy Gladding showed me hers and it looked funny. I didn't see what the big deal was. I wished I had a big brother like Rob to tell me things. Dan never told me anything about sex. Maybe he didn't know.

"I've seen dogs do it, too," Bruce said. "I guess all animals do it. That's how they have babies."

I lost interest in the subject. "Let's watch the game."

Luke lounged in the porch swing enjoying his celebratory drink and nightly cigar. The Glendale Bombers won the game with a walk-off single in the bottom of the ninth. "Tomorrow night," he said.

I nodded. "The Pattonburg place in the pits."

"This was Junior Rogers, Alex Buckner and Everett Smithton?"

"Yeah. Glen Smithton and Aaron Farmer were there, too, but they didn't say much."

"And you just happened to overhear this conversation?" Luke's eyes bored into mine.

"Not exactly." I couldn't see how to extricate myself.

"Tell me exactly."

"It all goes back to last Saturday and Malcolm Carroll." I explained how the men were teasing Malcolm and what Bruce and I did to rescue him.

Luke grinned at me. "Pretty good idea."

"So when we saw them at the game, we got under the bleachers to hear them talk."

Luke chuckled and shook his head. "Kids and their games."

"And they told Glen to watch what he said around Dan 'cause you're a cop."

"Anything else?"

"Well, they've decided to be friendly to Malcolm so they can use him sometime."

Luke frowned. "What for?"

"I don't know. Alex just said Malcolm might come in handy because he believes what you tell him."

Luke puffed on his cigar. "I don't like the sound of that."

"And they're watching somebody, and Mr. Buckner and Mr. Rogers are getting a crew together. Bruce said they're planning to rob a bank."

Luke chuckled. "I doubt that. Could be a pit crew, I suppose. I'll tell the county about the drag race. Don't want anyone getting hurt. Including you, son." Luke ruffled my hair. "If they'd caught you, no telling what they might've done. I don't think they're dangerous, but you never know. Now you run along to bed."

EIGHT

Flames lit the entire street making it easy to identify the volunteer firemen. Anton Paternik manned the water gun on the roaring pumper truck sitting in the middle of the highway, aiming a stream of water at the base of the fire. From the hydrant at the south end of the block, Porter Harmon and Darren Matlock wrestled with the hose snaking through the farm equipment. With a large wrench, Vinny Valetti turned the nut at the top of the hydrant to open the water flow. Fire engulfed Markmann's International Harvester dealership only half a block off the square.

The shrilling town whistle vaulted me from bed even before the phone clamored. By the time Luke returned from downstairs, even Mom was dressed and ready to go.

When we learned of the location, we knew the town faced a serious threat as the fire could spread to businesses around the square. Luke roared off down the street, siren wailing. Mom drove to Grandma Jenkins house to park, and we walked the two blocks to the Methodist Church's parking lot.

Highway K9 bisected Glendale from north to south and included the square's west side. The fire blazed in the middle of the block just south of the square. An alley backed Saulk's Appliance which faced the square. Markmann's dealership sat next to the alley and had a large lot beside it on the corner full of farming equipment.

Across the street from Saulk's Appliance, Kern's Grocery, a two-story brick building with the Chamber of Commerce upstairs, faced the square. Tony's Market came next beside the church's parking lot. The church itself faced the dealership's display of farm equipment across the street. Luke's car blocked traffic south of the church and another patrol car did the same at the north end of the block.

Here the firemen worked in a much more confined space than they had at Valetti's Mill, and the crowd, much closer to the fire, felt the heat of the inferno. Flames threatened only the Co-op office near Valetti's, but now sparks flew over businesses on the square's south side including the two-story Saulk's Department Store across the alley from the repair shop. Street lights illuminated the scene, while at the mill fire, the firemen were only black figures against the flames. Mom and I joined a group of neighbors.

"Bet it started in the shop," Mr. Gladding said.

"Markmann repaired my tractor," Mr. Herrick said. "His shop was spotless."

"Still. Lots of oil and gasoline around. Only takes a bit of carelessness. I should know." Gene Gladding owned an auto repair business.

"Grain dust. Only takes a spark. Oil and gas. Just another spark?" Mr. Herrick snorted. "Carelessness must be contagious."

From where we stood in the church's parking lot, the fire roared directly across the street with black smoke rising above the flames and the acrid stench of burning rubber surrounding us. People packed the church's lawn and sat in its front arches. Others lined the sidewalk in front of Tony's Market and the grocery.

"Hey, Mike." Pete elbowed through the crowd to my side. "Saw you and Bruce at the game."

"Yeah, and I've got something to tell you."

A dull explosion within the fire reverberated off the close buildings.

"Gas tank," Bob Valetti said.

"Say, Bob, how'd you come out on your insurance?" Mr. Parkinson said.

"It won't cover everything, but I've enough to build smaller. Old place was too big, anyway."

"Hope Windy has good coverage," Mrs. Gladding said.

"Wonder whose equipment was in for repair," Mom said.

Mrs. Gladding snorted. "Well, they just kissed it goodbye."

"Vinny fighting the fire?" Mr. Parkinson asked Bob Valetti.

"Somewhere. I lost track of him."

"He played a good game tonight. Drove in that winning run."

"Isn't that Windy?" Mr. Gladding pointed across the street. "What's he doing?"

"Trying to get equipment away from the fire," Bob Valetti said. "Let's go help him."

The three men sprinted across the street to the lot holding farm implements. Others soon joined them including Everett Smithton and Junior Rogers. I searched the crowd for Alex Buckner without success. One man lifted the tongue of a cultivator and the other men pushed it out into the side street. Soon the street was littered with cultivators and harrows and plows. A large hay baler required two men at the tongue and four men to push, but it, too, landed in the street.

"Look down beyond the shop." Mom pointed. "That must be the Pattonburg Department."

Another stream of water soared skyward to fall onto the flames.

"Looks like an ambulance over there." I pointed beyond the equipment parking lot.

"It's usual to have one at a fire," Mrs. Parkinson said, "in case there's an emergency."

"They've set up another hose in the alley, too," Mrs. Valetti said. "I wonder where Vinny is."

The pumper truck withdrew, its tanks spent, and another firetruck stopped at the north end of the street.

"That's the Harrington truck," Mrs. Gladding said.

"Most of those men played in the game earlier," Mom said. "They've got to be tired, but here they are helping their rivals."

The Harrington crew unrolled a hose and attached it to the hydrant near Kern's Grocery. One man tried to open the hydrant but couldn't get the mechanism to turn. Another joined him and between the two of them, water finally filled the hose. Now four hoses gushed water onto the fire.

"The men are having trouble moving equipment," Mrs. Parkinson said.

"The fire hose is in their way." I watched Bob Valetti climb onto the tractor nearest the fire.

"He can't start it," Mrs. Gladding said. "Key's probably in the office and only a lump by now."

Four men lined up behind the tractor and pushed it into the street in front of the church. The crowd cheered. One of the firemen intercepted Bob Valetti and pointed to the rear of the repair shop. Bob ran in that direction.

"Where's he going?" Mrs. Valetti's voice rose. "Where's Vinny?"

"Now, Lavon." Mrs. Parkinson put her hand on Mrs. Valetti's arm. "I'm sure he's alright."

"I haven't seen him for ages." Mrs. Valetti shook off Mrs. Parkinson's hand. "I've got to go see."

Mom took Lavon's arm. "You can't do anything. You'd only be in the way."

Several minutes later, I recognized the shriek of the local ambulance as it left the scene.

Mr. Gladding gasped. "Someone's on the way to the hospital."

"Is it Vinny?" Mrs. Valetti's voice cracked.

"I don't know, dear, but I see Bob across the street."

Bob Valetti darted across the street to his wife. "They're taking him to Pattonburg. We've got to go." He took her hand and the two pushed through the crowd.

"What happened?" Mrs. Gladding called after them, but they disappeared from view.

Under attack from four sides, the fire slowly admitted defeat while the spectators buzzed with speculation about Vinny Valetti's injuries. Soon only the building's skeleton stood over the blackened ruins while the firemen concentrated their aim on flare-ups. The Harrington crew turned off the hydrant, unhooked their hose and rolled it up to store. They disbanded to converse with their counterparts.

I observed Luke consulting with Leroy Beach, head of the volunteers and owner of the movie theater on the square. One of Pattonburg's squads abandoned the conflict and packed up to leave. Windy Markmann wandered around, hand on his forehead, surveying the destruction. With the excitement over, the onlookers drifted away to return to their beds.

"Might as well stay up," Mrs. Parkinson said. "Got to be at work in an hour. Probably have some of these hungry men in for breakfast at the café."

Pete returned to my side. I hadn't noticed his departure. "Where've you been?"

"Around the other side. The Pattonburg guys had their hose up the alley beside the creamery, so I sat on the creamery's dock to watch. Saw them work on Vinny."

"You shouldn't run off like that," Mrs. Parkinson scolded. "I had no idea where you were."

It seemed to me that she hadn't worried about Pete's disappearance. Both parents worked during the day leaving Pete alone to do as he wished, and he took advantage of their lack of supervision.

"You wanted to tell me something," Pete said.

"Not here." I looked around to see who might've heard. "I'll be over later."

The Parkinsons departed but Mom still stood looking across the street like she waited for something.

"Where's Dan?" I thought that might be why she remained.

"With Dean at the parsonage." Rev. Norris lived behind the church.

Then Luke separated from the group of men and walked slowly across the street to us. "I'll probably be home for breakfast," he said. "Once we get this tractor off the highway, we can open the road for Saturday traffic. Beach's men will stay to monitor the situation, but all that equipment on the side street needs to be moved back."

"There's no hurry," Mom said. "Just block off that street for the time being."

Luke ran his fingers through his hair. "This would happen on a Saturday morning. It's hectic enough patrolling the streets without a tourist attraction like this."

"I've been waiting," Mom said. "About Vinny."

"Critical condition." Luke shook his head. "He ran into the shop for some reason. Beam fell on him. He was lucky two other guys saw it happen and got him out of there."

"Injuries?"

"He's probably got a concussion though he regained consciousness before the ambulance left. He's got a compound leg fracture and some burns, too. I'm glad the ambulance was here. He got immediate attention."

"What started the fire," I said.

"Don't know. They'll investigate."

Mom let me sleep late. When I stumbled downstairs, she focused her attention on a magazine with pictures of Queen Elizabeth's coronation enabling me to escape after a quick snack. I biked to Pete's house with Duke loping along beside me and told him about overhearing the conversation at the ballpark, and he whined around a bit about my revealing our secret to Bruce. We set out for the square, pausing to inspect the ruins of Markmann's dealership along with disheartened farmers in town for Saturday shopping.

We left our bikes at the Methodist church and joined the throngs on the square in search of Bruce. As he missed the excitement of the fire, Bruce wished to see the destruction firsthand, so we returned to the roped off debris. Windy Markmann and one of his employees busied themselves moving farm equipment from the side street back onto the lot.

"How'd he get that tractor started?" I wondered.

"Probably hotwired it." Bruce pointed to two men who wandered through the debris taking pictures and making notes in a book. "Who are those guys?"

"Insurance men?" Pete said.

"Could be fire investigators," I suggested.

"Let's find some shade." Pete pointed to the lawn of the Reynolds Community Home across the street from the church.

"Okay." Bruce led the way. "I saw Mr. Hrabrosky on the square this afternoon."

"He's back from the convention." Pete sprawled on the grass. "Bet he's got some new commie lies to print in his *Little Red Books*."

"Where was he? What was he doing?" Duke and I joined Pete on the grass.

"He came out of the movie theater with Leroy Beach. Stood on the sidewalk and talked for a while."

"About what?" Pete asked.

"Couldn't hear."

"So Beach is a commie, too?" Pete's eyebrows rose.

"He did show that movie *High Noon*," I said. "Mom read that it was anti-American. Had a communist writer."

"That makes three. Hrabrosky, Paternik and Beach." Pete counted them off on his fingers.

I shook my head. "I don't think Mr. Paternik is a communist."

Pete leaned toward me. "He speaks with an accent. He thinks Mr. Hrabrosky is a swell guy."

"Doesn't prove anything," I said. "He sponsors the town team and his son Anton plays outfield. Mr. Beach plays, too, and he's the volunteer fire chief."

"Exactly." Pete nodded. "That's what communists do. They get into our hallowed institutions."

Bruce and I laughed.

"Hallowed institutions?" Bruce said. "Where'd you get that?"

"From the radio. Some guy talking about the communist threat. They're sneaky. Likely to be leaders of the community, he said."

"They must meet secretly at night," Bruce said.

I shrugged. "I can't be out after dark."

"Me neither." Pete sighed. "We can't follow Hrabrosky in his car. So what do we do?"

"Why not just watch him on the square? See who he talks to and such," Bruce suggested.

"Yeah." I nodded. "That way we can keep an eye on Malcolm, too. Keep him away from those bullies."

"What's Luke doing about the drag race?" Bruce asked.

"He said he'll tell the county guys as it's out of his jurisdiction. I hope he remembers."

NINE

That long-ago season, the weeks passed with summer sameness as even vacation established a routine. Monday and Wednesday I biked to the pool in mid-morning for swim lessons. After reviewing the Australian crawl, I learned the back stroke and the butterfly. Dan advanced to the lifesaving class as being a lifeguard was part of his duties as a cabin leader at church camp. Tuesdays I biked to Mrs. Evan's house for my piano lesson and Thursday I played baseball at the city park. Mom commandeered Dan and me on Fridays to pick first strawberries then cherries and finally peas and carrots at the Horlacher farm, all of which she packaged to freeze and put in our locker at Louie's.

Each afternoon, Pete and I haunted the square and noted Mr. Hrabosky's chats with Mr. DeCarlo at Tony's Market, the Mayor Mr. Kennedy, Windy Markmann, Mr. Simmons at the hardware store and Mr. Wayford at the five and dime. We suspected more and more people belonged to the communist cell in our town.

We could spot Mr. Hrabosky easily. He invariably wore a suit and hat even on the hottest days. From hips to shoulders, he was a stout oblong. He had a square, ruddy face with a narrow mouth, a prominent nose, and dark piercing eyes. Of average height, he leaned forward and strode purposefully down the street. Mr. Rogers said Hrabosky was a foreigner, but he sounded American when he spoke as he had no accent. We noticed Mr. Hrabosky entering Wayford Variety Store carrying a package one afternoon and decided to follow him.

Mr. Wayford came down from the office. "Hello, Emile."

"Leonard." The men shook hands.

"You didn't need to make the delivery yourself."

"I wanted to see you," Mr. Hrabosky said. "You still keep these under the counter?"

"Have to. Otherwise they'd disappear. Customers know to ask for them."

Pete and I fingered through the shoelaces in brown, black and white.

"I have a special this month. A follow-up on our government crime fighters. Now I have experience." Mr. Hrabosky chuckled.

"You're courting trouble, Emile. I wish you wouldn't call attention to yourself."

"Someone has to stop him. He's gaining power. Controlling congressmen. Influencing legislation."

"Maybe. But, Emile, he can investigate and threaten you."

"I know he's a bully. But I break no laws. They haven't questioned you yet. They might this time."

"I have nothing to tell them. I break no laws, either. I can think anyway I want."

"I wanted you to be forewarned. They can be quite intimidating. See you Saturday evening?"

"I'll be there."

"Good. And Leonard, you take care."

Mr. Wayford spotted us. "Can I help you boys?"

"I think brown," I said, "but I'm not sure of the length."

"For your sneakers?"

"Oh, no. For my dress shoes at home."

"I suggest you measure first and then come back."

"Sure, Mr. Wayford. Thank you."

We left the store in time to see Mr. Hrabosky's blue Buick turn south.

"That's not the way to the office," Pete said.

"Let's follow."

Two blocks later, we discovered the car in front of Tony's Market.

"We can't go in," I said.

"Over there." Pete pointed to what was left of the International Harvester dealership.

Several men and a bulldozer worked at tossing debris into a large dumpster. The lot originally covered with farm implements sat empty. We watched the men work from the Methodist Church's parking lot.

"I think he delivered some *Little Red Books* to Mr. Wayford," Pete said.

"Uh huh. Must've written about J. Edgar Hoover again."

"And there's a meeting tonight. Wish we could find out about that."

Mr. Hrabosky left the market carrying an empty box.

"He left more of those books for Mr. DeCarlo to sell."

"There's a whole nest of commies in this town," Pete said, "and we can't do anything about it."

Besides tailing Mr. Hrabosky, Pete and I kept watch over Malcolm, but we didn't see Alex Buckner and his buddies in town. They seemed to be lying low since the county sheriff broke up their drag race. They attended the Bombers games but ignored Malcolm. Having escaped without being detected under the bleachers, Bruce and I decided the risk was too great to attempt eavesdropping again, but Pete and I overheard town gossip in our efforts to keep Malcolm safe. We learned that Mrs. Beach was expecting, that the Saulks were traveling to Paris and that Coach James's oldest son got a ticket for drunk driving.

"He drinks too much," Mr. Paternik told Mr. Simmons.

Pete and I were shopping for a bell for my bike at the hardware to keep an eye on Malcolm who mopped the floor.

"I'm sure Clyde James will deal with that."

"He's a good man," Mr. Paternik said. "You know Vinny told my Anton he went into the fire to rescue someone."

"I heard that, too," Mr. Simmons said. "Thought it looked like Windy Markmann."

"But Windy, he says no."

"If he was there, how'd he get out?"

"Vinny. He's certain," Mr. Paternik said. "Not seeing ghosts."

"Poor Vinny. Pins in his leg. Hobbling around on crutches. He won't be playing more ball this summer."

"Might not next summer, either. Still will have operations for his burns."

"My wife heard at bridge that Windy was in financial trouble before the fire," Mr. Simmons said.

"No. I've not heard that."

"Borrowed to expand. Couldn't make the payments."

"So sent all the equipment back?"

"That's what she heard. Still owes interest on the loan. Some people think he set the fire to collect the insurance."

"But was electrical fire," Mr. Paternik said.

"That's what the investigators say but people still talk."

One Thursday, Clark Davenport brought his cousin Beau to the park to play ball with us.

Beau pointed at Charlie Whitley and said, "We don't play with niggers."

A stunned silence followed.

"Charlie's one of our best players," Gary Kennedy said.

"Guess you haven't heard about Jackie Robinson," I said. "If it's good enough for the Dodgers, it's good enough for us."

"Where you from, anyway?" Pete said.

"Goose Creek, South Carolina."

Everyone laughed and hooted.

Bruce stepped forward. "That explains a lot."

Beau's face flushed and he stuck out his jaw. "What do you mean?"

Bruce jabbed Beau in the chest with his index finger. "You come from a backward small town full of rednecks."

Beau pushed Bruce back. "Don't neither."

"Do, too." Bruce shoved Beau as members of the team encircled the two expecting a fight.

"Take that back." Beau clenched his fists.

"Won't."

Beau threw a haymaker that missed badly and he fell onto the grass.

Hands on his hips, Bruce said, "Can't fight, neither."

Beau scrambled to his feet and charged, catching Bruce around the waist and throwing him to the ground. The team circled the combatants, shouting encouragement as first one and then the other seemed to be winning. Finally, Bruce had Beau's body in a scissor hold with a choke hold around his neck.

"Say uncle," Bruce demanded.

Beau struggled to extricate himself. "Won't."

Bruce tightened his choke hold as Beau fought to pull Bruce's arm away.

"Say it."

Beau's lower lip trembled and he whispered, "Uncle."

"I can't hear you," Bruce said. "Louder."

"Uncle," Beau shouted.

Bruce released his holds.

Beau got to his feet and brushed off his clothing. "Still ain't playin' with no nigger."

"Nobody asked you to play," Pete said.

Beau waved to his cousin. "Come on, Clark," he said. "Let's go."

Clark shook his head. "You go. I'm playing ball with my friends."

"I'm gonna tell my dad."

"Go ahead. See if I care."

Beau turned his back and walked away.

"Will you get in trouble?" Gary said.

Clark shrugged. "Maybe, but it's worth it."

After the game, I pedaled to Grandma Jenkins's house to deliver a blouse Mom repaired for her. I liked Grandma's house with it screened-in front porch shaded by huge catalpa trees along the street. I lounged in the porch swing with a book whenever I had time.

The two-story edifice had a leaded glass window in the front door, pocket doors to close off rooms and crown molding in the dining and living rooms. The house was so old that the kitchen floor slanted to the north. A cistern sat in back and a carriage house containing a buggy hugged the alley. A huge room upstairs held trunks packed with old-fashioned clothes that Mom often altered for us to wear as Halloween costumes.

On Wednesdays, I walked from school to Grandma Jenkins's house for lunch as our school had no cafeteria. Town kids went home for lunch while the country kids ate their sack lunches at school. Grandma Jenkins didn't talk down to me. We talked science, history and books. She read *Huckleberry Finn* when I did so we could discuss the book. I could ask her questions knowing she'd give me a straight answer, but I found out something surprising about Grandma on Memorial Day. While visiting relatives' graves, I asked where Grandpa Jenkins was buried.

"Why, he isn't dead," Mom said.

"He isn't?" I found this astonishing. "Then where is he?"

"He lives in Baldwin City with his wife."

"But Grandma Jenkins is . . ."

"This happened long ago," Mom said. "I was about your age. Evan five years older. Dad had an affair with a woman working at the courthouse. When she became pregnant, he emptied the bank account and left town with her."

"What did Grandma do?" Dan asked.

"Divorced him. It was quite a scandal. The town's sympathies lay with my mother. She got the house and the business."

"She owns a business?" I said.

"Not any more. She sold it. You know Saulk's Appliance?"

"Sure."

"It used to be Jenkins Appliance."

"Holy Toledo."

"What's Grandpa's name?" Dan asked.

"Elmer. Elmer Jenkins. I haven't seen or heard from him in over twenty-five years."

I couldn't imagine how I'd feel if Luke did something like that and I never saw him again.

"Then Grandma has money?" Dan said.

"She's made some shrewd investments. Owns some property."

"But I thought she supported herself by selling Avon," Dan said.

Mom chuckled. "She needs something to do. It keeps her busy and she gets to visit with people."

All my life I'd felt sorry for Grandma Jenkins as a poor widow who supported herself on the paltry earnings from Avon sales. I no longer worried about taking food out of her mouth when she offered to make me lunch.

Mom called during lunch asking me to get some hamburger at Louie's on my way home. I dropped by the library first to check out two Zane Grey books. Louie's Zero Locker was next door. Like many people, we didn't own a freezer but rented space at Louie's. A lady I recognized as Windy Markmann's wife talked to Louie's wife at the counter.

"I know it's that Vinny Valetti and Anton Paternik." Mrs. Markmann clutched the edge of the counter, her knuckles white. "We've lost everything and now these vicious lies."

"Everyone knows it was an electrical fire. It was in the newspaper. And you'll get back on your feet."

"Yes, we will." Mrs. Markmann pulled keys from her purse. "Emile Hrabosky has proved himself a true friend, not like some other people."

"Now, Louise, you have many friends willing to help."

"But it's Emile who acts on his beliefs while our good Christian friends sit on their hands and talk behind our backs." Mrs. Markmann sighed. "Listen to me going on. I'm sorry. I shouldn't have sounded off on you like that. I'm just blowing off steam."

"It helps to do that at times."

Mrs. Markmann picked up a package from the counter. "Now look what I've done."

"Just a little puddle from the meat. Happens all the time." Louie's wife wiped the countertop. "And you have a good afternoon, Louise."

The door closed behind Mrs. Markmann and Louie's wife looked down at me. "Your mother called to say you'd be by without a key."

"Yes, ma'am."

"Do you know your number?"

"Two hundred twenty."

"Second row near the end." She took a jacket from a hook and put it on. "You have a jacket?"

"No, ma'am."

"We'll hurry then." She took a key from a drawer. "Come on."

Inside the freezer I could see my breath and goosebumps rose on my bare arms and legs. She quickly led me to our locker and opened it for me. There among the frozen packages of beef were the results of our labor at Horlacher's farm, but urged by the frigid temperature, I ignored the packages of fruit and vegetables to lift one of hamburger.

We quickly retreated to the warmth of the office. I set off for home with my bike's basket full of hamburger, books and my ball glove and my mind full of questions about Emile Hrabosky.

TEN

"Where've you been?" Pete stood at our door.

"Picking cucumbers for Mom to make pickles."

"It's been uncovered. We've got to go."

A Corvette, Chevrolet's new sports car, hid under canvas as it was trucked into town. The truck sat in the alley behind the Glendale Motors dealership next to the post office just north of the square until after dark. Police cars blocked off the alley while men unloaded the car to display it on the showroom floor. Paper covered the front windows to prevent a glimpse of the long-anticipated fantastic new ride.

We made it to the square in record time to find a line stretching from the square to the dealership.

"They're only letting in six at a time," Mr. Herrick told me.

"And you only get five minutes," Mrs. Herrick added.

We joined the end of the line next to Leroy Beach, his wife, and their boy Sonny, a classmate of ours.

"They still have paper over the windows," Sonny said. "Can't see it 'til you get inside."

Mr. Saulk and his wife joined the line behind us. "Leroy, you going to be the one to buy it?"

"Don't believe it's a family car," Mr. Beach replied. "Besides, I'd have to mortgage my house."

"Only a few in town can afford it." Mr. Saulk lit a cigarette.

"Why'd he get one in, then?" Mrs. Beach asked.

Mr. Beach smiled at his wife. "Publicity, dear."

"I want to sit in it," Sonny said.

"What's going on?" someone shouted.

"Alex Buckner and Everett Smithton trying to crowd in," a man further down the line replied.

"Let them in," Mr. Beach said. "Don't want them back here causing trouble for the next half hour."

I jumped and strained but couldn't see what was happening. People at the front of the line started to shout.

"Don't push me!" someone yelled.

"They've gone inside," another said.

"Listen. They're honking the horn."

Someone laid on the horn and didn't let up.

"Wish we could see what they're doing." Mr. Saulk puffed on his cigarette.

Suddenly, the horn fell silent and a series of thumps followed.

"What's that banging noise?" Mrs. Beach clutched her husband's arm.

"Don't know. Slamming doors?"

"Could be the hood or the trunk," Mr. Saulk said.

"Can't anyone do something?" Mrs. Beach said.

Pete pointed to the corner. "Here comes Luke."

I stepped to the curb to see past the crowd. Lights flashing, Luke's car roared around the corner and abruptly stopped in front of the dealership. Luke stepped from the car and left it running in the middle of the street. He marched to the door and disappeared inside.

"He'll get them straightened out." Mr. Saulk flipped his cigarette into the street.

"Wish they'd take down that paper so we could see what's happening," Mrs. Beach said.

"George Buckner needs to have a talk with his son." Mr. Beach removed his hat and wiped his forehead with a handkerchief.

"George isn't much of a role model," Mr. Saulk commented.

Alex Buckner and Everett Smithton exited the dealership and swaggered off down the street laughing. Luke followed.

"You let them go?" someone said.

Luke nodded. "Mr. Turnbow doesn't want to press charges. No damage done."

"A crowd in town tomorrow," a man said. "Better have someone here for the day."

"Good idea." Luke laughed. "Here I was inside and I didn't even look at the car."

"Well, go on back in," a lady said. "We'll wait."

The red Corvette was worth the long wait. Dan was crazy about hotrods, but I'd take a Corvette over a hotrod any day of the week.

The Bombers played the Pattonburg Miners that evening, the toughest of the four Pattonburg teams. With Kirkpatrick on the mound for the Bombers, I feared we had little chance of a win. Luke chose to stay in town, so Mom and I drove out to the Horlacher farm and rode to the game with them. Dan begged to ride with Glen Smithton and Mom give in to his entreaties. When Glen Smithton showed up with Aaron Farmer but no Dan, Mom sent me over to ask Glen about Dan. Bruce went with me for moral support as Alex Buckner, Everett Smithton and Junior Rogers sat in front of Glen.

"It's the germs I was talkin' about." Alex whooped. "You lookin' for that retard? Malcolm ain't here."

"I just wanted to ask Glen about—"

"You can't talk to Glen. Right, Ev?"

"That's right." Everett elbowed Alex. "Glen is unavailable for comment."

"Come here, kid." Alex grabbed me around the neck, bent me over and gave me a noogie. It didn't hurt anything but my pride.

"Scoot over, Ev. Make room for the friggin' little punk."

Alex sat me down beside him. When I looked up, Bruce sat on the other side of Alex with Junior Rogers's arm around his neck.

"I'm glad you joined us." Alex smirked at me. "We need to be friends, you see. Like me and the boys are tight with Malcolm now."

"Your brother's our friend," Everett said.

"He's just a bit frosted right now." Alex laughed. "Can't take teasing. But you, you got spunk."

Junior snickered. "Spunk like a skunk."

"Your old man rousted us this afternoon," Everett said.

"Interfered with our fun." Alex tightened his grip around me so that I leaned into his chest. "Just like you and your friggin' little pal did on the square when we was teasing Mal."

"Runs in the damned family," Junior said.

"We ain't hurtin' nobody." Alex turned me loose. "We ain't hurtin' you or Mal or that friggin' car."

"Bruce. Mike," Ed Horlacher barked. "Come with me."

A hand on our shoulders, Ed led us away.

"We're not finished," Alex called after us.

"I want you boys to avoid that group."

"Mom wanted me to ask Glen about Dan," I explained.

"Then she made a mistake. She should've done it herself. They wouldn't have harassed her."

Ed left us to find our seats and returned to the dugout. He played outfield in the game in place of Vinny Valetti.

On Saturday, the lines were even longer to see the Corvette as so many people came to town, but a cop at the door prevented any serious incidents. Dan avoided the Smithtons and hung out with Dean Norris. Bruce and I crept around the square fearing Alex Buckner would jump out at us from any doorway, but our fears were unfounded. We all went to the movie *Peter Pan* that night, and it spawned a week's worth of swordfights.

Sunday afternoon, Pete and I lounged on the front porch with Duke listening to the Cardinals play the Dodgers. We turned up the volume on the cabinet radio in the living room and sat in the old Adirondack chairs each with a glass of lemonade. Vinegar Bend Mizell pitched for the Cards and Pete said he'd have to be good with a name like that. Stan Musial led off with a double in the second inning when Dan burst out the door.

Dan covered his ears. "Do you have to have that so loud?"

"We can barely hear it," I said.

"Go in the house, then."

"It's too hot."

"Just a minute." Dan slammed back into the house.

"What's he doing?" Pete asked.

I shrugged. "Don't know."

Dan soon returned with his radio. "This'll be better." He plugged it into the outlet on the house that we use for Christmas lights. "I'll turn the other one off."

After that, we often used Dan's radio on the porch not only to listen to baseball but to *Perry Mason*, *The Inner Sanctum*, *Sky King* and *Father Knows Best*. I had yet to use Dan's new glove.

July ushered in summer humidity which made the swimming pool a popular place. Mom and Luke spent evenings on the shaded front porch listening to the radio, talking to neighbors, and watching me and the neighborhood kids play until darkness settled over the block.

The required shower refreshed me before the torture of the bed. Nightly, we suffered in misery, tossing and turning on our sweat-soaked sheets. Mom and Luke placed a box fan in their bedroom's east window to draw in the cooler night air. On the west side of the house, our bedroom baked, and the little oscillating fan we were allotted pushed the hot air around and little else.

Under a clear blue sky, heat radiated from the pavement during the July Fourth parade. No breeze stirred the American flag carried by the mayor dressed as a minuteman and accompanied by a drummer and a fife player. Lady Liberty on her float wilted and insisted on fanning herself rather than holding high the beacon of freedom.

The high school band marched in shorts and T-shirts and women in sundresses and hats and men in shirts and ties watched the parade from the shade of the oaks on the courthouse lawn. Even the group containing George and Alex Buckner, Kelvin and Junior Rogers and the Smithtons seemed subdued, but to my dismay, Malcolm Carroll watched the spectacle with them.

The town invited everyone to picnic in the park and offered free admittance to the pool. After changing clothes and gathering our supplies, we lunched with our neighbors, Grandma Jenkins, Aunt and Uncle Jenkins and Ricky in the park. We spent a dull hour waiting so we wouldn't get cramps and drown before Mom allowed us to enjoy a swim while the others stretched out on blankets to talk and rest.

A bunch of us boys were involved in a furious cannonball contest when shouting erupted in the pool house. Pete, Gary and I interrupted our game to investigate. The pool manager, a college kid home for the summer, faced Alex Buckner, Everett Smithton and Junior Rogers.

"I'll say it again," the manager stated. "You can't come in."

"The hell I can't. Open the damned gate," Alex shouted. "It's a friggin' public pool. I ain't gonna let some officious little prick tell me what I can do."

"You're over eighteen." The manager attempted to swing the counter door closed.

Alex pushed the door back. "It's free to the public."

"Eighteen and under only. I went to school with you. I know how old you are."

"And I remember you, you nerdy little shit. I'll come over the damned counter and show you who's boss."

I looked around for help, but no adults were in the pool area. I couldn't go out the gate. I ran back to the pool. The eight-foot chain link fence surrounding the pool was often scaled by boys skinny dipping at night. If it could be climbed to get in, the opposite was possible. Though clinging to the chain with my bare toes hurt a bit, I made it over and ran down the hill to the park, calling for Luke who sat up.

"Come on," I panted. "It's Alex Buckner again."

Luke ran up the hill to the pool house with me close behind him.

"They saw you coming," the manager said.

"Any damage?"

"Sprung the hinges on the counter door but I can fix that." He turned to me. "Thanks, Mike."

After dinner, all the neighborhood kids assembled on the street with lit punks. Snakes crawled emitting black smoke. Rockets shot into the air. Tin cans with cherry bombs under them flew skyward. Firecrackers thrown at another's feet resulted in screams and laughter and a few altercations. Sparklers, fountains and Roman candles glowed after dark. Then parents began calling.

"Time to come in."

"A storm's coming. Better get home."

The dark cloud in the west had escaped my notice, but now lightning lit the block turning startled faces white. The booming thunder found fleeing children dashing for the shelter of home. Safe on the porch, Dan and I watched sheets of rain pound the neighborhood while Mom and Luke scurried to secure Dan's radio and close windows. Blowing through quickly, nature's fireworks overshadowed the puny efforts of man, but the hoped-for heat relief failed to materialize.

Luke pulled us from bed the next morning. "I've a job for you today."

Dan groaned. "It's my last day before church camp. I wanted to sleep in."

"I made a discovery when I went out for the newspaper."

"We'll clean up the street," I said thinking of the abandoned fountains, sparklers and debris left from our celebration.

"Someone else can do that," Luke said. "Our house was egged."

"Bet I know who did it," I said.

"I want it cleaned by lunchtime."

After breakfast, Dan and I faced the Herculean task of removing dried egg from the front of the house. Luckily, no one had aimed at the second story.

ELEVEN

We stood in front of the Presbyterian Church staring south to the Glendale Motors dealership as it went up in flames. The all-to-familiar scene played out. The pumper truck sat in the alley behind the building while Leroy Beach, Porter Harmon and Darren Matlock manned the hose at the building's front. Harold Turnbow, owner of the dealership, and his son Chevy, the Bomber's third baseman, arrived and ran to the service department door. Soon the overhead doors rose and two cars emerged.

"Nice of them to think of customers," Mr. Parkinson said.

"The Corvette." Pete's voice broke.

Flames and smoke obscured the red sports car.

"It's a goner." I pointed. "Look at Mr. Turnbow."

Harold and Chevy hurried to the car closest to the flames, tire iron in hand. With one quick swing, Harold broke the driver's window, opened the door and climbed in while Chevy pushed.

"He needs help." Mr. Murphy dashed across the street followed by Mr. Parkinson and Mr. Valetti. They pushed the car across the street into the empty telephone company parking lot. Others soon joined to help remove the new cars from the display lot.

The Pattonburg crew pulled in, siren wailing, and quickly hooked up another hose to the hydrant on the corner.

"This isn't right," Mrs. Murphy said.

Mrs. Parkinson puffed on her cigarette. "What do you mean? It's neighbor helping neighbor."

"I'm talking about the fire. We haven't had a fire in years. Now three in a little over three months?"

"Yeah." Mrs. Kennedy nodded. "What will they blame this one on? Lightning? I think they were set."

"But why would anyone be setting fires?" Mom asked.

"It's got to be someone from out of town," Mrs. Kennedy declared. "No one we know would do such a thing."

"Someone with a grudge against the whole town." Mrs. Parkinson drew on her cigarette.

"We need a full time fire department." Mrs. Beach joined the conversation. "No telling who's next."

"Something must be done," Mrs. Kennedy said.

"Well, get your husband in gear. As mayor he should get a move on." Mrs. Parkinson dropped her cigarette and crushed it with the toe of her shoe.

"I hope no one else gets hurt," Mom said.

Mrs. Parkinson pulled on Pete's arm. "Step back. Here comes the Harrington crew."

"They played a make-up game with the Pattonburg Miners tonight," Mrs. Murphy said.

"Poor men have got to be tired," Mom said.

Luke moved his patrol car to let the firetruck through. It stopped directly in front of us blocking our view.

Pete tugged on my arm. "Let's cross the street and work our way to the back."

I looked up at Mom. "Okay if I go?"

Mom nodded. "But keep out of the way."

We trotted north about thirty yards, crossed the street and cut between two houses to reach the alley. People crowded the mouth of the alley, so we elbowed through them and meandered left along a high lilac hedge. Five or six new cars sat across the street and a few men still moved among them pushing them out of the firemen's way.

"Look." Pete pointed.

A man raised a crowbar and smashed the rear window of a car.

"Hey!" I shouted without thinking.

The man turned in our direction. Pete jerked me back into the lilacs.

"That's Junior Rogers," Pete whispered. "I don't think he saw us."

We watched through the lilac branches.

"That's Everett Smithton with him," I whispered. "He's grabbed the crowbar."

"They're yelling at each other."

Junior attempted to get the crowbar back from Everett who refused. Junior punched Everett in the face. Everett threw down the crowbar and retaliated. The two men fell behind a car.

"Damn it!" Pete cursed softly.

The Harrington firetruck drove down our street to the alley behind the dealership to relieve the pumper truck, and we lost track of Junior and Everett. With four hoses aiming at the blaze, the firemen had the upper hand and the flames slowly died. Pete and I retraced our route back to the Presbyterian Church.

"An expensive car like that," Mr. Parkinson said, "hope he had it insured."

"It was a beautiful thing," Mr. Murphy said.

Sitting within the framework of the building, the skeleton of the red Corvette smoked.

"I wish Dan was here," I said.

"You have a piano lesson today." Mom took me by the shoulder. "Let's get you home and to bed."

The piano lesson didn't go well. The Fourth of July and seeing Dan off to camp interfered with my practice, and lack of sleep ruined my concentration. After lunch, Pete and I biked to Glendale Motors to inspect the ruins. Neatly arranged in rows, the new cars with their broken windows again sat in front of the undamaged service area. Two men used plastic sheeting and tape to cover the gaping holes where the windows had been. Sheeting covered the rear window of a black Buick.

"That's the one Junior broke," Pete said.

"There's Mr. Hrabrosky with Harold Turnbow." The two men stood in front of the blackened building watching two other men take pictures and make notes.

"Insurance guys," Pete said.

Mr. Turnbow shook hands with Mr. Hrabosky and they strolled toward the square.

Pete nodded toward them. "Where are they going?"

"Let's see."

We biked past the two men and stopped at the Rexall Drug. The men reached the corner and crossed to enter the bank.

Pete frowned and shook his head. “That’s strange.”

“Maybe one of them owes the other money.”

“Must be a lot to have to go to the bank.”

Pete went into the Rexall to get Cokes while Duke and I kept an eye on the bank for the two men to reappear. When they did, they shook hands again and parted. Mr. Turnbow walked back to his decimated dealership and Mr. Hrabosky headed east.

Pete looked at me with a raised eyebrow.

“Awfully hot to be riding around following him,” I said.

But it wasn’t necessary. The blue leviathan chugged to the corner, turned north for a block and then went east.

“Going to the office,” Pete said.

We abandoned the square to listen to the Cardinals’ game at Pete’s house.

“My dad says nothing’s better on a hot day than a nice cold beer.” Pete opened the refrigerator door and pulled out a bottle of Budweiser.

“Your dad lets you drink beer?”

“Now and then.” Pete opened the bottle.

I remembered that Pete claimed Mrs. Gladding let him climb her pear tree, so I doubted his word.

He must’ve seen the skeptical look on my face as he said, “He pours half a glass for me at supper sometimes. I’ll get you a glass.”

The Cards came to bat in the fifth inning leading two to one over Chicago. Enos Slaughter led off. Pete handed the glass to me and I absently took a sip. Holy Toledo! With effort, I kept my face neutral. What awful stuff! And people really drank it?

“We’re supporting the Cards by drinking Bud.” Pete tipped up his bottle and flopped into a chair.

By game’s end, I managed to finish my glass, but I still wondered how Anheuser-Busch could sell the stuff. I took the alley home and our neighbor Mrs. Gensill flagged me down.

“I’ve got to water my plants,” she said, “but I can’t get the hose onto the faucet.”

"I'll fix it. Don't worry." I immediately discovered the problem. The little rubber washer was stuck at an angle which prevented attaching the hose to the faucet. I put it back into place and attached the hose. "I can water for you," I said.

"No, but thank you, Mike. I like tending my flowers. You go on into the house. I baked cookies today. They're on the kitchen cabinet."

I noticed the questioning look on old Mrs. Gensill's face and wondered if she smelled the beer on my breath. The chocolate chip cookies were right where she said they would be and beside them rested a *Little Red Book*. Holy cow! Mrs. Gensill was a commie, too. I grabbed two cookies and biked home to brush my teeth and use mouthwash.

No one noticed me at dinner as Luke talked about the emergency city council meeting held that afternoon.

"Everyone questioned the findings of the previous fires." Luke took another helping of potato salad. "Bob swore grain dust couldn't have burned down the mill, and Windy declared his building had no electrical problem. Harold believes his fire was set. Merchants from around the square packed the room."

"Anyone have a solution?" Mom asked.

"Leroy Beach on the council wants me to increase police patrols at night."

Mom took another sliced tomato. "How can you do that?"

"Well, I requested overtime pay to finance twelve-hour shifts, but Crosby Kennedy said the town can't afford it. They've had to reimburse both Pattonburg and Harrington for fighting the fires."

"Why not use the contingency fund?"

Luke, his first hamburger gone, looked around for another. "That's what they've been using."

Mom passed the plate of hamburgers to Luke. "Then transfer funds from another service like street repair."

"Leonard Wayford suggested hiring guards, but the council rejected that even if the merchants paid for it themselves. Crosby felt it would be a liability problem."

"So they're doing nothing?" Mom rose and picked up her dinner plate.

"Earnest Simmons came up with the idea of the merchants themselves patrolling."

Mom chuckled and cut into the cherry pie. "I can just see that."

"I said it'd have to be coordinated through the police department. We got twelve volunteers. Now I have to make up a schedule. Problem is we've no way to communicate with each other."

"At night, just honking your horn would get attention."

"I'm afraid some of these volunteers like Ryan Saulk intend to be armed. I don't want some innocent resident shot."

"So the Saulk boys were there?"

"They occupy most of the south side. They've got a lot to lose."

Mom distributed slices of cherry pie. "But what about the fire department?"

"They set up a committee to report in two weeks not only on a yearly budget but the initial start-up costs for a permanent department. A new station, new equipment, salaries for full-time employees."

"Sounds like a lot of money." Mom waved her fork at Luke.

"And it would mean raising the mill levy. Would have to be voted on and you know how people feel about taxes."

"But this is important."

"All of it takes time. Even if taxes are raised, a station has to be built, equipment purchased, firemen hired. It may be two years down the road."

"Better get started then." Mom picked up her pie plate. "Anyone for more?"

"Maybe half a piece," Luke said. "Harold Turnbow has a mess. Can't sell cars until the windows are replaced and he gets new keys. He said someone busted out the back window on one of the Buicks."

"Junior Rogers." I blurted it out without thinking. I'd been listening to the conversation go back and forth, looking first left and then right as though I was watching a tennis match, but now I'd ruined the rhythm by calling attention to myself.

"Junior Rogers." Luke searched my face. "You saw Junior Rogers smash the window."

"Yes, sir."

"You and anyone else?"

"Pete Parkinson."

"Let's have the whole story."

"Well, Pete wanted to see the fire from the back. Mom said I could go."

Mom nodded. "That's right."

"So we crossed the street, went between two houses to the alley. Lots of people were there so we moved down the street along that lilac hedge."

"The one at Ziglar's house," Luke said.

"Um huh. Anyway, we saw Junior smash it with a crowbar. Then Everett Smithton took the crowbar away from him and they got into a fight. Then the Harrington firetruck blocked our view."

Luke rubbed his chin. "I'll need to speak to Pete."

"We don't want Junior knowing we saw him," I said.

Luke studied my face. "Ed told me about the incident at the ballpark. Maybe we can get an adult to verify this. Did you recognize any of the people in the alley?"

I scratched my head to think. "I remember Steve Saulk and that Brent guy from the auto parts store. Maybe Pete knows more."

And he did.

TWELVE

By the next evening, Luke found two other witnesses, so Pete and I were off the hook. Mr. Turnbow said he wouldn't press charges if Junior paid for the window and its installation. Luke said Everett's nose was swollen and he had a black eye. Junior looked better with only a bruised cheek. Junior said he couldn't pay as he didn't have a job and his dad refused to help him out. Luke considered arresting Junior but decided to see if something could be worked out. He took Junior to see Mr. Turnbow. A deal was made. Junior would work at Glendale Motors for a month to pay for the window.

Following our morning baseball game, Pete and I rode to Glendale Motors to see Junior work. He and several other men carted rubble to a big truck to be hauled to the city dump. The Corvette's skeleton had vanished.

"Must've taken it to the junk yard," Pete said.

"We won't have any trouble with Junior for a month. That leaves Alex and Everett."

"There goes Mr. Hrabosky." The blue behemoth sailed by creating a breeze.

We followed on our bikes. Mr. Hrabosky parked on the courthouse side of the street and walked across the street to the café.

"Lunch. Let's put our bikes in the shade and see who he meets," I said.

We left our bikes on the courthouse lawn and entered the café. Mr. Hrabosky sat in a booth with the guy who ran Roman's Market.

"Roman Barberini," Pete murmured.

We ordered Cokes to go, left the café, and again moved to the awning shade of Ziggy's Jewelry to wait for Mr. Hrabosky.

"Another commie," Pete said.

"They can't all be commies," I said. "Maybe Mr. Hrabosky just knows a lot of people."

"They wouldn't lunch with him unless they believed like he does."

I thought about that as I sipped my Coke. "That's not true. Look, Pete, my mom's family all loves Ike and they're glad he's president while dad's family thinks Ike will ruin the country. They still talk to each other, even share a meal now and then."

"It's not the same thing. That's just politics."

"There's Alex Buckner." I pointed across to the courthouse lawn.

"Our bikes!"

I held Pete back. "I'm not going over there."

About halfway across the lawn, Alex stopped and scanned the buildings on our side of the street.

"Did he see us?" Pete said.

"Don't think so."

Alex backtracked a bit and headed to the street.

"He's crossing," Pete said.

"No. He's stopped by Mr. Hrabosky's car."

"What's he doing?"

"I can't tell. He bent over. Picking up something, I guess."

Alex straightened, turned around and resumed his stroll across the courthouse lawn. He crossed the street and entered Meyer's Drug.

Pete pushed me. "Let's get our bikes."

We scrambled across the street.

"Look. Mr. Hrabosky has a flat tire."

Pete's eyes widened. "Alex did it."

"We should tell Mr. Hrabosky."

"Not me." Pete picked up his bike. "I don't want Alex Buckner after me."

"Yeah." I followed Pete. "I already have enough trouble with him."

"Let's see what happens."

We walked our bikes to the far side of the courthouse and waited for Mr. Hrabosky to appear. He exited the café with Roman Barberini and stood talking for a few minutes. The men shook hands. Mr. Hrabosky crossed the street to his car, stopped by the driver's door and scanned the square. He took off his suit coat and hat and put them into the car then opened the trunk and took out a jack. We watched him change the tire. He examined the flat, shook his head and put it into the trunk. After scanning the square again, he drove away.

"How do you suppose Alex did it," I said.

"Maybe a knife."

That night when Luke told Mom that someone slashed Mr. Hrabosky's tire, I kept my mouth shut.

The next morning, Mom and I picked tomatoes at Horlacher's farm. It took longer than usual without Dan to help. The whole week seemed strange with Dan at church camp. Alone in my room at night, I found sleep avoided me. Without Dan at meals, conversation lacked color and often bored me. The house felt empty, devoid of sound and action. I looked forward to his return that afternoon. I truly missed him when we returned home with a bushel of tomatoes because Mom recruited me to help her prepare them for canning.

"I'll start the water," Mom said. "Run upstairs and get Dan's radio."

When I got back, the pot of water had begun to boil.

"I'll give you the easy job." Mom handed me a big slotted spoon. "Put the tomatoes into the water like this. When the skin splits, take the tomato out and put it into this bowl."

I filled the bottom of the pot with tomatoes. Steam rose to the kitchen ceiling and soon sweat rolled down my forehead into my eyes. When the bowl was full, Mom took it and gave me another empty one. She sat at the table to skin and core the tomatoes.

I wiped my forehead with a dish towel. "What are you going to make?"

"Stewed tomatoes, some spaghetti sauce, chili sauce. Keep those tomatoes coming." She put another big pot onto the stove, filled it with Mason jars and water and lit the flame under it.

An angry man's voice blared from the radio and was answered by a softer, hesitant one.

"That was . . . well . . . it was years ago."

"But you admit you were once a member of the Communist Party."

"I wasn't a member. I . . . well . . . I went to a few meetings . . . just to see . . . you know . . . to see what it was all about."

"And who invited you to these meetings?"

"I don't remember."

"I'll remind you that you are under—"

Mom changed the station.

"Is that the senator?" I said. "You know, the one after communists?"

"McCarthy." Tomato juice covered Mom's hands.

"Who was the other guy?"

"I don't know."

"Do we have communists here in Glendale?"

Mom chuckled. "I don't think so."

"Pete said some guy on the radio said they were everywhere. That they could be the mayor or on the school board."

"You asked me before about communists. Why are you so interested?'

I wiped my forehead again. "I hear people talk."

"Don't you worry about it." She exchanged bowls again. "Put in more tomatoes."

I filled the pot again. "Would Luke know if there were communists here?"

"I doubt it." She changed the radio station again. "I want to listen to my soap."

We worked to *One Man's Family* on the radio. When all the tomatoes were skinned and cored, Mom released me.

"I prepared onions, green peppers and spices yesterday," she said. "I can do the rest on my own. Once you practice, you can run along."

Dan came home looking different. I couldn't put my finger on the change. Maybe he'd grown taller or heavier or his face assumed a more angular shape. His voice seemed lower. Maybe all those changes had been happening to him and I didn't notice.

He threw his duffel onto his bed and left for Smithton's garage with barely an acknowledgement of my existence. Pete had a dental appointment in Pattonburg and I didn't dare patrol the square on my own, so I spent the afternoon at the swimming pool.

Dan finally noticed me at dinner. "My cabin had five kids your age."

Mom placed a platter of fried chicken onto the table. "What were your responsibilities?"

Dan grabbed a drumstick. "Oh, get them up and to breakfast in the morning. Go with them to classes to make them behave."

I buttered my corn on the cob. "What classes?"

"Swimming, archery, crafts, that kind of stuff." Dan piled sliced tomatoes onto his plate. "And of course Bible classes. I'll teach swimming next year."

Luke held a chicken breast. "You'll go next year, Mike."

"Will Bruce go?"

"I don't know," Mom said. "He does a lot of work at the farm."

"Glen told me all about the fire." Butter from his ear of corn ran down Dan's chin. "Wish I'd been here."

"He tell you about Junior Rogers?" I said.

"Yeah. Said two men saw him break the window. Now he has to work a month for Turnbow."

"Well, I told Dad—"

"That's enough talk." Luke frowned and shook his head at me. "Finish up. We've a game tonight."

The regular bat boy was on vacation, so Bruce and I took over his job. Vinny Valetti lounged in the dugout with Chevy Turnbow, the third baseman, and outfielder Anton Paternik.

"Wish I'd been able to help fight your dad's fire," Vinny said to Chevy.

"You wouldn't have made a difference. Fire had too much of a head start." Chevy picked up his glove and left for the field.

"I see coach has Steve Saulk in center," Vinny said.

"You've left a big hole in our lineup." Anton punched Vinny's shoulder.

"Not my fault."

"I know that, but the Pattonburg Gorillas are tough. We'll get a lot of fly balls with Horlacher pitching. Hope Steve's up to the task."

I noticed Windy Markmann approach Gideon McKinley, the captain.

"Hey, Gid."

"Windy. How you doing?"

"Not so good." Windy shifted his weight as though he was nervous. "I've already told the others. I have to pull out as a sponsor."

Gideon scuffed the dirt with his cleats. "Damn, Windy. That'll put us in a fix."

"Sorry about that, but I just can't afford it." Windy sighed. "Damned hard to admit it but I'm strapped."

"Any chance that'll change? We hate to lose you."

"Insurance company is stalling." Windy fanned a moth away. "Once that comes through I may be okay but that could be months away."

"What's the problem with the insurance?"

"This rumor someone started that I was in the building."

Vinny lunged to his feet. "If you're going to talk about me, might as well do it to my face."

Windy turned to Vinny. "Fine by me." He stepped forward. "Why're you trying to ruin me?"

"I said what I saw."

"You're mistaken. I wasn't there."

Vinny stood his ground. "I'm not prone to hallucinations."

"Can't you admit you could be wrong? That through the flames and smoke you saw an image you thought was a person?"

"It was a person."

Windy held his hands out, palms up. "Look, Vinny, I know there are questions about these fires. Some now think they were arson. Turnbow's positive his was set. There may have been a person there but it wasn't me."

"Sure looked like you."

"Vinny." Windy shook his head and put his hands into his pockets. "The whole town saw me out moving machinery off the lot. How could it have been me you saw?"

Vinny looked confused. "I don't know. You could've got out and then moved the implements."

"Two others went in to save you. They saw no one."

"You must've been gone by then."

"Damn, you are hardheaded and stubborn. These lies are—"

"Don't call my friend a liar." Anton stood beside Vinny.

"I didn't call him a liar." Windy wiped a hand across his mouth. "He's mistaken, that's all."

Gideon McKinley touched Windy's elbow. "We've a game to play here."

"Oh, what's the use?" Windy tried again. "Please, Vinny, think about what I said. If you don't, I'll . . ."

"You'll what?"

"Forget it." Windy waved off the question and left the dugout.

"We'd get the little monsters to sleep and sneak out." Dan's soft voice came to me through the darkness.

"What'd you do?" I lay on my stomach petting Duke's head.

"Wasn't much to do. Camp's in the middle of nowhere. Woods all around. Mostly we'd light a campfire and sit around talking."

"About what?"

"Normal stuff. School, home, sports. The guys from the city always talked about girls. I wouldn't want to live in the city."

Though I couldn't see him in the dark, I leaned up on my elbow to look in Dan's direction. "Why not?"

"Too much fighting. Those guys talked tough. I think life in the city is more complicated than what we've got here."

"Alex Buckner talks tough."

"Yeah. He and Everett and Junior. They only think they're tough. Put them up against some city guys and they'd learn what tough really is."

"That night you were supposed to ride to the game with Glen. What happened?"

"They got to talking about the old man. Made me mad."

I'd never heard Dan call Luke that before. "Luke only did his job."

"I know. When I went over there this afternoon, they talked about how fair Luke is. Didn't arrest Junior when he could've. Worked out a deal with Turnbow instead."

"That's Luke."

"Everett said Luke caught him doing donuts in the snow on the square last winter. He only stopped him, warned him and sent him home."

THIRTEEN

That Sunday, the churches held a luncheon potluck on the courthouse lawn to benefit Glendale's fire victims. The Methodist board voted to participate over the objections of Clyde James. Even Mr. Hrabosky attended with his wife who sat in a wheelchair. Farmers from the surrounding countryside who didn't even belong to Glendale churches donated food and joined in the effort. The Catholic Church set up several games of chance which attracted large numbers of attendees but the cake walk was the most successful of all. The beer stand did a brisk business. When dance music played over the loud speaker system and couples began waltzing around the lawn, some of the Baptists packed up and left, but nothing spoiled the holiday mood—not even Alex Buckner's riding through the crowd on a motorcycle.

"Mr. Hrabosky talked to a lot of people Sunday."

"I was too busy to notice," Pete said.

We were on the square as usual waiting for Mr. Hrabosky to leave the café. I sat on the sidewalk, leaned back against Ziggy's Jewelry and watched Duke lap up the water I'd given him. "Every time I looked over, someone was there talking to him and his wife."

"Mom says she has Parkinsons."

"What's that?"

"I don't know." Pete sat down beside me. "I only remember it 'cause it's my last name."

"Even my grandma talked to them." I rubbed Duke's head as he flopped down beside me. "She's no communist."

"Think we ought to quit following him?"

"Well, it's pretty boring. He never does anything."

"What are communists supposed to do?"

"I don't know. That senator guy says they want to overthrow the government."

Pete frowned as he pulled on his straw. "How will they do that?"

I shrugged. "With guns, I guess."

"Never saw Mr. Hrabosky with a gun." Pete repositioned his straw in his Coke cup. "Besides, the army would whip their butt."

"Maybe they start small. Overthrow the city government." I finished my Coke.

"Why would they want to do that?"

"Why, to take over the businesses."

"But most of the guys Mr. Hrabosky talks to already own the businesses."

"Never thought of that."

"Should we follow him today?"

"What's the use?" I threw my cup into the trash can at the curb. "He'll go back to his office."

Mr. Hrabosky came out of the café followed by Kelvin Rogers.

"Goddammit. Don't you walk away from me," Mr. Rogers yelled.

Mr. Hrabosky stopped and stood with his back to us.

"That's a damned lie." Mr. Rogers clenched his fists, his face wine-red.

Mr. Hrabosky said something we couldn't hear.

"Just what a damned Jew would say," Rogers said.

Mr. Hrabosky said something else.

"You fuckin' cheated and you know it."

Mr. Hrabosky replied.

"I won't let you get away with it." Mr. Rogers lunged at Mr. Hrabosky but was intercepted by Mr. Simmons who stepped from the café.

"Kelvin." Mr. Simmons held Mr. Rogers back. "You're making a fool of yourself."

"I know what's going on," Mr. Rogers said. "You're all in this together."

"Another of your conspiracy theories," Mr. Simmons said. "You need to drop this."

Mr. Rogers shook off Mr. Simmons's hands. "The hell I will." He stalked away.

Mr. Simmons and Mr. Hrabosky spoke for a few minutes and shook hands. Mr. Hrabosky drove away.

"What in the world?" I said.

"Thought he'd blow a gasket."

"Let's find out what that was about." I put Duke's water bowl in my bike's basket.

"How?"

"Mr. Simmons knows." I mounted up. "Let's ask him."

We rode down the sidewalk to catch up with Mr. Simmons.

"Hi, Mr. Simmons." I dismounted to walk beside him.

"Mike. Pete." Mr. Simmons paused to blow his nose. "Summer cold."

"We were in front of the jewelry store," I said. "Why was Mr. Rogers shouting at Mr. Hrabosky?"

"Oh, that." Mr. Simmons resumed his walk. "Last year Kelvin sued Emile and lost. He claims Emile bribed the judge."

"Did he?" Pete said.

"Not at all." Mr. Simmons shook his head. "Kelvin lost fair and square but he won't let it go."

"Is Mr. Hrabosky Jewish?" Pete said.

"Well." Mr. Simmons stopped. "Depends on how you define the term."

"What do you mean?" I said.

"See, Emile's family lived in Hungary, but because they were Jewish, they had trouble. So they came to America."

"So he is Jewish," Pete said.

"Some people would say so." Mr. Simmons resumed his walk. "But Emile abandoned Judaism long ago. I don't believe he holds with any religion."

"Oh." I remembered what Grandma said. "Does that mean he doesn't believe in God?"

"You'd have to ask him." Mr. Simmons opened the door to his hardware store.

"Thanks, Mr. Simmons," I said.

"Good afternoon, boys."

"Communists are atheists," I told Pete. "They don't believe in God." I noticed Alex Buckner at the end of the block with Everett Smithton and Malcolm Carroll.

"Maybe we should go the other way," Pete said.

"What are they doing?"

"Looks like they're showing Malcolm something in a magazine."

"Hotrod stuff, I suppose."

"There's your brother."

Dan and Glen Smithton joined the group.

"Come on. They won't bother us with Dan there."

As we approached, I noticed the wide grin on Malcolm's face but Dan looked uncomfortable.

"See here, Mal?" Alex pointed to the magazine. "That's called her pussy. That's where you put it in and give it to her good."

I got a glimpse of the picture.

Malcolm giggled. "Give it to her good."

I looked at Dan who turned away.

"Oh, you want to see, too?" Alex thrust the magazine at me.

I turned my bike around and pedaled as fast as I could back to the hardware store with Duke running to keep up. "Mr. Simmons! Mr. Simmons! It's Malcolm. They're showing him dirty pictures."

Mr. Simmons ran to me. "Where?"

"At the end of the block."

Mr. Simmons's eyes shifted back and forth. "Pour some paint on the floor."

"What?"

"Do as I say. I'll be right back."

I watched him run down the street. He said to pour paint on the floor. I shrugged. I took a quart of paint from the shelf, found the opener at the counter and splashed some of the contents onto the floor. I grabbed Duke's collar and pulled him away from the paint.

Mr. Simmons came in with Malcolm. "I'm so glad to have found you," he said. "I've got an emergency. See where I accidentally spilled the paint?"

"Oh, I can clean it up," Malcolm said. "I'll get my rags." He shuffled to the back of the store.

"Thanks, Mike." Mr. Simmons patted my back. "We need to take good care of Malcolm."

"Mr. Simmons called," Luke said at dinner. "I'm proud of you, Mike. As for you, young man, what were you thinking?"

"It was an accident, Dad," Dan said. "Glen and I were headed to the auto parts store when we saw Everett. We didn't know what Alex was doing."

"That's right, Dad," I said. "I saw Glen and Dan join the group just before I got there."

"What should you have done?" Luke said.

Dan shrugged. "I couldn't stop them. I wanted to leave."

"And you should have," Mom said.

"Mike went for help," Luke said. "What kind of reputation do you want in this town? You get an award at graduation and then hang around in a group showing pictures of naked women to Malcolm? I hope you're ashamed of yourself."

Dan stared at his plate. "I won't go to the garage again, okay?"

"I think it's for the best," Mom said.

"I have enough to do without getting calls from the merchants around the square about what you're doing." Luke drank some iced tea. "We've had another burglary."

"Who?" Mom said.

"Saulk. Their neighbor went over to water plants and discovered a broken window." Luke reached for the mashed potatoes.

"What'd they take?" I said.

"The television but we'll have to wait for them to get home to see if anything else is missing."

"Didn't they take Kirkpatrick's television, too?" Mom said.

Luke nodded. "They seem to like televisions."

"The Kirkpatricks were on vacation, too," Mom said.

"It's a problem," Luke said. "Everyone in town knows when someone goes on vacation."

"The Saulks even had their itinerary printed in the *Glendale Courier*," Mom said.

"We ought to get a television," Dan said.

"We might like to get one," Luke said, "but things we need come first."

I took the last of the sliced tomatoes. "What do we need?"

"A washer and dryer are on my list," Mom said.

"And we may have other expenses." Luke looked around for dessert. "The council got the committee report about establishing a fire department."

Mom cut into a cherry cobbler. "How much would it cost us?"

"Figures aren't exact but it looks like it might raise our property tax about three hundred dollars."

"I know a fire department is necessary, but I could get a washer and dryer for less than that." Mom distributed the cherry cobbler.

"Maybe we won't have another fire," I said.

Luke forked into his cobbler. "Bound to happen. Turnbow's fire was caused by emptying an ashtray into a trash can. Look how many people smoke."

"What did Harold say about the results of the investigation?" Mom said.

"He stood there with a cigarette in his hand and said nobody emptied the ashtray." Luke finished his iced tea. "He claims emptying ashtrays is done first thing in the morning before the dealership opens."

That week, Mom took us to Horlacher's to pick sweet corn. She would blanch it, cut the corn off the cob and freeze it. Bruce joined us to help and we finished in no time.

"Can Mike stay for the day?" Bruce said.

"What about it, Mom?" I said. "I can ride to the game with Bruce and meet you there."

"Thelma, would that be okay with you?" Mom said.

"We'd be glad to have him," Mrs. Horlacher said.

"Dan can help me shuck the corn," Mom said. "Mike, you be sure to do whatever you're told."

"First, boys, I want you to help Ed with the milk," Mrs. Horlacher said. "After that, you can take over the vegetable stand."

"Come on." Bruce led me to their car. "We gotta drive to the barn."

"Your dad lets you drive?"

"Just around the farm."

I sat in the passenger's seat wondering if Bruce's claims were more truthful than Pete's. At the barn, Mr. Horlacher removed the car's back seat and loaded four ten-gallon milk cans to go to the creamery in town. We walked back to the house.

"Only two customers still picking," Mrs. Horlacher said. "When they're finished, put up the closed sign."

We lounged on the grass and I told Bruce about Alex and the naked pictures. "Alex told Dan that he was going to teach me to mind my own business."

"You better be careful."

"Here comes Mrs. Murphy."

Mrs. Murphy pulled a child's wagon full of corn and watermelons. Bruce and I helped her load the produce and the wagon. She paid and drove away. Only one car remained in the parking area.

"That's a nice car," I said.

"Pontiac two-door," Bruce said. "I think they're from Pattonburg."

We walked around the car to see it from all sides.

"Keys are in it," Bruce said.

"You wouldn't."

"I got an idea." He opened the driver's door and pushed down the lock.

"But the other door's locked. They won't be able to get in."

Bruce grinned. "I know."

We sat back on the grass to wait. Soon an older couple loaded with bags emerged from the garden and Bruce tallied their produce bill.

"Only two thirty, sir."

"And worth every bit." The man counted out his change.

"We'll help you put it into the car." Bruce picked up two bags and left me to get the others.

"I'll open the trunk." The man tried to open the driver's door. "Oh, dear. It's locked and the keys are in it."

Bruce winked at me. "I'll get it open, sir." He ran into a shed and returned with a looped wire. "We've had others do the same thing." He put the wire in through the top of the window, angled the loop around the lock and popped it up. "There you go, sir."

The man gave Bruce a quarter for his help.

Bruce waved goodbye to them. "I always get a tip that way," he said.

After we closed the vegetable stand, Bruce's mother reminded him to work with Blackie. Bruce explained that Blackie was his 4-H project. We walked to the pasture past the barn where short, stocky black cattle and taller black and white ones grazed. Bruce said the black ones were Angus beef cattle and the others were milk cows.

He clapped his hands and called, "Yo, Blackie." One of the Angus prickled up his ears and walked to us. I backed away a bit as he looked pretty big up close. Bruce said he was a steer and explained about castrating which I knew about as we had Duke fixed. Bruce petted him a little then said," Come on, Blackie," and the steer followed us to the barn as gentle as a pet dog.

We brushed him, soaped him down and rinsed him off, and all the while, he stood there contemplating us with his beautiful black eyes framed by long lashes. Bruce led him around on a halter, posing him at various times, as he planned to show him at the fair. When we left, Blackie called after us as though we were abandoning him.

After lunch, we swam in the creek where some beaver dammed it off and later I got to help with the milking before dinner. I wished I lived on a farm and got to do all the things Bruce did every day.

FOURTEEN

I remember that long-ago evening when Luke said change was coming. He came into our bedroom for a serious talk about sex. I felt repulsed and fascinated at the same time. Mom noticed that Dan was experiencing wet dreams, and Luke explained how this was normal and told all about the urges Dan might have and how he should handle them. Luke said I should hear this, too, as it would happen to me. That scared me. I didn't want to have urges. I didn't want things to be different. Everything was fine the way it was. Why couldn't it stay the same? If change happened all the time, what could I count on? I told Bruce what Luke said and he shrugged it off. He said his brother told him all about it, and it was part of growing up. He looked forward to it and I should, too. I didn't tell Pete. He would've laughed.

Luke rattled the newspaper. "North and South Korea have signed a truce."

"The war ends?" Mom said.

"I guess so."

"About time." Mom buttered some toast. "Now our boys can come home."

"Not all of them," Luke said. "There's a zone between the two countries that will have to be patrolled."

"So we'll leave some troops there?" Mom placed a plate of toast onto the table. "I wonder how long they'll have to stay."

Luke folded the newspaper and handed it to me so I could check the sports page. "Probably forever," he said. "Gid told me we have a new sponsor for the team."

I knew he meant Gideon McKinley, the team captain. “Who?”

“The new sponsor prefers to remain anonymous. Windy told Gid this person came to him and volunteered.”

“Any idea who it is?” Mom said.

Luke sipped his coffee. “I have a suspicion.”

Mom’s eyebrows rose. “Oh.”

“Who is it?” Dan said.

“If he wants to remain anonymous,” Luke said, “we’ll honor his wish.”

“Will you be patrolling again tonight?” Mom said.

Luke nodded. “Until we catch the burglars. Now that we have a list of people on vacation, we know which houses to watch.”

“Who’s on vacation?” I said.

“Let’s see.” Luke finished his coffee. “The Murphys. Davenports, Jameses, Millers, Waylords.” He shrugged. “That’s all I remember.”

“You boys be quiet this afternoon so your dad can sleep.”

Pete and I sat in the awning’s shade in front of Ziggy’s Jewelry again.

“We swam in the creek,” I said. “The beavers built a dam so there’s a deep pool.”

“Did you see the beavers?”

“Only for a bit. One sounded an alarm and they all disappeared. Bruce has a vine that you can swing on and drop into the water.”

Pete slurped his Coke. “Suppose we can bike out there and go swimming?”

“We’d have to ask.” I petted Duke. “It’s private property.”

“Why not just do it and say sorry later?”

“’Cause it’s Bruce and he’s our friend, that’s why.” I sipped my Coke. “He has this black steer that follows him around like a puppy. We brushed and washed him.”

“He taking him to the fair?”

“Yeah. And I got to help milk the cows.”

Pete’s eyes widened. “You milked a cow?”

"They have a machine that does that, but first the cow's udder has to be washed."

"Udder?"

"That's the bag that hangs down under the cow where the teats are. You know, where the milk comes out."

"Oh." Pete nodded toward the café. "There he is."

Mr. Hrabosky walked to his car, turned and waved at us.

"Uh oh," I said. "He saw us."

"So what. We're not doing anything."

Mr. Hrabosky started the Buick and backed from the curb.

"He's turning left. That's not the way to his office." I stowed Duke's water dish and mounted up.

Two blocks later, we found the Buick at Tony's Market again.

"Over there in the shade." Pete pointed to the community house across from the Methodist Church. "He won't notice us there."

We sat under an elm on the community house lawn.

"He must be good friends with Mr. DeCarlo," I said.

"Yeah, but we already knew that Mr. DeCarlo is one of them. We ought to go to my house and listen to the game."

"The Cards are only three games out," I said.

"He's getting into his car."

We watched Mr. Hrabosky pull away from the curb. When he reached the corner, he waved to us.

"We're busted," Pete said. "He's got to know we're following him."

"Guess we'll have to lie low for a while." I hesitated about going to Pete's house as he might force a beer on me again. "Luke's patrolling at night to catch burglars. We could help him."

"How? We can't go out at night."

"We can watch the houses where people are on vacation," I said. "Burglars often case the houses in the daylight and come back at night."

"Who's on vacation?"

"Luke mentioned some at breakfast. Burglars would go for the biggest houses. That would be Waylords or Davenports."

"I know where Mr. Wayford lives," Pete said, "but his stuff is probably as old as he is."

"I'll bet he has a television. That's what the burglars like."

"Do you know where Davenports live?"

"No, but we can find out."

"You going to ask somebody?"

"No. We'll look in the telephone book at the hardware store. We're on the good side of Mr. Simmons."

Malcolm stood outside Simmons Hardware talking to someone. By the time we identified that someone as Alex Buckner, it was too late to turn around.

"Ah, my nemesis," Alex said.

I didn't know what a nemesis was but assumed he didn't call us his friends.

"Hey, Malcolm," Pete said.

"Hey, yourself." Malcolm grinned.

Duke sniffed at Alex's leg, but when Alex bent to pet him, Duke backed away and growled.

"Got your attack dog with you, I see," Alex said.

"Duke isn't an attack dog," I said.

"He growled at me."

I held Duke by his collar. "I guess he doesn't like you."

Mr. Simmons came from the store. "Time to go to work, Malcolm."

"Sure." Malcolm followed Mr. Simmons into the store.

"Where do you think you're going?" Alex blocked the hardware store's door. Duke bared his teeth and a rumble emanated from his chest. Alex moved away. "You need to keep that dog on a leash." He turned and walked away.

I knelt to pet Duke. "Good boy."

"I'll bet if we trained him, Duke could be an attack dog," Pete said.

"He may look kind of like a German Shepherd, but he's just a mutt."

"I'm sure glad he was with us."

Inside the store, Malcolm used a feather duster to clean the display of paint cans. He interrupted his work to pet Duke. "Duke growled," he said.

I nodded. "He sure did."

"He never growls at me."

"He likes you."

"He doesn't like Alex?"

"I guess not."

"Say, Malcolm, what was Alex talking to you about?" Pete said.

Malcolm resumed his dusting. "Bad people."

I believed Alex might be an expert on the subject. "Like who?"

Malcolm shrugged. "Somebody called commie, I think. He said the cops were after commie and I should watch out for him but I don't know what he looks like."

"Don't worry, Malcolm. Pete and I will look for him. We know what he looks like."

"Good," Malcolm said. "I don't like bad guys."

We used the telephone book and got an address on Carbon Drive for the Davenport house in the north end of town. Once we crossed the highway that ran east and west three blocks north of the square, we found most houses of brick, stone or stucco rather than wood. Homes with attached garages sat on larger landscaped lots. The further north we biked the larger the lots. The Davenport home rested far back from the street on a lot the size of a football field. I knew Clark Davenport from Sunday school and baseball, but the opulence of his home stunned me into silence. A long drive led to a three-car garage attached to a two-story stone house which by my standards could be called a mansion.

"We can't stay here," I said. "We'd stick out like a sore thumb."

"We can watch from the corner," Pete said. "What're we looking for?"

"Somebody coming by looking the place over."

We loitered on the corner waiting for something to happen.

"How did Clark's dad get so much money?" Pete said.

"Luke said his dad was in real estate and Clark's dad inherited a bunch so he doesn't have to work much."

"Here comes the mailman."

"Say, he'd know who was on vacation."

"Think he's the burglar?"

"Could be." We watched him deliver mail from house to house.

"He's not looking the place over," Pete said.

"Wouldn't have to. He's seen it every day for years."

Time passed and few cars travelled the street.

"This is boring," Pete said.

"Wonder what Luke does when he's on a stakeout."

"At least he's in a car. Can listen to the radio."

"Here comes someone." I knelt beside my bike as though I was adjusting the chain.

"He slowed down," Pete said. "Acting like he's looking for an address."

"He's scanning the place. An old black Ford. Did you recognize him?"

"No. Two men."

The car drove on and turned the corner.

"We need a license plate number," I said.

"Maybe they'll come back."

"If they do, we can't be here. Let's move down the street a bit."

"There's shade on the other side."

We crossed the street and stopped in the shade of a mulberry tree. Duke stretched out on the grass.

"Look at that." Pete pointed down the street.

"It's Mr. Hrabosky."

Half a block away, the blue Buick turned up a driveway.

"Wonder who lives there," Pete said.

"Here comes the black Ford." I knelt to adjust my chain again. "Get the tag number." I heard the car pass and looked over my shoulder after it.

"P1C493," Pete and I said together.

"We need to write that down so we don't forget it," I said.

"No paper."

Mr. Hrabosky's blue Buick stopped at the street and turned south away from us.

"Let's go to that house and ask for paper. Then we'll find out who lives there," I said.

We walked our bikes down the street and up the drive. The name on the mailbox said Markmann.

"Windy's place," Pete said.

Mrs. Whitley, Charlie's mother, answered the doorbell wearing an apron. "Why, it's Mike and Pete. Surprised to see you boys up here."

"We need paper and a pencil, Mrs. Whitley. Got to write something down," I said.

"Sure. I got a pad right here on the telephone table." She handed it to me and I quickly wrote down the license number.

"We only see Charlie at baseball this summer," Pete said.

"He cuts lawns to earn money." Mrs. Whitley chuckled. "But he do love baseball. Takes Thursday mornings off to play."

"He's a good player," I said.

"I know what happened at the ballpark," Mrs. Whitley said. "I 'preciate what you did."

"Clark's cousin was in the wrong, that's all," Pete said.

"I see you got your dog with you."

"Oh, I'm out of water for him. Could you?" I held out the water jar.

"Glad to." Mrs. Whitley took the jar and disappeared into the house.

"My mom says Windy had the choice of letting Mrs. Whitley go or dropping the ball club, and he chose to keep her," Pete said.

"I didn't know she worked here."

"Charlie's dad is gone a lot working on the railroad."

Now Luke worked odd hours. He came home for lunch then slept until seven or eight when we'd have dinner. Afterward, he left to patrol until dawn, ate breakfast at the café, and worked at the office until noon. I sympathized with Charlie who must've missed his dad terribly. Working all those hours, Luke prevented burglaries during that week.

I told Mom about seeing Mrs. Whitley at the Markmann's house, and she said Mrs. Whitley had worked there a long time. Mom said everyone in town knew about the incident at the ballpark.

When I asked why she'd never mentioned it, she said we'd done the right thing, although she didn't hold with fighting, and she'd have mentioned it if I hadn't done what she expected.

Now locusts sang in the evenings, a sure sign August waited in the wings. Lawns, once green and springy underfoot, browned into needle-sharp blades that crunched under my sneakers. Saturday crowds avoided the afternoon and arrived early to finish before noon or waited until evening to shop and see a movie.

Mom approved of the movie *Shane* starring Alan Ladd, so she took Dan and me and Grandma Jenkins to see it. The cattlemen tried to force the homesteaders off their land. They hired a gunfighter, played by Jack Palance, who killed one of the homesteaders and frightened some of them into leaving. Shane, an ex-gunfighter who worked for one of the homesteaders, rode into town and killed the gunman and two of the cattlemen. Though he was injured, he rode away. A lot more happened, but that's the gist of it. I liked *Shane*, and it generated more gunfights than *High Noon* did.

FIFTEEN

I sobbed on Mom's shoulder as we stood on the courthouse lawn and watched flames gut the Glendale Theater. I thought of all the cartoons, shorts, serials and movies I enjoyed in the darkness as the projector's light flickered above me. It would flicker no more and I cried for all the town and I had lost. I wasn't alone. Many of the spectators around me wiped their eyes and blew their noses. Unwanted, devastating change came to Glendale.

A new phenomenon, the mill fire excited and fascinated the townspeople. Flames devouring the International Harvester dealership still intrigued onlookers but contained the added element of danger. When Glendale Motors burned, fascination turned to fear and anger. The destruction of the theater struck at Glendale's heart, one of the town's major draws on the square. I didn't buy flour from the mill or farm machinery from Windy or a Corvette from Mr. Turnbow, but most weekends I purchased a ticket at the Glendale Theater.

"Come, Mike," Mom said, "it's not the end of the world." She handed me a tissue.

I wiped my eyes, blew my nose and hiccupped a couple of times. Something sat on my chest, something so heavy I could hardly breathe. I glared at the spectacle in front of me—the inferno, the firemen and their ineffective hoses, the water arcing into the air, the smell of burning wood, the snapping of the flames, the heat on my face. I turned my back.

"I want to go home," I said.

Mom put her arm around my shoulders. "I think that's a good idea. Come, Dan." She took his hand.

The three of us trudged across the courthouse lawn to the car on the other side of the square. Home in my bed, I curled up with my arm around Duke and let sleep overtake me.

"By the time they had the fire out, no one was left on the square but Janice Beach and her son," Luke said at breakfast. "Everyone had seen more than enough."

"Poor Janice with a child on the way." Mom dished up scrambled eggs. "And Leroy fighting the fire."

"Sonny's in my class at school," I said.

"Leroy's dad owned the theater before him," Mom said. "It's been on the square for as long as I can remember."

"It's a blow to all the businesses," Luke said. "People come to town not only to shop but to stay for a movie."

"What about the night patrols?" Mom said. "Did anyone see anything?"

"I haven't checked with them yet."

I spilled my juice when the phone rang.

"Now who can that be?" Mom answered the phone. "Just a second. Luke." She held out the receiver.

I watched Luke's face turn dark. "Another burglary," he said as he hung up the phone. "Wayford's house. Mrs. Matlock discovered it."

"They used the fire as a distraction," Mom said.

"Does that mean they set it?" Dan said.

"Not necessarily." Luke grabbed his hat. "But someone in town knew we'd all be at the fire."

"Maybe someone in town called someone out of town," I said.

Luke's eyes settled on me. "That's a possibility." He nodded. "Got to run." He kissed Mom's cheek and was out the door.

I thought of the paper in my room with the license tag number on it.

"Once you boys practice, I want you out of the house," Mom said. "I've got to finish my flower arrangements and take them to the fairgrounds and your dad needs to sleep this afternoon."

"We can help take the flowers out," Dan said.

Mom nodded. "Okay. We'll see about that at lunch. Now go on with you."

"Let's walk to the square," Dan said once we finished our practice.

The invitation surprised me. "Okay."

We sauntered up the street in silence for several minutes.

"What've you been doing this summer?" Dan said.

"Not much." I hesitated to tell him about spying on Mr. Hrabosky. "Pete and I watched the Davenport house to see if anyone planned to rob it."

Dan grinned. "Find out anything?"

"One car came by twice. Slowed down and looked the place over. We got its license number."

"You should tell Luke."

"He's been so busy."

"There's Mr. Horlacher." Dan pointed to their old car parked at the creamery. Mr. Horlacher hefted a can of milk onto the roller rack and it glided into the building. We walked over to say hello.

"Guess we missed last night's excitement," Mr. Horlacher said.

"If you've seen one fire, you saw this one," Dan said.

"A real shame." Mr. Horlacher slammed the car's back door. "We're terribly busy today. Everyone taking projects to the fair. Judging tomorrow."

"What're you taking?" Dan said.

"Thelma's canned goods. Rob and Bruce's steers. Madge has a pig. I've got to get home to pick corn and peaches. Your mom doing her flowers?"

"Yeah. We'll take them out this afternoon," I said.

"Well, drop by the 4-H barn and say hello to Bruce." Mr. Horlacher started his car and pulled away.

"I wonder how they'll get those animals to the fair," I said. "They don't have a truck."

"Neighbors, I suppose."

We walked past the county jail, an insurance office and a service station to the southeast corner of the square. The courthouse blocked our view of the Glendale Theater.

"Don't know if I want to look," Dan said.

I felt the same way, but the disaster pulled at us. We crossed the street and skirted the courthouse. Sawhorses blocked off the whole north side of the square. A crowd of people stared across the street at what was left of the theater. The blackened brick front stood, its door missing. The *Shane* poster on the theater's front still showed Alan Ladd's scorched face. The marquee, once bright with alternating lights, drooped over the sidewalk. Through the gaping front, I saw only a pile of charred rubble where the concession stand once perfumed the air with popcorn.

"Looks like it started in the back," someone said.

"Lots to burn in the old place," a lady said.

"Four fires," an old man said. "What's this world coming to?"

"Another burglary last night, too."

"And I thought Glendale was a safe place to live."

"Anyone seen Leroy?"

"He's at the insurance office waiting for the fire inspectors."

"How competent are these inspectors? Could they spot arson when they see it?"

Dan pulled me away from the hated sight. "It's almost time for lunch," he said and we started the walk home.

Luke came home to sleep about three that afternoon after an emergency city council meeting.

"Leroy Beach accused the council of dragging their feet," Luke said. "He said they might as well have burned down the theater themselves."

"That's a bit harsh," Mom said.

"He's angry. I understand that but the council looked over the committee recommendations and did nothing."

"Did they make any decisions today?"

"They're putting a bond issue on the ballot in November."

Mom sniffed. "That's months away."

"And they're borrowing money to hire six firefighters to man the station full time. Two on each eight-hour shift. Crosby has already posted the positions."

"That's some progress, I guess."

"They're also getting a used firetruck from Pattonburg. Making payments on it."

"Did anyone see anything last night?" I said.

"Earnest Simmons and Ryan Saulk were on patrol. They saw no one. The square was deserted."

"Did they question you about the burglaries?" Mom said.

"A bit. We've notified pawn shops about Saulk's jewelry and the various other things. Nothing's turned up yet."

"You need to sleep," Mom said. "The boys and I will get these arrangements to the fair."

"Don't put the window down," Mom said. "You'll ruin my arrangements."

Flowers filled the whole back seat of our car and their combined perfume overwhelmed me as I sat between Mom and Dan on our way to the fairgrounds. The county fairgrounds was east of town past the municipal golf course. Cars and trucks turned through the gate bringing exhibits to be judged. Cattle lowed, pigs squealed and horses whinnied as we drove past the livestock barns.

"I'll get as close as I can," Mom said, "but we may have to carry the flowers a ways."

She found a place to park near the chicken and rabbit barn.

"Each of you take one," Mom said. "It doesn't matter if you spill the water. I can get more."

I picked a small one with cosmos, marigolds, Queen Ann's lace and thistle and followed her. In the exhibit barn, people bustled back and forth checking in their entries. Mom told us where to place her arrangements and sent us back to the car for the rest. She said she'd be busy checking in her exhibits, and we should meet her at the car in half an hour. Dan and I set off for the 4-H barn. We found Bruce brushing his steer.

"This is Blackie," I told Dan. I picked up a brush to help Bruce, and Blackie swung his head around to gaze at me with soft, trusting eyes.

"I get to sleep here tonight," Bruce said, "on that cot over there."

"By yourself?"

"Rob will be here, too, and lots of 4-H kids."

"When is the judging?"

"Tomorrow morning. Ten o'clock."

I turned to Dan but he was gone. "Where'd Dan go?"

"He's over there talking to the Johnson girl. She has that big Hereford. Competition."

Blackie turned and shoved me with his nose. "Hey!"

Bruce laughed. "He wants you to brush some more."

I brushed to make Blackie happy. "Saw your dad in town this morning."

"He's in the crop barn. Said the movie theater burned down."

"Yeah and burglars hit the Wayford house."

"You and Pete still looking for the burglars?'

"When we have time."

"Time to go, Squirt." Dan waved me out of the barn.

Mom took Dan and me to the fair the next evening. Judges awarded her arrangements three grand championships and two blue ribbons. A grand champion ribbon hung on Blackie's stall. Bruce and I rode the Ferris wheel and the Tilt-a-Whirl, ate hotdogs and cotton candy and watched Mr. Horlacher compete in the tractor driving contest. Dan strolled around holding hands with the Johnson girl and tried to win a teddy bear for her at the ring toss. We left the fair late.

"Mom, Bruce said he sold Blackie for a lot of money," I said.

"That's nice."

"He sold him to Roman's Market."

"Uh huh."

"But they'll kill him."

"Yes." Mom didn't seem to be concerned.

"That's not right," I said.

"I don't know what you mean."

"It'd be like . . . like me selling Duke for somebody to kill and eat."

"Blackie isn't a pet, Mike."

"But Bruce treats him like one. He brushes and pets him. Washes him. Blackie has faith that Bruce won't hurt him."

"Farmers raise food for people to eat," Mom said. "That's why they raised Blackie. Bruce knew all along he would be sold."

"I still think it stinks," I said.

I knew then that I could never be a farmer. It couldn't be right to trick an animal into trusting you enough to follow you around like a pet then brutally betray that trust. For months, every time Mom served beef, I thought of Blackie, and years later I thought of him again when I read a short story about aliens invading Earth. They convinced people that they came to help and even had a book entitled "To Serve Mankind." Everyone wanted to visit their planet, and those who did never returned. The book turned out to be a cookbook.

SIXTEEN

"We should have Duke along in case we run into Alex." Pete leaned his bicycle against the big oak shading the park's swing set.

"It's too hot for him," I said. A south wind rustled the leaves but did nothing to relieve the oppressive heat. I wiped my sweaty forehead with my shirt sleeve.

Pete tested the teeter-totter. "Whose house are we watching today?"

"Hale. He owns the pool hall." I pulled down the opposite seat and straddled it. "Left for vacation yesterday."

"Nice that he's got this little park across the street."

"Didn't know it was here."

A jungle gym, sand box, and a couple of picnic tables decorated the shady park. A line of spirea shrubs separated the park from houses on both sides with a parking area off the alley in back. We were in the north end of town—unexplored territory for us. We lazily rode the teeter-totter up and down.

"I'll be glad when summer's over," I said.

"You're crazy." Pete pushed hard hoping to slam my end down to earth. "I want it to stretch forever."

"Too much has happened." I pushed back. "Fires and burglaries. Communists and Alex. I want things back to normal."

"But then school starts."

"So?" I held Pete up in the air before pushing off again. "That's normal."

Pete pointed to the street. "Look. There's the old Ford."

I twisted around to see. The car poked along up the street. When it turned the corner, I noticed a truck parked in the alley behind the corner house.

"See the truck?" I pointed. "I'll bet the truck is the burglars and the old Ford is a lookout."

"I can't see." Pete pushed his end of the teeter-totter up. "Hey! There's two guys carrying something to the truck."

"What is it?"

Perry strained to see over the shrubs. "I can't tell. Those bushes are in the way."

Pete boosted me up. "The robbers! In broad daylight! They're going back into the house."

"You recognize them?"

"Never got a good look."

"Let's see what's in the truck," Pete said.

We trotted to the parking lot off the alleyway. The pickup's bed faced us with the tailgate down, and a large object sat in the truck's bed covered by a tarp.

"Come on." Pete ran to the truck and I reluctantly followed. He vaulted onto the tailgate and stumbled forward. "Get up here," he said. "Let's uncover this."

I pulled myself up, grabbed one side of the tarp and lifted.

"It's a television," Pete said.

"Luke says the burglars like televisions." The huge cabinet model rose about four feet tall with a small twelve-inch screen.

"We found the burglar!"

I saw the man leave the house. "There he is! What'll we do?"

"Hide!" Pete crawled under the tarp and I joined him.

I heard the crunch of footsteps approach. The tailgate clanged closed. The footsteps came closer. The truck's door creaked as the man opened it. The truck bounced. The door slammed. The engine started and the truck lurched forward.

"We're trapped!" My voice cracked. I clutched the tarp with shaking hands and swallowed the bile which rose into my throat.

"We'll get out as soon as he stops." Pete's voice sounded shaky.

The truck slowed, turned and sped up. Soon I knew we were going fast as the tarp flapped in the breeze. We were headed away from Glendale! I wished I were home and had never cooked up the idea of watching for the burglars. My heart raced and muscles cramped with tension.

The truck sped north mile after mile. Sun baked the tarp, and sweat rolled down my cheeks. I leaned against the truck's cab with my knees pulled up to my chest and closed my eyes. Finally, the truck slowed and turned, and I heard gravel crunch and hit the undercarriage. We were out in the country headed to the burglar's hideout! I clutched the tarp and gasped for air. The truck braked, turned, bounced and stopped. The engine died. The truck bounced as the man opened the truck's door and slammed it. Footsteps crunched on gravel. The tailgate clanged down.

"Come help me with this," the man said.

"What 'cha got, Pa?" a female answered.

"Ray Hemphill's television. Having trouble with the vertical hold."

The tarp flipped back, and I looked into the startled faces of a man and a young girl. I recognized the man as one of the Harrington Harvesters' coaches, and the girl had held Dan's hand at the fair. It was Mr. Johnson and his daughter.

Mr. Johnson stepped back. "What in the world?"

"It's hard to explain," I stammered.

"Luke's boy, ain't it?"

"That's right, sir." I crawled from under the tarp and stood. "Come on, Pete."

"You are?" Mr. Johnson said.

"Pete Parkinson, sir." Pete scrambled to his feet.

"Your dad works at the auto parts store."

"Yes, sir."

"Well, get down from here and let's hear this explanation."

Mr. Johnson sat on the tailgate while I told him the whole story about watching for burglars.

"Well, don't that just beat all." Mr. Johnson laughed and slapped his knee. "Thought I was a burglar."

"And the black Ford was your lookout," I said. "We got its plate number."

"You did, huh. Playing detective." He laughed again. "Let's get this television in and I'll run you home."

"Can I go, too, Pa?" the young girl said.

Mr. Johnson elbowed me. "She's sweet on that brother of yours."

Pete and I rode in the back again. Mr. Johnson stopped at the park for our bikes. I dreaded facing Luke as the truck pulled to the curb in front of our house.

"Come on, boys." He led us to the porch.

Mom answered the door. "Mr. Johnson." She frowned at me. "Can I help you?"

"I don't suppose Luke's around."

"He's sleeping. He'll be patrolling all night."

"I believe he'll want to hear this."

"Just a minute." Mom left to get Luke and I wanted to sink through the porch floor.

"Mr. Johnson." Luke buttoned his shirt.

"Your boy has something to tell you."

I told the tale again and Luke didn't laugh.

"You realize you'd have been in real trouble if Mr. Johnson had been the burglar." Luke put his arm around my shoulders.

I nodded.

"I appreciate your trying to help." Luke hugged me tight then looked down into my upturned face. "I forbid you to do this again. You could've been in real danger."

"These two may be on to something," Mr. Johnson said. "They got the tag number of that old black Ford."

That Friday evening, Bruce and I sat in our favorite seats for the game against the Pattonburg Professors, mostly teachers from the college. The Bombers easily whipped them earlier in the season, but they were behind five to three in the sixth inning.

"They've lost their zip," Bruce said.

"Yeah."

The players usually laughed and glad-handed each other. Now they sat morosely on the bench, lumbered up to bat and slumped in the outfield. The summer fires hit the Bombers hard. Vinny Valetti hobbled around the dugout on crutches. Windy Markmann gave up his sponsorship. Chevy Turnbow, who played third base, missed an easy fly ball for an error. He seemed distracted for weeks after the Corvette burned. Leroy Beach, one of the Bomber's best hitters, had yet to get on base.

The stands, ordinarily packed for home games, stood half empty with no one making the normal hoots and catcalls. The game reflected the depressed spirit of Glendale's citizens.

Only one area seemed full of life. Alex Buckner, Junior Rogers and Everett Smithton laughed and cutup on the front row. Malcolm Carroll sat with them, a grin never leaving his face.

I nodded toward them. "Think we can spy on them again?"

"Nah."

Bruce seemed to lack his usual animation, too, and I wondered if selling Blackie had him a bit down.

I elbowed him. "Come on. I'd like to hear what they're saying."

Bruce pushed my arm back. "Haven't you been in enough trouble lately?"

"I haven't been in trouble. Luke never even scolded me."

"If you want to go, go on." Bruce waved his arm toward the far end of the bleachers. "Nobody's stopping you."

"Come with me," I said.

"Ha." Bruce gave me a withering look. "You're afraid to go alone."

"Am not."

"Are."

"Not."

"I dare you."

Well, that did it. "Okay, I will."

I jumped down from the bleachers and skirted the back to reach the area where they sat. With the stands so empty, more light poured in under the bleachers leaving little shadow in which to hide. My heart beat in my throat as I crawled near to them. Malcolm sat between Junior and Alex with Everett behind them.

"She likes you. I can tell," Alex said.

"Yeah. She smiled and said 'Hi, Malcolm'," Junior said.

Malcolm giggled and shifted around on his bleacher seat. "She always does that."

"Go over there and sit with her." Alex tugged on Malcolm's arm.

I remembered the time Alex bought Malcolm an ice cream cone at the game. He told his friends they could use Malcolm because he believes what he's told. Now they were talking down to him, teasing him, and he didn't even realize it.

"I'll bet she'll let you feel her boobs," Everett said.

Malcolm giggled again. "My dad says to leave girls alone."

"What does he know?" Alex said. "Bet he doesn't even let you jerk off."

"What's that?"

Alex and his friends snickered. Junior stomped his feet and slapped Malcolm's back. I smelled the sulphur of a match, and soon cigarette smoke wafted down.

"If you don't know," Everett said, "we ain't gonna explain it to you."

"Go over there, Mal. She'll jerk it off for you," Alex said.

"I can't."

"I give up," Alex said. "You'll never get any pussy."

"I already have a cat."

The group howled and stomped their feet on the wooden bleachers.

"He has a cat."

"What a tickle."

"Mal, you're a hoot."

Someone dropped a lit cigarette which landed on my shorts. I brushed it off and scooted back.

"Maybe he likes boys," Junior said.

"You like boys, Mal?" Alex said.

"Yes. I like lots of people."

"He means for sex, Mal," Everett said.

"For sex? Why would I do that?"

"Sex is fun, Mal," Alex said. "It gets your rocks off."

"I don't have any rocks."

The group shrieked with laughter again.

"Rocks in the head is all," Junior said.

"Malcolm, I need you." It was Mr. Simmons.

"Is something wrong?"

"Nothing's wrong. I want you to sit with me," Mr. Simmons said.

"Sure." Malcolm got to his feet, and for an instant, I stared out at Mr. Simmons before Malcolm shuffled away with him. Everett moved down to take Malcolm's place.

"Somebody's always ruinin' our fun," Junior said.

"Say, we haven't heard anything from your old man lately," Alex said.

"He's been watchin'," Junior said. "Tryin' to scare him off."

"Is it workin'?" Everett said.

"Doesn't seem to be." Junior snorted. "Guy must be too friggin' dumb to get it."

"What's he plan to do?" Alex said.

"He figures it takes more than just one person. He wants to get a group together and get the guy to leave."

"This game is friggin' awful," Everett said.

"Let's go play pool," Junior said.

"Yeah. I could use a beer," Alex said.

"I'll never get one at the pool hall," Everett said.

"Hale's out of town," Alex said. "Arnold's runnin' the bar. He don't care if you ain't twenty-one. He'll sell you a beer."

The group sauntered away. I lay flat on the ground as they strolled by the back of the bleachers on the way to their car.

Walking back to my seat, I reviewed the conversation. Mr. Rogers watched someone and wanted him to leave. Why? Well, so he could rob him, that's why. Mr. Rogers was the mastermind behind the burglaries. He wanted several people to help him rob the place. Luke ordered me to keep out of it. I decided to tell Pete. What about Malcolm? Mr. Simmons. I should tell him about Alex and his friends. Malcolm could get into a lot of trouble listening to them.

SEVENTEEN

Pete and I lounged on the courthouse lawn with Duke stretched out beside me.

"There goes the front wall," Pete said.

The brick facade of the Glendale Theater crashed to the street raising a dust cloud. The marquee lay in the back of a truck ready to go to the dump. The bricks littered the street and sidewalk, and men bent to pick them up and toss them with a clang into the truck.

I wiped sweat from my forehead with the tail of my shirt. "The inspectors say it was arson."

Pete frowned. "Leroy burned his own place?"

"Aw, come on." I punched Pete's shoulder. "He was home in bed when they called."

Pete flopped onto his stomach, his chin on his hands. "Maybe he hired someone."

I rubbed Duke's soft ears and thought about that. "Doesn't sound like something he'd do. He's on the ball team and the city council. Heads up the fire volunteers."

"My dad says you can never tell about people," Pete said.

"Like Mr. Rogers," I said. "He works for the city. Who'd figure him for a burglar?"

"He knows his way around town, that's for sure."

"So do guys who work for the electric and gas companies."

"And the telephone guys." Pete sat up. "Look at Duke."

Duke's ears were forward, his gaze focused on a squirrel hunting around the courthouse lawn. From a crouch, he sprang into action, legs flashing beneath him as he dashed after the small rodent. The squirrel leaped up an oak tree and turned to chatter at his pursuer.

Pete and I laughed. "I wonder what he'd do with a squirrel if he caught one," I said.

"He's pretty fast."

"Come, Duke." I whistled. Duke barked once at the squirrel and walked back to me. I hugged him and buried my face in his fur. "Good boy." I picked up my bike.

"Where you going?" Pete said.

"Hardware store. Got to talk to Mr. Simmons."

When we got to the store, I looked around but didn't see Malcolm. Duke flopped down on the wooden floor near a fan, and Pete looked over an assortment of rubber handlebar accessories.

"Hello, boys." Mr. Simmons seemed glad to see us. "What can I help you with today?"

"It's Malcolm," I said.

"He's not here today," Mr. Simmons said. "Over at Saulk's Appliance."

"I didn't want to see him," I said.

"What is it then?" Mr. Simmons crossed his arms.

"Well . . . uh . . . you see . . ." I stared down at my feet.

Mr. Simmons shook my shoulder. "Is he in trouble?"

"No, at least not yet."

"What's going on? Out with it, boy."

I looked up into Mr. Simmons's face. "You see, it's about Alex Buckner and the others."

"Oh. I saw him sitting with them at the game." Mr. Simmons shook his head. "I don't like for Malcolm to associate with that group."

"I know," I said, "and you got him away. But you don't know what they were telling him."

"And you do?"

I nodded. "I listened under the bleachers."

Mr. Simmons put his hand on my shoulder. "So tell me."

"Well . . . uh . . . you see, I don't talk the way they do." And I told him about the conversation as best I could.

"I don't like this at all," Mr. Simmons said. "They'll get Malcolm into trouble. He has several jobs around the square, and we do our best to take care of him. I'll talk to the others and his dad. Oh, and Hrabrosky, too. He cleans the presses for him."

"I knew you'd want to know."

"Thanks for telling me. You hear anything else, let me know."

We stopped at Tony's Market for an ice cream bar and sat in front of the store to enjoy it while Duke lapped up his water.

"Cards have a late game," Pete said.

"I know. They're on the coast."

"Let's go to the pool then listen to the game."

When we reached the community house across from the Methodist Church, a squirrel scampered across the street, and Duke dashed after it. Brakes squealed. A thud. Duke yelped. I threw my bike to the sidewalk and sprinted around the big blue car. Duke lay in the street thrashing around and trying to stand. He howled in sharp bursts. A bone in his back leg poked through his fur and blood spurted from the rupture. I knelt beside him and grasped his head. His body quivered as though he was cold, and he whimpered. Someone was screaming and yelling, but I didn't realize it was me. The driver grabbed me. I pounded on his chest, screaming at him.

He shook me. "Get in the car, I said." He shoved me into the back seat and lay Duke onto the seat beside me. My eyes filled with tears so I couldn't see where we were going, but Mr. Hrabrosky left rubber to get there. "We'll get him to the vet," he said.

Blood spurted from Duke's leg, and I wrapped my hand around it to stop the flow. Everything afterward was a blur. Mr. Hrabosky carried Duke into the vet's office and I followed. They told me to wait in the reception area. Luke came but they still wouldn't let me in to see Duke. Luke talked to Mr. Hrabosky and walked him to his car. The vet took Luke into his office. Empty and numb, I sat stiffly in a chair awaiting the terrible news.

"Let's go," Luke said when he came from the office.

"I want to see Duke."

"He's sedated." Luke grabbed my arm and guided me to the door. "He's getting a blood transfusion."

I struggled to turn around. "But is he okay?"

"I'll take you home."

Fresh tears rolled down my cheeks. "I want to stay with him."

Luke opened the car door. "Get in the car."

I slumped into the passenger's seat and slammed the door.

As Luke started the car and pulled away, I turned for a last look at the vet's office.

"You can't stay with Duke," Luke said. "He'll need an x-ray and then Jim will know if he can save the leg."

"Save the leg?"

"He may have to amputate. Depends on how badly it's broken."

"No! No! He can't do that," I sobbed.

"Dogs can get around on three legs," Luke said. "Jim will call and let us know."

I wiped my face with my shirt tail. "That damned Mr. Hrabosky and his big car."

"Mike. Mr. Hrabosky didn't hit Duke on purpose. He feels terrible about this."

"He should."

"You straighten up right this minute, young man. I'll not let you say a bad word about Emile Hrabosky. He's done more than anyone else would. He got Duke to the vet and his back seat and suit are bloody. He offered to pay Duke's vet bill. He's a fine man."

I kept the rest of my opinion to myself.

"Where's your bike?"

"Don't know. Maybe at the Reynolds Community Home."

It lay on the grass. Luke put it into the trunk and left the trunk lid open.

At home, Mom hugged me. "I'm so sorry, honey. Duke will be fine, don't you worry."

"When will the vet call?"

"Jim said about seven." Luke climbed the stairs. "I've got to get some sleep."

"We'll be quiet," Mom said. "You get out of those clothes, Mike. I'll need to soak them."

I looked down at the blood on my shorts..

"And shower, too," Mom said. "Just be as quiet as you can."

Holding my bloodstained clothes, I tiptoed down the stairs fifteen minutes later, my hair still wet from the shower.

"I'll take those." Mom held out her hand for my clothes. "Do you want something to eat?"

"No. What time is it?"

"A little after four."

Three hours. The vet would call in three hours.

Mom brushed the hair from my forehead. "Why don't you read a book? That'll take your mind off things."

"I could listen to the Cardinals," I said.

Mom shook her head. "Your dad's trying to sleep."

"At Pete's house, then."

"Okay."

"I'll be back before seven."

The Parkinson's door stood open and I could hear the game through the screen.

"Hey, Pete," I called.

"Come on in."

Pete lay on the floor in front of an oscillating fan. "My suit's still wet from the pool. Can't sit in a chair."

"Any score?"

"One to nothing, Cards." Pete sat up. "Boy, you sure told Mr. Hrabosky off."

"I did?"

"You called him every name in the book. I didn't know you could cuss like that."

"I don't remember it."

"You called him a damned son-of-a-bitch, a creepy asshole. You even used the F word." Pete examined my face. "How's Duke?"

I shrugged. "They may take his leg off." My lip trembled and tears filled my eyes. "Blood was all over." A tear coursed down my cheek. I wiped it away.

"I know just the thing for you." Pete leaped to his feet. "In the kitchen." He returned with a juice glass full of amber liquid. "My dad says when he's feeling down, a little whiskey cheers him up."

It burned going down, but the physical pain somehow made me feel better.

"Mr. Hrabosky said he was taking Duke to the vet, and I should call Luke," Pete said. "So I went to Tony's and called your mom."

"I don't want to think about it anymore," I said. "Let's just listen to the game."

By the end of the game, I'd emptied the glass. The ground beneath my feet shifted constantly on my way home, and attempting to anticipate its next move made me dizzy. From the alley, I saw our backyard where Duke should be waiting to welcome me home. My stomach lurched. I leaned over Mrs. Gensill's fence and upchucked into her flowers. My head swam and sweat popped out on my forehead. I seemed to be bobbing up and down on huge ocean waves. I closed my eyed and clutched the fence.

"Mike," Mom said. "Are you all right?" She put her arm around me and I leaned on her. "Mrs. Gensill called. Said you were sick."

"Yeah."

Mom sniffed. "You've been drinking."

"Just a glass."

"Let's get you home." Mom guided me down the alleyway and into the house. "Shh! Don't wake your dad."

She helped me up the stairs to bed. The next I knew my room was dark, and I heard quiet voices in the hallway. Duke! The vet must've called hours ago. Sitting up made my head spin. My bedroom door opened and Mom came in.

"Luke's gone to work." She sat on the edge of my bed. "I thought you'd like to know about Duke."

"What'd he say?"

"Jim thinks he can fix Duke's leg. He'll operate in the morning and do his best."

"But there's still a chance he'll . . ."

"Yes." Mom brushed the hair back from my forehead. "If he gets in there and it's worse than he expected, but he sounded very optimistic. Now you go back to sleep. We'll talk about your behavior tomorrow."

I felt almost normal in the morning.

"Mike, I want you out hoeing my flowers." Mom cleared the breakfast table. "After that, you can practice, but you're not to leave the premises until your dad talks to you."

"What's going on?" Dan said.

"Mike's in a spot of trouble," Mom said.

"About Duke?"

"No." Mom ran water to wash the dishes. "He went to Pete's house and drowned his sorrows in whiskey."

Dan looked at me with widened eyes and a smirk on his face. "No kidding? You get drunk, Squirt?"

"Got sick," I said.

"After you practice," Mom said to Dan, "you can drive over to my mom's house and mow her lawn."

I attacked the few weeds in Mom's flower garden as though they were my enemy. Across town, the vet was cutting into Duke's leg, and I promised God I'd never touch another drop of whiskey if Duke came home with all four legs.

Luke came home for lunch, grabbed my arm and sat me down hard in a chair. He paced back and forth in front of me, his face a mottled red.

"I don't know where to start."

"I won't do it again. Promise."

"You will apologize to Mr. Hrabrosky." Luke jabbed a finger at me. "Half the neighborhood heard you screaming at him including Rev. Norris."

"Oh." I hadn't thought of that.

"As for you and Pete, you are not allowed to go to his house when his parents aren't home."

"Okay."

"You want to listen to the games, he can come over here. I've talked to Pete's dad and Pete about this. I don't know what consequences Pete faces, but you will spend the afternoon at the library writing a report on the effects of alcohol."

That didn't sound so bad. "Okay."

"Have you heard anything about Duke?" Mom said.

"I went by and talked to Jim," Luke said. "Everything went well. Duke has a pin in his leg and will probably limp."

"I want to see him," I said.

"Seems you're all tied up this afternoon," Luke said.

"When can we bring him home?" Mom said.

"Jim wants to keep him for a couple of days."

"I'll drive Mike to the plant to apologize to Emile when Dan gets back with the car."

"Where is he?"

"He went over to Mom's to mow her lawn."

"Shouldn't he be back?"

"Why, I suppose so. I'll call."

Grandma Jenkins reported that Dan left her house over an hour ago. Mom called Rev. Norris who said Dan picked up Dean. They were going to Nick's Drive-In. I wasn't the only Martin boy in trouble that afternoon.

EIGHTEEN

"That's the last game of the summer." I threw the old ball glove into my bike's basket. The season ended and I never did get to use Dan's new glove.

"We got over two weeks before school begins," Pete said. "Why we quitting now?"

"Mr. Meadow's gotta get his football boys in shape."

Pete put his glove with mine. "Your dad said you got sick."

"Yeah."

"I got whipped." Pete rubbed his behind.

"No kidding?"

"What about you?"

"I had to apologize to Mr. Hrabosky."

"What'd he say?"

"He was nice." I walked my bike to the street. "Said he understood I was upset."

"Where you going?"

"To see Duke."

"Okay."

The vet's office was on the highway west of town, a long ride on a hot August morning. We rode out Antelope to the cemetery road marking the city limits then north to the highway.

"I don't like riding on the highway," Pete said.

"Keep far over on the shoulder."

That half mile stretched forever with the hot sun punishing me and the turbulence of passing vehicles whipping at me.

The vet's door opened and Dr. Buchman's elderly assistant Mrs. Duffy emerged, key in hand. "Oh, Mike," she said. "I was just leaving for lunch."

"I want to see Duke."

Mrs. Duffy looked at her ancient truck and then back to the office door. “Well, since you’ve ridden all this way.”

She led us into the office, through an examination room, and back to a row of cages. Duke lay on his side on the floor of his cage, his right leg encased in plaster and his whole hip shaved. He weakly thumped his tail twice. Tape held a needle into his paw and a long tube stretched from it up to a bottle hung from a wire.

Mrs. Duffy opened the cage door. “He’s still a bit doped up to keep him from trying to stand.”

I reached in, rubbed his soft ear and stroked his thick coat.

“We’ve got him on antibiotics to keep down the risk of infection,” Mrs. Duffy said. “He should go home tomorrow afternoon. Tell Luke to come. He’ll need to be carried.”

I put my arms around Duke’s head and hugged him. “Tomorrow.”

“I’ve got to get to lunch.” Mrs. Duffy shut the cage door. We followed her from the office and she locked the door. “Put your bikes in my truck. I’ll give you a lift into town.”

She dropped us off at the service station where the highways intersected north of the square.

“I’d better get home for lunch,” I said.

“I got a dollar,” Pete said. “Let’s eat at the café. You can call your mom from there.”

After lunch, we sat in the shade on the courthouse lawn to finish our drinks. A front loader rumbled through the theater ruins lifting debris into a truck.

“My dad says we gotta get a television now,” Pete said.

“Won’t be the same.” I lay back on my elbows. “Itty-bitty picture. Black and white.”

“Yeah.” Pete sighed. “But it’s on every night and free. You can watch in your pajamas.”

“By yourself.” I pulled on my straw to finish my drink. “Won’t be any friends there to laugh with you.”

“Gotta watch commercials, too.”

“I hope Mr. Beach rebuilds,” I said. “I’d go to the movies even if we had a television.”

“Let’s go to the pool. Won’t be long until it closes.”

We cut over a block to ride home for our suits. I heard the roar of a large vehicle and looked back. A red firetruck rumbled past.

"The new truck," Pete yelled.

We pedaled hard to keep it in sight. When we got to the station, a fireman backed the truck into place.

"Want to look her over, boys?" a man said.

"Oh, boy!"

We abandoned our bikes to climb onto the truck. Pete took the steering wheel. "Wow! This is high up."

"Are you one of the new fireman?" I said.

"No. We're from Pattonburg. Just delivering the truck."

Darren Matlock, one of Glendale's volunteers, dashed through the door. "Sorry I'm late. Meant to be here when you arrived."

"Just got here. You Leroy Beach?"

"No. Darren Matlock."

"Joe Lake." The two men shook hands.

"Leroy's tied up at the insurance office," Darren said. "Seems the insurance company refuses to pay until he's cleared of arson."

"Sure a rash of fires here," Mr. Lake said.

"The state investigators are reviewing the previous findings for inconsistencies." Darren wiped his forehead with a handkerchief. "Seems we may have a firebug in town."

We hung around as Mr. Lake showed Darren all the neat features of the truck.

"Bet I could drive that firetruck," Pete said as we left.

"I wouldn't mind that," I said, "but I don't want to fight fires."

"I might." Pete slowed to ride beside me. "I want to do something exciting when I grow up. What about you?"

I shrugged. "I'd really like to play baseball."

As we neared Smithton's Garage, I recognized a familiar figure.

"Dan isn't supposed to be there," I told Pete.

"You gonna tell on him?"

"No. He knows I saw him. If I keep it to myself, he'll owe me one."

Mom, Dan and I picked peaches in the Horlacher orchard the next morning. Back at home, Mom put me to work dipping the peaches into the boiling water as I had experience. From the pot, the peaches went into cold water and the skins sloughed off. Dan and Mom halved, seeded and sliced the peaches. When we finished, Mom sent us off to practice while she finished the canning. I looked forward to peach cobbler at dinner.

I hung around the house all afternoon waiting for Luke to come home so we could get Duke from the vet's. Mom created enough steam in the kitchen to loosen wallpaper if it had any.

"When will Luke be home?"

"Good grief." Mom brushed the hair off my forehead. "You asked that ten minutes ago."

"Well?"

"I don't know. He had lunch with Sheriff Gilliland. Something about catching the burglars."

"He hasn't called?"

"No." She turned me around and checked the back of my hair. "You'll need a haircut before school starts. I've scheduled a physical to update your shots and a dental appointment, too."

"Ah, Mom."

"You've grown this summer. Since it seems you've nothing to do, go up and try on your jeans. See if they still fit. We may have to do some shopping."

I attempted to zip up the third pair when I heard Luke's car pull into the driveway. I fell down trying to get the jeans off, donned my shorts and thundered down the stairs.

Luke laughed. "Better slow down. You'll hurt yourself or someone else."

"Take this old blanket." Mom handed it to me and she gave Luke an envelope. "I called to see how much it was."

I beat Luke out the door.

"Spread that blanket over the back seat," Luke said.

By the time I finished, Luke started the car and I took the shotgun seat.

"I met with Sheriff Gilliland today," Luke said.

"Mom told me."

"It was about that old black Ford you and Pete saw."

"No kidding?"

"We've run the plate. Belongs to a guy out by Cougar Creek in the county. He's got a record. Probably one of our suspects."

"What'll you do?"

"Gilliland and I have a plan. Right now, all we have is a suspicion. Can't get a warrant on that."

"You gonna set him up?"

"Something like that. You keep your mouth shut about it. Don't want to warn him off."

"Okay."

"Maybe I shouldn't have told you, but I think you deserve to know. It was fine work, son. You'd make a good detective. You notice things and you use your head." Luke chuckled. "Usually, that is. Here we are."

Mrs. Duffy put us in one of the examination rooms. Soon Dr. Buchman carried Duke in and laid him onto the table. Duke's tail whacked the table enthusiastically and he gave a half-bark. I put my arms around his head and he licked my face.

"He's a smart dog," Dr. Buchman said. "I got him onto his feet this morning. He put that foot down and yelped. Hasn't done it since."

"Any special instructions?" Luke said.

"Keep him off his feet as much as possible. He'll have trouble with stairs."

"He sleeps upstairs in the boys' room."

"Probably have to be carried up." The vet handed Luke a small envelope. "This packet contains pain killers for only two days. You know how to give him pills?"

"Sure," I said. "Had to do that when you fixed him."

"And this little bottle is antibiotics. Pill's so small you can do both at the same time. Morning and evening for a week. Start tonight."

I sniffed. "He smells."

"Needs a bath," the vet said. "Tie a plastic bag over the cast so you don't get it wet. Bring him back next Friday. We'll do an x-ray to see how he's healing."

Luke carried Duke to the car. I got into the back seat and held Duke's head in my lap.

"I'll be right back." Luke returned to the vet's office.

When he came back, I said, "Why'd you go back in?"

Luke started the engine. "To pay the bill."

"But you said Mr. Hrabosky offered to pay."

Luke checked for traffic and then turned onto the highway. "We couldn't let him do that."

"Why not?"

"For several reasons. It wasn't his fault. Duke ran out in front of him."

"Yeah. So?"

"Mr. Hrabosky already has a ruined suit, you know." Luke signaled to go through town. "And after you called him all those awful names, well, your mom paid with the money she'd saved for a washer and dryer."

"Oh."

"Don't let her know I told you."

This knowledge tempered the joy I felt at having Duke back. After dinner, Luke slept before he left to patrol and Rev. Norris and Dean picked Dan up to go to the game. I bathed Duke and gave him his pills. Mom and I skipped the Friday evening ballgame. Instead, we relaxed on the front porch with Duke and listened to *Fibber McGee and Molly* and *The Jack Benny Show.*

Duke limped down the three steps from the porch to the front lawn to do his business then stood at the bottom of the steps and whined.

"We'll have to help him," Mom said.

She took his shoulders and I maneuvered his hindquarters up the three steps.

"We'll never get him upstairs," I said.

"He'll have to stay down for the night." Mom sat back onto the swing.

"He'll whine all night. I should sleep out here with him."

"On the porch? I don't know, Mike."

"Besides, it's cooler here than in my room."

Mom seemed to think about that for a minute. "Mosquitoes will bother you."

"Haven't heard a one tonight."

"But sleeping on a wooden floor?"

"Let's take the mattress off my bed."

"You are determined, aren't you?" Mom got to her feet. "Well, I suppose it would be okay."

We managed to scoot the twin mattress down the stairs and out the door. I ran back for my pillow.

"I don't like the idea of your sleeping out here by yourself," Mom said.

"People have been sleeping in the park this summer."

"The city sponsors that on Thursday nights."

"Why haven't we done that?"

"We can't go. Luke needs to be near a phone. And those people don't sleep alone."

"I'm not alone. Duke's here."

"Let's bring Dan's mattress down. He can sleep with you."

"Okay."

We tugged and shoved the mattress onto the porch.

"Now you'll be alone in the house," I said.

Mom sat and chugged some iced tea. "Luke will catch the burglars soon and we'll be back to normal."

A car turned down our street and pulled to the curb at our house.

Dan got out of the car. "Thanks for the ride." Coming up the steps, he paused to examine the scene. "What's going on?'

"Duke can't get up the stairs so we're sleeping here to keep him company," I said.

"Neat." Dan flopped onto his mattress.

"Wash up and brush your teeth," Mom said. "You can sleep in your shorts."

Dan and I talked a bit. He said thanks for not telling on him about being at Smithton's Garage. The Bombers lost again and Malcolm sat with Alex Buckner and his buddies at the game. Mr. Simmons must not have been there. I asked about the Johnson girl and Dan said he saw her at the game. I wondered if he sat with her but didn't ask. The unfamiliar setting kept me awake for some time but I slept well.

NINETEEN

I spent the weekend with Duke leaving him only to attend Sunday school and church. I fed him, made sure he had water, gave him his pills and used a sheet of plywood to make a ramp for him. Instead of bouncing around as he usually did, Duke lay stretched out on the porch only getting up to eat or do his business. I helped him when he needed it but mostly sat beside him and read a book. Dan and I continued to sleep on the porch to keep Duke company. Luke said Duke was okay and that the pain pills were making him lethargic. Sure enough, when the pain pills were gone, Duke perked up. He walked around the yard keeping his injured leg raised, held his head up to gaze around instead of sleeping, and followed me around in the house.

I was surprised to see Luke at the breakfast table Monday morning reading the newspaper.

"You're home," I said.

"We caught the burglars last night."

"Where?"

"Earnest Simmons's house. When we learned he'd be out of town for a week, we made some arrangements with him."

"Cereal this morning." Mom sat a bowl in front of me.

"How'd you catch them?" Dan said.

"Simmons gave us a key to his side door. I've been inside the house for the last three nights."

I filled my cereal bowl. "Who was it?"

"Just who we thought. Victor Slobetz who owns that old Ford you saw and his son. They broke into the house a little before three and started carting things out to a truck. Sheriff Gilliland blocked the drive and we had them pinned between us."

"They're in jail?" Dan said.

"Uh huh." Luke finished his coffee. "As soon as the judge is up, we'll get a warrant to search their properties."

"I'm so glad your schedule will be back to normal," Mom said.

"We'd have caught them sooner or later, but the plate number you and Pete supplied helped. I'll catch a couple hours sleep then meet the county boys to serve those warrants." Luke slowly climbed the stairs.

"Time to mow your grandma's lawn again," Mom said. "And Dan, you drive straight over there and back. No side trips."

"Okay." Dan put his cereal bowl into the sink.

"Mike, you and I have some deadheading and weed pulling to do."

Both the *Pattonburg Sun* and the *Glendale Courier* printed long articles about the apprehension of the burglars who were found to have robbed other homes in the county. Law enforcement credited Pete and me but refused to release our names. Luke said it was for our protection. Instead, the newspapers printed this paragraph:

A couple of enterprising young men playing detective thought the burglars might locate a house to rob during the day and look it over. They noticed a car doing that, wrote down the license tag number and gave it to police. The tag number led to Victor Slobetz. Law enforcement is grateful to these alert fine citizens."

I cut out the articles and saved them.

The next day, Mom went into full get-ready-for-school mode. She went through my closet, had me try things on and decided what to keep and what to give to the community closet. She brought down a box of Dan's old clothes and had me try them on. Several shirts fit but none of the pants as my waist was narrower and my legs longer. She washed and ironed and hung the shirts in my closet and made a list of what I needed. Finished with me, she moved on to Dan's closet.

List in hand, we stopped at the community closet to donate clothes and buy a few. Saulk's Department Store beckoned us. Inside, a riches of clothing and shoes tempted me beneath swirling ceiling fans. A helpful clerk measured my waist and inseam and found jeans to fit. An hour later, we approached the checkout counter loaded down with everything on Mom's list.

The clerk listed the apparel and tallied the total. Mom gave her the cash. The clerk put the cash and list into a container, shoved it into a pneumatic tube, and with a swish, it disappeared. A few minutes later, the metal container returned with Mom's change and a receipt. We carried our loot to the car and stopped at Rexall Drug for an ice cream soda.

Satisfied that we'd be decently clothed, Mom took us to get our books. I carried a spelling book, a grammar text, and one book each for math, social studies and science to the counter. Dan's books were more interesting—algebra, biology, American government, American literature, speech and debate. We added notebooks, pencils and pens and Dan's required clothing for physical education. We finished the week with our doctor and dental appointments and got a haircut.

The high school held open house Thursday evening and we all went. Glendale High stood in the north end of town next to Hawthorne Elementary and Stephen Crane Junior High. The separate gymnasium/auditorium sat next door to the three-story brick building.

The school's hardwood floors gleamed and groaned underfoot and the smell of fresh paint and polish greeted us. We followed Dan's schedule to the second floor where he had his homeroom across from the large study hall/assembly room reserved as a base for upperclassmen. Back to the first floor and the large music room where the band practiced then to the third floor for biology and algebra. Dan would eat lunch at home as the school had no cafeteria. After lunch, Dan had American government on the second floor, went outside to the gym for physical education and back to the second floor for American literature. We met all of Dan's teachers and visited with Gideon McKinley, the principal. High school excited me and I envied Dan. He got to move from one classroom to another, had six different teachers and even got to go outside to get to the gym. I'd be stuck in one room with one teacher all day.

The Glendale Bombers played their final game of a disappointing season the next night. I hadn't seen Bruce in over a week, so we had a lot to talk about. Luke took Leroy Beach's position in the outfield and received several backslaps and handshakes from his teammates over arresting the burglars.
In the fourth inning, a foul ball line drive clipped the bat boy whose mother drove him home, so Bruce and I took his place. The heckling began in the sixth inning.

"McKinley, you're a sorry shit for a coach."

I searched the stands for the loudmouth. Most spectators' eyes looked at the end of the stands and there sat George Buckner, Kelvin Rogers and Alex Buckner with his two shadows.

"Wonder who yelled that," Bruce said.

"Better not be George Buckner," I said. "He's the custodian at the high school. Has to work with Mr. McKinley." I watched George lean to Kelvin and say something.

"My mother could coach better'n you, McKinley," Kelvin bellowed.

"Looks like Mr. Rogers is Buckner's mouthpiece," Bruce said.

"You got shit for a team." Alex added his voice.

"You're a lousy principal, too," Junior Rogers yelled.

The heckling continued through the seventh inning and spread to every player on the Glendale team. The Bombers came to bat at the bottom of the eighth inning with Anton Paternik leading off.

"Well, if it ain't can't-hit-Paternik." Kelvin Rogers stood at the backstop.

Junior Rogers joined his father. "Hey, Anton, you need glasses."

"That was a strike, you dumbass." George Buckner joined the heckling.

"I think George Buckner is drunk again," I said.

Bruce shoved a bat into the rack. "Wish they'd shut up."

Alex Buckner joined the group at the backstop. "Vanderwell, you can't run worth a damn."

"Hey, Chevy. They oughta call you by your real name—Asshole."

Alex Buckner pointed. "There's our hero police chief."

"Having kids do his job, I hear," George Buckner screamed.

Ed Horlacher stood, turned and glared at the group.

"Sit down, lack a whore." George Buckner roared with laughter.

"Windy's going over," Bruce said.

Windy Markmann approached the group. George Buckner shook his head at something Windy said. Kelvin Rogers turned and poked Windy in the chest. Bob Valetti joined the group and voices were raised.

"You're disturbing everyone," Bob Valetti said. "Why don't you sit down and enjoy the game?"

"We're just havin' a bit of fun," Kelvin Rogers said.

"No one here thinks this is fun," Windy said.

Kelvin turned to the crowd. "You havin' fun?"

"No they ain't," Alex said, "'cause this team's shit."

"Your language is inappropriate," Bob said.

"It's a friggin' ball game," Junior said.

"You should leave." Windy pointed toward the exit.

"You and what army'll make us?" George put his hands on his hips.

Windy took George's arm. George jerked away and shoved Windy back into the fenced backstop. Windy pushed off the fence and grabbed George again.

"Leave him alone." Kelvin Rogers slugged Windy who staggered backward wiping his bloodied mouth. Bob Valetti retaliated and Kelvin went to his knees. Kelvin drove forward, caught Bob low, and Bob's head hit the wooden bleachers as he went down.

Ed Horlacher charged from the dugout, trotted around the chain link backstop and grabbed George's arm as he prepared to hit Windy again. Ed caught George with an uppercut laying him out flat in the dust. Alex vaulted from the stands onto Ed's back. Ed leaned forward and flipped Alex over his head onto George.

The Pattonburg Miners left the field to watch the fight. Glendale's players abandoned the dugout. Spectators stood to scream and yell at the combatants. So many people lined the fence that I couldn't see, so I climbed the chain link to watch.

Mr. Simmons led Bob Valetti away, blood streaking the back of his shirt. Coming to the aid of his father, Vinny Valetti swung his crutch and caught Junior Rogers across the shoulders. Junior tripped over Simmons and went down. Everett Smithton walloped Vinny who staggered back into the fence and sat down. Windy punched Everett whose nose gushed bright red blood down his chin. Everett stumbled into Alex who helped him sit down.

Luke stood on the third row of the bleachers banging a bat against the seat. "Stop it! Stop this right now." He pounded the bleachers with the bat until he had everyone's attention. "We'll call this a draw. Rogers. Buckner. I'd advise you to leave. The whole team's here. You're outnumbered."

Kelvin helped George to his feet and they careened away. Alex gave a napkin to Everett who held it to his nose. Junior Rogers loped after his father.

"Still a shitty team," Alex said as he led Everett away.

Windy helped Vinny to his feet. "You okay, kid?"

"Yeah, sure. Broke my crutch." He held it up.

"Use me as your crutch." Vinny put his arm over Windy's shoulder. "We'll see how your dad's doing."

Vinny looked at Windy. "Your mouth's bleeding."

"Probably have some loose teeth, too."

Glendale lost the game.

"How's Duke?" Pete said.

"He's putting some weight on the leg," I said. "Vet says he's healing well."

"A few guys got some healing to do from that fight last night," Pete said. "You had a front row seat."

We sat on the courthouse steps Saturday afternoon eating ice cream cones. "Quite a fight."

"Half the time I couldn't see. Too many people."

"Luke said Bob Valetti had ten stiches."

Chocolate ice cream ran down Pete's chin. "I think Luke should've given our names to the newspaper."

"You want to be a hero, huh?" I bit into my cone.

"Sure. Why not?"

"Luke says not everybody likes heroes."

Pete snorted. "Everybody knows it was us, anyway."

"Maybe here but not in Pattonburg." I finished the last of my cone.

"You get your books?"

"Yeah. We toured the high school, too."

"You went?" Pete finished his cone and wiped his chin.

"Yeah. It's a great place. I can't wait to get there."

"There's Bruce's dad." Pete nodded toward Wayford's Variety.

Ed Horlacher carrying a big box followed a short, slim woman to a car. Wavy blonde hair fell to her shoulders above a colorfully flowered sundress. Her yellow hat's floppy brim flapped in the breeze. She opened the car's trunk and Ed lowered the box into it. They exchanged a few words.

"That's Mrs. Brackett," I said. "She's a neighbor of his and her husband's on the ball team."

"He's hot for her," Pete said.

I punched Pete's arm. "No, he's not."

"Just watch."

Ed leaned toward Mrs. Brackett and said something. They both laughed. Ed caressed her arm and she put her hand over his. She turned away, opened the car door and sat behind the wheel. Ed hung onto the car door and leaned in.

"Bet he kissed her," Pete said.

"He wouldn't."

Ed closed the car door and walked away.

I couldn't believe Mr. Horlacher would cheat on his wife, but the whole incident made me doubt the rightness of the world. It also made me doubt myself as I realized two people could see the same event and reach different conclusions, and my take on the event could be wrong. At church when I looked at Mr. Horlacher singing in the choir with his wife, he appeared different somehow as though I truly saw him for the first time.

TWENTY

A front pushed through with a brief shower, cleaned the humidity from the air and left behind cotton ball clouds in a bright blue sky. Having helped Mom put up preserves all day, Grandma Jenkins joined us for dinner and relaxed on the front porch in the evening. We listened to an episode of *Gunsmoke* before Dan tuned in XERF out of Del Rio, Texas, with Wolfman Jack. Luke lit his evening cigar as Mr. Hrabosky's blue Buick pulled to the curb. He wore golf clothes and I almost didn't recognize him without his suit and hat. Duke watched him come up the walk.

"Good evening, folks," Mr. Hrabosky said.

"Emile." Luke stood. "Come on up and sit awhile."

Mr. Hrabosky stepped to the porch. "How's Duke doing?"

"Pretty good," I said. "Dr. Buchman said he's healing well."

Mr. Hrabosky leaned down to pet Duke. "He's a fine looking animal."

Duke's tail thumped on the porch floor.

"Good idea about the ramp," Mr. Hrabosky said. "You do that yourself?"

"Yes, sir."

"And I understand you're good at playing detective, too."

I felt my face flush. "Got lucky, I guess."

"Would you like an iced tea?" Mom said.

"That'd sure hit the spot."

"Sit here, Emile." Luke pointed to the chair beside him. "You've been on the course?"

"Beautiful day for it." Mr. Hrabosky sat and pulled a pack of cigarettes from his shirt pocket. "Okay if I smoke?"

"Sure." Luke moved the ashtray to the table beside Mr. Hrabosky. "I'm enjoying a cigar myself."

Mom returned with a tall glass of iced tea. "Here you go."

"Thanks, Joan."

"Have you heard from Alice lately?"

"Her girls are back in school," Mr. Hrabosky said. "They plan to visit us at Thanksgiving."

"I'll look forward to seeing them." Mom returned to her seat on the swing. "It's been ten years."

"They don't return to the States often enough for Margaret and me." Mr. Hrabosky turned to Luke. "The FBI's back in town."

"They dropped by the office." Luke knocked the ash from his cigar. "Asked questions about your associations like they did last time. Afraid I couldn't come up with anything they wanted to hear."

Mr. Hrabosky pulled on his cigarette and blew smoke at the ceiling. "They're determined to get me for something even if they have to make it up."

"Is this because of your last pamphlet?" Grandma said.

"I'm sure of it." Mr. Hrabosky coughed to clear his throat.

"I thought your facts were compelling," Grandma said. "Hoover is creating a police state."

"We need to convince our congress of that," Mr. Hrabosky said. "Earnest Simmons and Tony DeCarlo tell me the FBI has questioned them. They own the two locations in town that sell my work."

"Was there a problem?" Luke puffed on his cigar.

"They asked for the names of customers," Mr. Hrabosky said. "At first they refused, but the officers returned and threatened them with jail time."

"So they've got my name," Grandma said.

"I'm afraid so, Iona."

"What will they do?"

"I don't know. They may question you but you've done nothing illegal." Mr. Hrabosky puffed on his cigarette. "None of us have. It's pure harassment."

"More proof of Hoover's misuse of power," Grandma said.

"Something else." Mr. Hrabosky sipped his iced tea. "I'm being followed and it's not the FBI."

This got my attention and I wished to be anywhere else.

"Who is it?" Luke said.

Mr. Hrabosky turned to me with a smile. "I've seen enough of Mike and his friend Pete Parkinson to suspect they were following me, but I assumed they were playing some spy game. What about it, Mike?"

"Well . . . it was something like that. Like playing detective."

Mr. Hrabosky laughed. "Just as I thought. I'm sorry my life is so dull and spying on me wasn't more exciting for you."

Luke frowned at me. "I'll talk to you about this later."

"It's Kelvin Rogers, mostly." Mr. Hrabosky crushed out his cigarette. "He's still angry that I didn't have to pay for his foundation work. If I'd known he'd do this, I would've just paid for it to avoid the trouble."

"What's he doing?" Luke said.

"He sits at the end of my drive. Sometimes it's one of his friends. When I leave, they follow me. Doesn't happen all the time, you see. But often. And they want me to see them. One night we went to a concert in Pattonburg, and Rogers followed us clear to the college."

"That's all he does? Follows you?"

"He doesn't try to pass or even tailgate but he's there. I think he's writing the threatening notes, too."

"Notes?"

"The first one was in my mailbox. Luckily, Margaret didn't see it. Now I check the mailbox every morning on the way to work."

Luke rubbed his chin. "What do these notes say?"

Mr. Hrabosky glanced at Mom and Grandma. "Mostly name calling. Filthy language. Now they've shown up at the plant."

"Have you kept them?" Luke said.

"The first ones I threw away," Mr. Hrabosky said. "I have a few in my office desk."

"I'll come by tomorrow and get them. What would be a good time?"

"I get to the office about eight. It's probably nothing and I'm letting my nerves get to me." Mr. Hrabosky rose. "I'm on edge with this and the FBI."

"I'll see what I can do, Emile." Luke rose and the two men shook hands.

"Thanks. I better get home. Good night, Joan, Iona. You, too, boys."

I watched Mr. Hrabosky leave and remembered what Mr. Simmons said about the lawsuit.

"Mike."

Luke's sharp voice pulled me back to my own situation.

"I want an explanation."

"Well . . . I." I decided to start at the beginning. "Do you remember the Sunday Dan skipped church and you found him in the park?"

"Of course."

"After church, I went to Tony's. Mr. Rogers was there. Well . . . I don't remember everything word for word."

"That's okay."

"He asked Mr. DeCarlo if he was an atheist or something."

Grandma said, "You asked me about that."

"He said communists were atheists and Senator McCarthy was after them. Then he said Mr. Hrabosky was a communist and the FBI was investigating him."

"Emile isn't a communist," Grandma said.

"Go on," Luke said.

"He called him a foreigner, a liar, and a Jew. Said his printing business should burn down with him in it."

"Did he threaten to burn it down himself?" Luke said.

I shook my head. "I don't think so."

"But why were you following Mr. Hrabosky?" Mom said.

"Well . . . I told Pete about it. We thought we'd be helping the FBI. We'd be heroes."

That got a chuckle from everyone.

"You've quite an imagination, Squirt," Dan said.

"So that's why you kept questioning me about communists," Mom said.

Grandma Jenkins squirmed in her seat like a hen settling onto her nest. "Emile isn't a communist. Let me tell you a bit about him. He was born in Philadelphia about 1890, I guess as he's my age. His Jewish parents came here to escape persecution in Hungary. He grew up poor but he's made quite a success of his life."

"His daughter Alice was one of my best friends growing up," Mom said. "In the summer, we had wonderful swim parties at her house—slumber parties, too. That was before Margaret got sick."

"Margaret still buys Avon from me," Grandma said, "so I visit her every month or so. I like reading Emile's *Little Red Books*. Don't agree with everything he says but he has interesting ideas."

"I never knew you read those," Mom said.

Grandma smiled at Mom. "Guess you don't know everything about me, dear."

"What interesting ideas?" Mom said.

"Okay, let's see." Grandma chewed on her lip. "Government sponsored universal health care. He says it's the government's responsibility because of the clause in the preamble to the constitution about promoting the general welfare."

Luke frowned. "How would that work?"

"Everyone would pay a tax to go into a fund to pay for health care," Grandma said.

Luke shook his head. "It'll never fly. Republicans will never raise taxes."

"But if he's not a communist," I said, "what is he?"

"A socialist," Grandma said.

"What's that?"

"Not sure I can answer that." Grandma leaned forward. "From what I've read, Emile supports democracy. That's one reason he's so upset about Hoover. Thinks he's interfering with the democratic process in our government."

"That doesn't explain what a socialist is," Mom said.

"I'm not good at explaining it." Grandma bit her lip and frowned. "It's not only health care. Emile wants everyone to have a livable wage, a good place to life, enough food. He's concerned about clean water and air."

"Sounds great," Luke said. "How do we do all that?"

"Pass laws," Grandma said. "Make sure companies don't pollute. Provide housing for those who need it."

"Pie in the sky," Luke said. "Everybody on welfare?"

Grandma shook her head. "Said I wasn't good at explaining it."

"Maybe I should read some of Emile's writing," Mom said.

"Can't you do anything about this FBI persecution of Emile?" Grandma said.

"I can't interfere with the feds," Luke said.

"Hoover must be real paranoid to harass an obscure publisher in Glendale, Kansas," Mom said.

"Rogers is a bigger worry than the FBI," Luke said. "He's a loudmouth hothead and a bigot, too. That fight at the ball park shows he has a violent streak."

"Has he broken the law?" Mom said.

"Following Emile. Writing threatening notes." Luke shook his head. "I can't arrest him for that."

"What would this town do without Emile?" Grandma said. "You know he wrote a thousand dollar check at that Sunday fundraiser on the courthouse lawn."

"He took Windy's place as sponsor of the team," Luke said.

"I thought he wanted to be anonymous," Mom said.

"Everybody knows it was him," Grandma said.

"He bought a share of Windy's dealership so he can rebuild," Luke said. "Windy can buy it back when the insurance comes through and he gets back on his feet."

"And he co-signed Turnbow's loan," Grandma said.

"I imagine he'll help Leroy, too," Luke said. "That's just the kind of man he is."

Luke turned to me. "Now, Mike. Dan, you, too. Don't be telling others about what went on here tonight. Got it?"

"Got it," Dan said.

"Promise," I said.

So Mr. Hrabosky not only wasn't a communist, he was better than the bank about helping people.

"It's Pete." Mom held the phone out to me.

I reminded myself again. Don't mention Mr. Hrabosky or Kelvin Rogers or the FBI. I found keeping this secret difficult.

"School starts next week," Pete said. "We've got to do it now."

He wanted to bike out to the creek where Bruce and I swam.

"I'll call Bruce," I said, "and I'll have to ask my mom."

"Call me back."

Bruce said he'd join us and Mom nodded okay, so after lunch, we set out for the two-mile ride. The paved first mile had no shoulder so we rode single file. As we passed the Brackett farm, I noticed Ed Horlacher's car in the drive. The sight punched me in the stomach, and I hoped Pete hadn't seen it. It puzzled me. He was over there. Did that prove he was having an affair? If he was, wouldn't he hide his car? Further down the road, two men worked in a hayfield. I recognized Ed Horlacher and Mr. Brackett. With renewed energy, I zipped past Pete.

"Come on, slowpoke."

Bruce waited for us at the end of his drive. After a quarter mile, the pavement ended and the county road turned to gravel at the top of a long hill leading down to the bridge over the creek. We flew down the hill faster than we could pedal.

"Look!" Pete rode with no hands on the handlebars.

I released the handlebars and followed suit. Wind whistled past my ears and I laughed with unrestrained delight. The next instant, I flew through the air, landed hard and skidded through the gravel. I gasped for air as agony slammed my body. I drew a ragged breath and sobbed.

"You okay?" Bruce knelt beside me.

I moaned in reply.

"Roll over." Bruce pushed me.

I flopped onto my back with a groan.

"What happened?" Pete said.

"Hell of a crash. He's hurt bad. I'll go for help."

I lay crying in the road.

"Damn." Pete grabbed the front of my shirt. "Come on. Sit up." He pulled.

I leaned forward and sobbed. Flecked with dirt and gravel, whitish jelly-looking patches on my legs oozed blood.

"Took the skin clean off," Pete said. "Your arms, too."

I lifted my arm to see. The whole forearm bled. I hiccupped several times trying to quit crying as a car stopped beside us.

"My goodness," a voice said.

I looked up. Mrs. Herrick, my teacher for the coming year, knelt beside me. I wanted to be at my best for her, to impress her, and here I sat a bloody mess with a dirty, tear-streaked face. Fine impression I made.

"I'll drive you home," Mrs. Herrick said.

"My bike."

"We'll put it in the trunk." Mrs. Herrick held out her hand.

"It's got a bent rim," Bruce said.

I took Mrs. Herrick's hand and Bruce helped me to stand.

More pain followed as Mom cleaned my cuts and scrapes and picked gravel out of them. She applied an ointment and bandaged me. School began in four days after the Labor Day weekend. I couldn't imagine putting on long pants.

TWENTY-ONE

Misery dominated the following day as every move brought pain. Bruises across my ribs prevented breathing deeply. My knees and elbows refused to bend without sending me new torments. So when the whistle blew that night announcing a new tragedy, I turned over in my bed believing no new blaze could be worse than losing the movie theater. I was wrong.

"It's the high school!"

Luke's panicked voice jerked me out of bed. Moving as quickly as my battered body would allow, I threw on a shirt and shorts and crept down the stairs after Dan. Mom soon followed.

"One minute, boys," Mom said. She quickly dialed a number and waited. "It's the high school . . . okay . . . We'll be on Gillette's lawn." She hung up and dialed again. "Mom." Her voice broke. "It's the high school . . . five minutes."

We hurried to the car.

"We'll pick up my mother," Mom said. "And I called the Horlachers."

She backed down the drive, hit the street and left rubber.

"Maybe it's just a small fire," Dan said.

"I hope so." She took a corner a bit fast.

I hit my arm on the car door. "Ow."

"Sorry, Mike." She didn't slow down.

Grandma Jenkins waited at the curb in front of her house and climbed into the back seat with me.

"Goodness," she said, "you've enough gauze wrapped around you to be a mummy. Maybe he shouldn't be out, Joan."

"He can always stay in the car if it gets to be too much for him," Mom said.

"I'm fine." I would watch this fire even if it hurt.

A police car blocked the street two blocks south of the high school, so Mom turned east for a block then back north. She parked behind other cars which just arrived and disgorged their passengers. We joined the throng charging to the scene. Homes lined the street across from the high school and people crowded their lawns and porches. Flames shot from the left side of the building.

Mom said, “That’s the home ec room.”

“Maybe they can hold it there,” a man said.

“It’s next to the stairwell,” a lady said. “If it goes up that . . . well.”

“We need to get to Gillette’s lawn,” Mom said. “Follow me.”

“There’s Dean,” Dan said. “Okay if I stay with him?”

Mom nodded. “You know where we’ll be.”

The firemen shot water through the windows onto the fire. One fireman broke the front door’s window and entered the building. He returned hurriedly and pointed back at the building as he yelled out a command. The second truck, hose finally attached to a hydrant, quickly directed their stream through the front door.

“Where’s the pumper?” a man said.

“Other side shooting water through the music room.”

Dan joined us with Rev. Norris and his family. Flames now flickered on the second floor.

“Look!”

“That’s my homeroom,” Dan said.

“It’s spreading,” Mrs. Norris said.

Rev. Norris placed a hand on my shoulder. “How’re you feeling, son?”

“Awful.” After a day of physical misery, I now suffered mental and emotional anguish. All those classrooms in which I’d never sit, the beautiful polished hardwood floors, the towering windows looking out on the street—all gone? Where would Dan go to school Tuesday?

Windows shattered on the second floor and flames shot out. The firemen raised their aim.

“Teachers worked all day getting things ready for the opening,” Mrs. Norris said.

“What will the district do?” a man said. “They won’t be able to use the building even if they put out the fire.”

"Why not?" a woman asked.

"Smoke and water damage," the man said. "Probably structural damage, too."

"I found you," Mrs. Horlacher said. "Oh, Joan."

Mom hugged Thelma. "We spent four wonderful years in that beautiful old building."

The two women stood with their arms around each other.

"I graduated from this building forty-three years ago," Grandma said.

Mom put her arm over Grandma's shoulders and the three women faced the fire together, their faces lit by the flames and tears in their eyes.

"Hi, Mike," Bruce said. "How're you feeling?"

"Lousy."

"Rob's really upset. First football game's less than a week away."

The Harrington crew pulled in from the north and stopped beside the gymnasium. With practiced coordination, they attached their hose to the hydrant across the street and opened fire on the high school's north side.

"There's no fire there," a lady said.

"Prevent it from spreading," a man said.

"Most of us graduated from this school," another man said.

"My God! What's that?"

A flash followed by an explosive whoosh lit the night, and orange flames billowed from windows on the north. The Harrington crew staggered back.

"Had to be an accelerant."

"You think it was set?"

"Why would anyone burn the school?"

"Guess someone likes to watch fires."

"A pyromaniac?"

"The movie theater was arson. Got to be the same guy."

"They've had a patrol out every night. No one's seen anything suspicious."

The Pattonburg firemen pulled to the south side of the high school.

"They've brought a ladder truck." Dan looked down at me. "You okay, Squirt?"

"Don't feel good."

"Mom." Dan pulled on her arm. "Mike's sick."

Mom felt my forehead. "You've got a fever. Better get you home."

"I thought it wasn't a good idea for him to be out," Grandma said.

At home, Mom examined my various wounds and reapplied ointment and bandages.

"I'll get you to the doctor in the morning," she said.

Dr. Hader redressed my injuries and complimented Mom on her nursing skill.

"I don't see any infection but he obviously has a bit," the doctor said. "We'll treat him for that. You should bring him back Tuesday."

"School starts then," Mom said.

"The board meets this afternoon to decide about that." The doctor wrote a prescription. "You heard about George Buckner, I suppose."

"No. What about him?"

"They found his body on the second floor near the principal's office."

"He died in the fire?"

"He wasn't burned. Probably smoke inhalation. They'll autopsy his body Tuesday."

"Did he set the fire?"

"No one knows. A fire extinguisher lay close to his body. He may have been fighting the fire. Or maybe he set the fire, got trapped and tried to fight his way out."

"Why was he in the building in the middle of the night?" Mom said.

Dr. Hader shrugged. "He was custodian there. Could have gone in to save it."

"Or to burn it."

"Too bad we can't ask him."

Mom filled the prescription at Rexall Drug. I sat at the counter with an ice cream cone and listened to the conversations around me.

"George obviously set it," a man said.

"That doesn't make sense. He was the custodian at the high school. He'd be out of a job," another man said.

"No, he wouldn't. They'd keep him on to help clean the debris away," a lady said.

"I heard the board wanted to fire him because of that brawl at the ball park," the first man said.

"Wasn't his fault. Windy shouldn't have grabbed him like that."

"Kelvin Rogers started it," the woman said.

"I've known George all my life," the second man said. "He wouldn't do it. He loved that school and the kids. Went to all their games."

"That's right," the woman said. "Their concerts and plays, too. George was a big supporter."

"He must've been trying to put the fire out."

"He hasn't been the same since his wife was killed in that car wreck," the woman said.

"Yeah. He didn't drink much when she was alive."

"And he loved the Bombers," the woman said.

"Then they kicked him off the team," the second man said.

"So he had it rough," the first man said. "I still say he set the fire. Now that he's gone, I bet we don't have another one."

"Let's go, Mike," Mom said.

"I want to see the school." I followed her from the store.

"Me, too."

We took the same route as the night before and parked closer this time.

"Are you sure you're up to this?" Mom said.

"I'm feeling better," I said. "Must be that shot the doc gave me and that stuff he put on makes it less painful to move."

We paused at the corner.

"Goodness gracious." Mom stared at the spectacle.

"Let's get closer."

We joined a group standing across from the school. Black streaks ran up the bricks on the south half of the high school. Windows gaped. The front door leaned against the top step, and I could see the charred classroom walls on the first and second floors. The third floor windows were broken, but it appeared that floor fared better than the ones below. The first floor on the north half of the building suffered the same fate as its neighbor, but the floors above it looked untouched.

"State fire inspectors are here," a man told Mom.

"I heard they called the other fires suspicious," a lady said.

"They didn't change the original finding much," another man said. "Just said suspicious but probably grain dust and so forth."

"You think George set them all?" the woman said.

"I don't think he set any of them," the first man said. "He was trying to put the fire out."

"Strange that he was in the building," the lady said.

"Nobody'll be going to school here Tuesday," another woman said.

"It'll have to be torn down," a man said.

"Where will the kids go to school?" Mom said. "My son's a freshman."

"I hear the board's going to decide what to do this afternoon," the man told Mom.

"That's Gideon McKinley," Mom said.

"Yes, he's been with the inspectors. Maybe he'll tell us something."

Behind me, a woman quietly cried.

"What's the back look like?" Mom said.

"The music room's missing windows." The man paused to blow his nose. "Has some fire damage but mostly water damage. Same for the study hall above it."

"It's a holiday weekend," someone said. "I'm surprised the inspectors showed up this fast."

"Five major fires in five months," Mom said. "They must've made it a priority."

"Something's going on at the gym," a woman said. "Coach Meadow's unlocking the door."

"Here comes Mr. Harris, the vo ag teacher."

Over the next few minutes, teachers straggled in separately and in groups.

"High school teachers' meeting," Mom said. "The news will be all over town when they finish."

I spent the afternoon on the couch listening to the Cards game. Every few minutes the phone rang as information leaked out about the teachers' meeting. Rumors and gossip reported temporary classrooms covering the football field, all games played away, practice at the city park, larger class sizes and an extended day to make up for days missed. Elementary and junior high classes start as planned, but the beginning of high school classes would be announced later. No one knew what the school board decided but that didn't prevent anyone from speculating.

TWENTY-TWO

Mom excused me from church attendance Sunday, and when Dan volunteered to stay with me, Mom said I was responsible enough to be home alone. Grandma Jenkins fried chicken for dinner using her ancient secret recipe.

"Dean's coming over to shoot baskets," Dan said.

Mom passed the scalloped potatoes. "You boys have about worn that Jayhawk off the backboard."

"I'm glad you use it," Luke said.

Dan buttered his bread. "I can't believe we're having football practice at the city park."

"I heard the board's already rented mobile classrooms," Grandma said. "Maybe they'll move them in Tuesday."

"A couple of weeks, you'll be back in school," Mom said.

Dan's lip twitched. "Won't be the same."

"Say, Luke," Grandma said, "what happened about those notes Emile was getting?"

"I've got them at the office." Luke held a drumstick. "Talked to Rogers who declares it isn't him. He did admit to tailing Emile several times, just for the fun of it, he said."

"There's no way to prove he wrote the notes?" Mom said.

Luke swallowed before he answered. "Get a handwriting sample. Have an expert compare it to the notes. Look for fingerprints."

"But you haven't done that?" Grandma said.

Luke shook his head. "No crime's been committed."

"Is the FBI still in town?" I said.

Luke took more scalloped potatoes. "The original agents left, but some financial guy is going over Emile's books."

Grandma snorted. "More harassment from Hoover."

"I'd like to get to the park earlier this year," Luke said. "What are you taking?"

"I haven't made anything," Mom said. "I thought we'd skip the Martin picnic this year."

"It's a Labor Day tradition," Luke said. "We always go. My aunt and uncle are coming from Springfield."

"But so much has happened with the school burning and George's death. And look at Mike. All those boys roughhouse and he can't swim in the pool."

"You have all afternoon to make something," Luke said, "and not peach cobbler again. Something really good like your mom's strawberry cake."

Mom's eyes blazed. "My peach cobbler isn't good enough for your family?"

"I didn't say that."

"They'd rather sit around and tell off-color jokes and drink," Mom said.

"They like to laugh and a couple of drinks never hurt anyone."

"It's more than a couple, and they smoke so much it gives me a headache. They're terrible role models for the boys."

Luke's mouth formed a straight line. "At least they aren't stick-in-the-muds like your family."

"Look who's being a terrible role model for the boys right now," Grandma said.

Luke stood and threw his napkin onto the table. "I don't need a lecture from my mother-in-law. We'll leave for the picnic at ten. All of you be ready." He stalked from the room.

Grandma sighed. "Sorry. I should've kept my mouth shut."

That night sleep eluded me. The voices across the hall alternated between strident and conciliatory. I lay in bed worried about what might happen. Would they get a divorce? If they did, what would happen to me? Then Alex Buckner popped into my head. He lost his mother in a car wreck. Now his dad was gone and he was all alone. I didn't like the guy but I felt sorry for him. The voices softened and I heard Mom giggle. Safe, I fell asleep.

I don't know how Mom did it, but I was excused from the Martin picnic, and this time Dan's request to stay with me was approved. I hadn't forgotten the fight with my cousin Jim at the last Martin get-together or the way Uncle Matthew turned me over his knee. I imagined Jim still remembered the incident and would seek revenge by ridiculing my inept bike riding and laughing at my injuries.

Pete came over in the afternoon to listen to the Card's game. We relaxed on the front porch with tall glasses of cold lemonade while Dan shot baskets with his friend Dean. Musial hit a two-run homer in the sixth to put the Cards on top. Chicago came up to bat when a car rumbled to a stop at the curb. Glen Smithton revved the engine twice and honked the horn. Dan ran down the drive to the car and leaned in to talk to Glen.

"It's a '32 Ford," Pete said.

The body of the car, only as wide as the narrow vertical grill, sat between the wheels which had no fenders. A dull primer coated the two-seater body. Dean walked slowly down the drive to stand beside Dan. Dan said something to Dean who shook his head and argued back. Dan shrugged his shoulders, opened the door and got into the car. Dean stepped back and the car roared down the street. Shoulders slumped, Dean shuffled down the sidewalk toward home.

I sighed. "Hope he gets home before Mom and Luke."

But he didn't. The Cards won the game to improve their record to seventy wins and fifty-four losses. Pete went home. I sat on the porch with Duke watching for Dan when Luke turned the corner. I prepared for the grilling to come.

Luke slammed out of the house and sat next to me. "Where's Dan?"

I shrugged. "Don't know."

Luke's eyes scanned my face. "Did you see him leave?"

"Yes." I rubbed my sweaty palms on my shorts.

Luke leaned toward me. "He didn't say where he was going?"

"No."

Luke rubbed his chin. "Did he leave with somebody?"

Well, I couldn't get out of that one. "Yes."

"Who?"

"Glen Smithton."

"In a car?"

"Yes."

Luke sat back in his chair and stared at the house across the street. "I thought Dean was coming over to shoot baskets."

"He did."

"Your brother went off with Glen Smithton and left Dean?"

"Yes."

Luke sighed deeply.

"How was the picnic?" I said.

"Oh, fine. Fine." Luke glanced up and down the street. "Everyone asked about you and Dan." He drummed his fingers on the chair's arm. "I'd better look for him." He clomped into the house.

I heard him tell Mom and the back door slammed. He backed down the drive like he was going to a fire. Dan was in trouble. Duke followed me into the house.

Mom washed dishes at the sink. "Did you practice today?"

"Sure."

Mom handed me a dish towel. "Your lesson tomorrow is at ten. Mrs. Murran will pick you up. I've talked to Mrs. Herrick about your lessons."

"Can't you drive me? Mrs. Murran is a terrible driver. She's so short she looks through the steering wheel."

"She'd be insulted if I did." Mom brushed the hair from my forehead. "Everyone knows her car and pulls over when they see her coming. She drives slowly and has never had an accident. You'll be fine."

"Couldn't I skip it?" I said. "It's the first day of school."

Mom frowned at me. "What's wrong? You always like your piano lessons."

"Dan's going to think I tattled on him."

"Your dad will straighten that out."

Half an hour passed before I heard the car come up the drive. Doors slammed and I recognized Luke's voice. The reply, a voice slightly higher, sounded like Luke, too. They both laughed as they came through the back door.

"He was at Smithton's Garage," Luke said.

Mom looked up from fixing sandwiches for supper. "He's not supposed to go there."

Luke chuckled. "The kid should be a lawyer. He's got us on a technicality."

"I don't understand." Mom wiped her hands on her apron.

"If you remember the conversation, Dan said he wouldn't go there."

Mom nodded. "That's right."

"You said you thought that best."

"I did."

Luke grinned. "We didn't forbid him to go. He didn't promise not to."

"You're splitting hairs," Mom said. "He said he wouldn't."

"And he meant it at the time, but the attraction is too strong." Luke's face lit up. "Glen's got this hotrod. You should see it." He went into a long description of the car.

Mom bit her lip as she listened. "I'm sure it's a great car but that's not the point. Glen Smithton is."

Luke shook his head. "The car is the whole point. Dan's not going to the garage to be friends with Glen. He's going because of the car."

Mom frowned. "And that's okay with you?"

"As long as he stays out of trouble."

Mom shook her head. "But leaving Dean like that."

"We went by. Dan apologized for his behavior."

I was as confused as Mom. Dan kept me awake that night extolling the virtues of Glen's car.

Mom redressed my wounds which were scabbing over and sent me off to school in shorts with a note for Mrs. Herrick. Tanned familiar faces greeted me and all wanted to hear about my accident. As he rode behind me down the hill and thus saw me fly and land, Bruce told the story multiple times in a way that made everyone laugh. I thought it funny, too, and rejoiced at being back among friends until recess. Mrs. Herrick refused to let me play dodgeball as one of my wounds might be hit. I sat under a tree while my classmates yelled, screamed and shrieked.

Even with the windows wide open and a fan stirring the air, we sweated through the afternoon. The principal Miss Walker announced that all students were allowed to wear shorts for the rest of the week due to the heat, and Mrs. Herrick took us to the shade of an elm for our history lesson.

Mom picked me up after school for my doctor's appointment. Dr. Hader said it was as he thought—the autopsy showed George Buckner died of smoke inhalation. Afterward, we drove by the high school where men carried furniture from the charred building to the gymnasium, and two mobile classrooms squatted on the football field.

"Dan and I took Duke to the vet today," Mom said.

Fear shot through me. "Did something happen to him?"

"No. Dr. Buchman removed his stitches. He's healing fine." Mom parked the car in the driveway.

Tail wagging, Duke limped out to greet us.

"All the bandages are gone." I sat on the ground to examine Duke's leg. A long red scar ran up the inside of it and short fuzzy hair grew back in from his foot to his hip. I hugged him. "A month from now you'll be back to normal." I hoped I would be, too.

"Luke's getting a new wheel for your bike," Mom said. "You can ride it to school tomorrow."

Heat drove us from the house to the porch after dinner Thursday evening. *Sky King* had just ended on the radio when Mr. Hrabosky's blue Buick pulled to the curb. He wore his usual suit and hat.

"How's Duke?" Mr. Hrabosky bent to pat Duke's head.

"Got his stitches out Tuesday," I said.

"Good."

"Have a seat, Emile," Luke said. "What's happened?"

Mr. Hrabosky removed his hat and sat heavily in the proffered chair. "They arrested me."

"The FBI?" Mom said.

"I'm out on bail like a common criminal." Mr. Hrabosky's hands shook as he lit a cigarette.

"What's the charge?" Luke said.

"Tax evasion." Mr. Hrabosky snorted. "It's ridiculous. I've always paid every penny I owe."

"What's Crosby advise?" Luke said.

"He's always been my lawyer," Mr. Hrabosky said, "but he thinks I need an expert on tax law. Recommended some law firm in Kansas City. It'll cost me a bundle to fight it."

"What's the alternative?" Mom said.

Mr. Hrabosky puffed on his cigarette. "I'll see what the lawyer suggests. Make some deal, I suppose."

"You'd have to plead guilty to do that," Luke said.

"Really?" Mr. Hrabosky examined his cigarette. "Then there's no alternative. I'll not say I'm guilty when I'm innocent."

"Is there a trial date?" Luke said.

"Not yet. Federal court. I don't even know what evidence they have to support the charges." Mr. Hrabosky sighed. "Margaret is so upset. Alice is in France. Henry's coming down from Chicago this weekend but he can't stay."

"Would it help if Mom and I dropped by for a visit?" Mom said.

"I'd appreciate it." Mr. Hrabosky crushed out his cigarette. "She needs someone to talk to besides me, and it'll probably be in the *Pattonburg Sun* in the morning."

"When do you see this lawyer?" Luke said.

"Monday. Crosby's driving up with me."

"If I can help," Luke said, "all you have to do is ask. About Rogers. Seen anything of him lately?"

"Not since you talked to him." Mr. Hrabosky took an envelope from his pocket. "I did get another note. Haven't opened it." He stood and gave the envelope to Luke. "Only fingerprints on this note are from the guy who wrote it."

TWENTY-THREE

"Lightning struck the Gladding's pear tree last night," Pete said.

A cool front created a series of storms which blew through during the night and dissipated the heat which had built all week. Now a chilly north wind blew.

"Guess Mrs. Gladding won't worry about us climbing her precious tree anymore," I said.

"The whole trunk's split. Two halves lying on the ground. It was so close it about knocked me out of bed."

"You need to copy my math homework?" I said.

"No. Mom made me do it," Pete said. "She says I've got to do homework when I get home from school. She'll forget about it by the end of the month. Let's walk up to the square."

"Okay, I'll tell Mom."

Scabs covered the wounds on my shins, thighs and forearms so bandages were unnecessary. Long pants and a long-sleeved shirt hid the unattractive crusty patches.

Twigs and small limbs littered lawns and the street, and we once detoured around a branch which lay across the sidewalk. We waved to two classmates who played jacks on the Bennett's porch, and watched Rev. Norris saw a large limb which had fallen in his yard. The half-block across from the Methodist Church lay barren. No farm machinery was displayed. The office and repair shop had vanished. A few weeds poked through the cracked and scarred concrete. Windy Markmann had yet to rebuild the International Harvester dealership.

Mr. Hrabosky's blue Buick sailed down the street, and I waved to him. He honked a return greeting.

"He got arrested, you know." Pete turned around and walked backward.

"Yeah, but I don't think he's guilty."

"How come?"

"He says he's not. He was at the house talking to Luke."

Pete shrugged. "All criminals say they're innocent."

"Grandma says it's all because he wrote about J. Edgar Hoover, and Hoover's sicking the FBI on him in revenge."

Pete returned to walk at my side. "I thought they wanted him because he was a communist."

I bumped Pete. "He's not a communist."

"You told me Rogers said he was."

"Rogers did say that, but you remember Mr. Simmons told us about the lawsuit Mr. Rogers lost. He's just mad at Mr. Hrabosky."

"I got to stop by the café and get some money from my mom," Pete said when we reached the square.

"Let's get an ice cream cone first."

"I don't have any money."

"I'll buy. You can pay me back," I said.

We loved the Rexall Drug's fountain which served sandwiches and chips as well as ice cream and drinks. Pete ordered his usual chocolate. I decided on pineapple.

"Let's sit with Malcolm." I pointed to a booth further back.

Malcolm saw us coming and grinned.

"Hi, Malcolm." Pete slid into the booth across from Malcolm.

"Hi, yourself. I'm having lunch." Malcolm pointed to his ham sandwich. "I'll get my ice cream after."

"Vanilla, I'll bet." I sat beside Pete.

"That's right." Malcolm bit into his sandwich and talked with his mouth full. "Did you know the big school burned?"

"Yeah. We saw it." Pete licked his ice cream cone.

Malcolm grinned. "I did, too." His grin vanished. "And George Buckner got killed."

"His funeral was yesterday," I said.

"I went," Malcolm said. "He was my friend."

"My mom went." Pete wiped chocolate from his chin. "She said a big crowd was there."

"Yeah. Big crowd." Malcolm popped a potato chip into his mouth.

"Luke and Mom went, too," I said.

"Probably most people went just to see what he looked like," Pete said.

"Maybe they thought they could tell by looking at him whether he set the fire or not," I said.

"No." Malcolm frowned. "He tried to put out the fire. He's a hero."

"Hey, Malcolm," Everett Smithton said.

Malcolm's face lit up. "Hey, yourself."

"Scoot over, germ." Junior Rogers butt-shoved me next to Pete.

"Why're you associatin' with these closet cases?" Everett sat next to Malcolm.

"Huh?"

"These guys are nobodies. People of no importance," Junior said.

"They're my friends."

"You need to be more selective in choosing friends, Mal," Everett said. "Like Emile Hrabosky."

"Yeah. You don't want criminals for friends," Junior said.

"Mr. Hra. Mr. H isn't a criminal," Malcolm said.

"He got arrested by the friggin' FBI," Everett said.

Junior nodded. "Tax evasion, they said."

"What's that?"

"It's when you don't pay your taxes," Everett said.

Malcolm shook his head. "I pay my taxes."

Junior sneered. "Mr. Hrabosky don't."

"You can tell by his name he's a crook." Everett stretched an arm over the booth's back.

"You oughta quit workin' for that friggin' man," Junior said.

"We told you before how bad he is," Everett said.

"My daddy says he's a good guy," Malcolm said.

Junior snorted. "Your daddy don't know nuthin', Mal."

Jammed between Junior and Pete, I squirmed.

"Am I crowdin' you?" Junior stood. "Go on. Get outta here. We don't want you germs around."

Pete and I took him up on the offer and left the drugstore. We stopped at the café where Pete's mom gave him fifty cents and he paid me back. We stood on the sidewalk and gazed at the vacancy where the theater once stood. The gap ruined the appearance of the entire block like a smile without front teeth.

"Fewer people are coming to town on Saturday," Pete said.

I surveyed the square. On Saturdays, finding a parking spot could be difficult, but today spaces sat empty.

"Leroy better rebuild soon," I said.

"Everybody's buying televisions, anyway," Pete said. "My dad's getting one next week when he gets paid."

"Wonder if we'll get one."

"You can come to my house to watch."

"Here comes Bruce," I said.

Bruce wore a pair of patched jeans and a shirt that must've belonged to his older brother. He needed a haircut, and I thought for the first time that his family didn't have much money.

"What're you doing?" Bruce said.

"Nothing much," I said.

"Let's walk up to the high school," Bruce said. "I haven't seen it since the fire."

"Okay," I said. "Did you go to the football game last night?"

"Yeah. Rob caught a pass for a touchdown," Bruce said.

"But they lost," Pete said as we crossed the street.

"Rob's playing both ways," Bruce said. "Linebacker on defense and tight end on offense."

"Must get awfully tired," I said.

We stopped to scrutinize Turnbow's ruined dealership. To the left, cars sat in front of the service area and a shed sported an office sign. The steel beams of the destroyed showroom and office building framed the empty sky.

"At least he has something left to begin again," Pete said. "Windy and Leroy have only vacant lots."

We crossed another street and passed the Presbyterian Church.

"Dan's playing football, too," I said.

"Yeah. Rob says he's not bad for a freshman," Bruce said. "There weren't many people at the game."

"With all the games played away, that's how it will be," I said.

"Beat you to the end of the block."

Pete took off running. Bruce soon passed him and I lagged behind.

Panting, Bruce leaned over, hands on his thighs. "What's the matter with you?" he said. "You can run faster than that."

"Not now," I said. "Wait until these scabs come off. I'll beat you by a mile."

We crossed the highway and passed the service station where gas was twenty cents a gallon. Alex Buckner's car sat at a pump and the attendant washed the car's windshield.

"We got trapped by Everett Smithton and Junior Rogers earlier," Pete said.

"What happened?" Bruce said.

Pete and I filled in the details.

"We got away," I said, "but they still had Malcolm cornered."

"Why are they so against Mr. Hrabosky?" Bruce said.

"Well, you see, Kelvin Rogers's house had foundation problems," I said. "He claimed the vibrations of Mr. Hrabosky's presses were the cause. He sued him and lost."

"So they're happy that Mr. Hrabosky's been arrested," Pete said.

We crossed another street to reach the high school. The empty brick building, its windows gone, seemed forlorn and abandoned, a derelict without hope. We sat on a low rock wall across the street from the vacant edifice and watched three men wander through the building.

"Luke said a structural engineer would inspect the school today," I said.

"Maybe it can be repaired," Bruce said.

"You think George Buckner set the fire?" Pete said.

Bruce shrugged. "Don't know."

"I do," I said.

"Really?" Bruce frowned at me. "Why?"

"Because he got kicked off the Bombers team."

"That's crazy," Pete said.

"You think so? He showed up drunk. Who stopped him from taking the field?"

"The coach," Bruce said. "Mr. McKinley."

"The principal of the high school. Who else?"

Bruce frowned. "Windy Markmann."

"And his implement dealership burned."

"No one would set fires because they got kicked off the team," Pete said.

"Who took George's place in the lineup?" I said.

"Why, Vinny Valetti," Bruce said. "And Valetti's Mill burned."

"Leroy Beach and Chevy Turnbow?"

"They're on the team, too," Bruce said. "Every fire is linked to the team."

"It's not proof," Pete said, "and the reason for doing it is weak."

I shrugged. "Okay, but it's still what I think."

"You going to tell Luke?" Bruce said.

"No."

"Why not?"

"I'm just a kid with crazy ideas," I said. "Besides, George is dead so what's the point?"

"I want to see the football field," Bruce said.

We trotted across the street to the path between the high school and Hawthorn Elementary to the field's metal bleachers. Eight mobile classrooms occupied the field in pairs facing a square area in the center. A crew of men laid forms for sidewalks between them while another group worked to string electric lines. A tractor with an auger dug a hole for an electric pole.

"They're ruining the field," Bruce said.

We ambled across the field pausing to inspect the work. Two men affixed skirting to a classroom. Another built steps. Each unit had two doors so I assumed two classrooms. The students would pass from one classroom to another through rain, snow and frigid temperatures.

"I hope they fix the school before we get here," Bruce said.

"I dropped by the high school this afternoon," Luke said at dinner that evening.

"What'd the engineer say?" Mom passed the chicken pot pie.

"Structural damage is critical but can be fixed. Cost may be prohibitive."

"Would it take very long?" Dan said.

"Don't know. The building is over fifty years old and not up to code."

"They should declare it a historic structure," Mom said.

Luke grinned at her. "I can see you'd disagree with McKinley. He's all for tearing it down. The superintendent's on the fence. Says he wants more information."

"About what?" Mom said.

"Costs. Compare costs to repair to costs to build," Luke said. "But McKinley makes good sense. Tear the whole thing down. Take out the trees. Get rid of the old gym and build anew."

Mom frowned. "It'd change the whole character of the school."

Luke continued, "Add a cafeteria which could also be used by the elementary."

"That'd be good," Dan said.

"There's even talk of buying that abandoned cheese factory over on Western Avenue and making it into a junior high."

"What would they do with the present building?" Mom said.

"Join it with the elementary and have only one."

This alarmed me. "Tear down Melville?"

Luke nodded "But that won't happen until you're in junior high."

"The whole thing sounds overly ambitious to me." Mom stood. "I'll get the pudding."

"None of it will happen immediately," Luke said. "They have to hire an architect and pass a bond issue. It may take two years."

Dan grimaced. "And I'll be stuck in those trailers until then."

TWENTY-FOUR

Summer pushed back in for a last hurrah but the nights remained cool. I climbed out of bed in the mornings before the sun rose, and darkness descended after dinner, ending outdoor play. Forecasters on the radio predicted an early, rainy fall, but fall meant only one thing to me—the World Series. My beloved Cardinals had a winning season going with Stan Musial hitting .437 and Enos Slaughter batting .395. Their record stood at 77-54 with twelve games to play. But the Dodgers looked like sure Series contenders with Jackie Robinson hitting .329 and Duke Snyder .336. They had a record of ninety-nine wins and only forty-three losses, the best in the majors, and they could end the season with one hundred ten wins. When the Cards were on radio, I dashed home from school to catch the end of the game and wished for more night games.

Mom and Grandma Jenkins put up apples, apple butter, apple sauce and apple jelly all day, so Grandma stayed for dinner.

"Duke needs a bath again." Mom passed the meatloaf. "First thing tomorrow, Mike."

Grandma spooned peas onto her plate. "He's healed nicely. Hardly limps at all."

"Most of the hair's grown back, too," I said.

Luke poured gravy onto his mashed potatoes. "How's football?"

"Fine." Dan wiped his mouth.

"What position do you play?" Grandma said.

"Running back."

"Does that mean you carry the ball?"

Dan nodded. "Sometimes, but I block, too."

Grandma's nose wrinkled. "I don't think much of football. Bunch of brutes trying to knock each other down."

Luke looked at her, his fork paused in midair. “It teaches teamwork and cooperation.”

“So does basketball and baseball and nobody gets hurt.”

“Unless the pitcher hits the batter,” I said.

Grandma nodded. “I guess what I mean is that the players don’t intend to hurt each other.”

“Emile called the office today,” Luke said.

“What’d he have to say?” Mom asked.

“Well, the FBI took pictures of his books and questioned his accountant, so the Kansas City firm is doing the same thing.”

“Any court date?” Grandma asked.

Luke shook his head. “They’re going through a discovery process. Emile said the lawyer’s investigator is photographing his bills and checks, too. Once they have copies of everything, a tax lawyer will sort through Emile’s finances.”

“The longer it takes the more it’ll cost,” Grandma said. “Poor Emile.”

“Did you stop by the high school today?” Mom said.

“Yea.” Luke glanced at Dan. “They’ll finish putting desks in over the weekend. Teachers begin work Monday. Looks like you’ll be back in class the following week.”

Dan grinned. “Great.”

“Now that the fire is officially arson, will they say George was to blame?” Mom said.

“An accelerant was used but they found no container,” Luke said. “Nothing on George to indicate he handled an accelerant. Guess we’ll never know.”

“I can’t see that he’d have a motive,” Grandma said.

I kept my theory to myself. “Maybe there won’t be any more fires.”

The phone rang and Mom left the table to answer it.

“No more fires would point to George as the firebug,” I said.

“It’s Ed Horlacher, Luke,” Mom called from the kitchen.

Luke left to answer the phone.

“More meatloaf, boys?” Grandma said.

Mom came back to the table with apple pie.

“Not for me,” I said to make sure I had room for the pie. “Do we have any ice cream?”

"Sorry." Mom placed a piece of pie onto my plate.

Luke resumed his seat. "Ed wants me to come out. Has something to tell me. Says he can't over the phone because of their party line."

"Can I go, too?" I said.

Luke looked at Mom.

"No harm in it," she said. "It's Friday night."

"Finish dessert first," Luke said.

"I picked apples until dark," Mr. Horlacher said as he opened the door. "Thelma and the kids went to the football game. Sure hate to miss seeing Rob play, but work comes first."

"He's getting his name in the papers," Luke said. "And he's only a junior."

"Come in. Come in. Have a seat."

"I brought Mike with me," Luke said.

"I thought Bruce might be home," I said.

"No, he went to the game. Can I get you a drink?"

Luke shook his head as he sat on the couch. "We just finished supper."

I sat beside Luke. "Bruce told me about Rob making a touchdown last week."

"It was a great catch. Rob's a good student, too. With his grades and athletic skill, he'll get a scholarship."

"Any idea where he'd like to go?" Luke said.

Mr. Horlacher shook his head. "Too early for that. Wherever he gets the best deal, I suppose."

"What can I help you with, Ed?"

Mr. Horlacher looked at me with a raised eyebrow.

Luke patted my back. "Mike knows to keep his mouth shut."

"Okay. See, my neighbor Andy Brackett has his mother-in-law living with him, a nosy old biddy who likes to listen in on phone conversations."

Luke nodded. "The hazard of a party line."

"Andy told me today about Kelvin Rogers forming a group to harass Emile Hrabosky."

"He's part of the group?"

Mr. Horlacher frowned. “I don’t think so, but he heard about it at the pool hall. Overheard some talk, I suppose.”

“Who was doing the talking?”

“I don’t know.” Mr. Horlacher sighed and massaged his calloused hands as though they ached. “I’m sorry to be so vague, but I thought I should tell you about it.”

“I’m glad you called.”

“Anyway, they’re meeting tomorrow night at the pool hall.”

Luke rubbed his chin. “I suppose I could watch to see who goes in. But then, the place is busy on Saturday night, and I wouldn’t know who’s in the group and who’s just a customer.”

“I thought Andy and I would shoot some pool tomorrow night and see what happens.”

“Didn’t know you shot pool.”

Mr. Horlacher smiled. “Used to be pretty good before Thelma got ahold of me.”

“I’d sure appreciate knowing what they’re up to.”

“Thought you might.”

“Rogers hasn’t done anything I can arrest him for,” Luke said. “Followed Emile some. Suspect he’s written a few threatening notes.”

Mr. Horlacher leaned forward. “I don’t understand this animosity. Is it only losing that lawsuit?”

Luke frowned. “It’s more than that. He wouldn’t have sued Emile if he didn’t dislike him in the first place.”

“But why dislike Emile? That printing plant of his provides employment. Adds to the tax base, too. And he’s a nice guy.”

Luke shrugged. “Who can explain bigotry? My boy here overheard Rogers call Emile a foreigner, a Jew and a communist. Said his plant should burn down with him in it.”

“I hope no one else in town feels that way.”

“Rogers looks at Emile, a guy with a funny name—“

Mr. Horlacher laughed. “Let’s don’t get into funny names.”

“—a poor guy who came from a foreign country and made good while Rogers, who had more advantages than Emile, is stuck in a nowhere job mowing lawns for the city. It makes him angry. But is he angry enough to be dangerous?”

“Maybe I’ll find out,” Mr. Horlacher said.

"He scored two touchdowns," Bruce said Saturday afternoon. "You should've seen him."

"Maybe I can go to the game with you next week," I said.

"The Pattonburg newspaper called. They want to interview Rob Monday afternoon for a feature article."

"That's nice," I said.

"There'll be pictures and everything. Comments from the coach and the other players."

"You going to be in the pictures?"

"No, but they'll talk to momma and poppa. They plan to put it in the newspaper next Friday before the game with Altoona."

"Let's get a hot chocolate."

Fall came in with a true cold front, and a brisk north wind whistled through the square. I hunched my shoulders and jammed my hands into my jacket pockets.

"If the quarterback was a better passer, Rob could've made three touchdowns," Bruce said. "He had over a hundred yards as it was."

"I'm glad they won the game."

We walked down the sidewalk in the usual manner, bumping each other, walking backward to talk and skipping every few steps. I opened the door to Rexall Drug and the warmth rushed out at me. We sat at the counter and ordered hot chocolate. I wrapped my hands around the cup to warm them.

"Did your dad tell you I was at your house last night?" I said.

"No. What for?"

"He wanted to talk to Luke."

"What about?"

I remembered I was to keep my mouth shut and wished I hadn't brought up the subject. "Nothing much. I didn't pay attention. He talked about Rob and college scholarships and his neighbors. Something about playing pool tonight."

"Momma won't like that."

"Luke says high school will start a week from Monday."

"Rob will be happy. Poppa's been making him pick apples," Bruce said. "They should finish today."

"Pete said his dad's buying a television today."

"Wish we had one." Bruce elbowed me. "Let's go to Saulk's and look at their sets."

"Okay."

Now a mist hung in the air and low clouds scurried across the sky. Wind swirled around us as though it couldn't decide which way it wanted to blow. I turned up my jacket collar.

"Look who's coming," Bruce said.

Dan sauntered toward us holding hands with the Johnson girl.

"Hey, Dan," Bruce said. "We're going to Saulk's to look at televisions."

Dan grinned. "Thinking of buying one?"

"Pete's dad is. He said I could watch at his house," I said.

"I saw Pete down the street," Dan said, "going into Ben Franklin's with his dad."

"Let's catch up with him," I said.

We ran down the sidewalk to the five and dime. I opened the door and ran into Alex Buckner coming out.

"Watch where you're goin', germ."

Alex shoved past me followed by Everett Smithton, Junior Rogers and Malcolm Carroll who ignored me. I watched the four climb into Alex's car.

"Close call," I said.

"Why's Malcolm running with those guys?" Bruce said. "They're trouble."

"Remember what Alex said about using Malcolm? I bet they've got something up their sleeve."

"There's Pete."

"Hi, guys," Pete said.

"Did your dad get the television?" I said.

"Yeah. It's big and heavy. A Silvertone. The salesman said it's one of the best."

"Can I watch tonight?" I said.

"Sure. Right now we only have rabbit ears. My dad bought an antenna and wire to put up on the roof tomorrow."

The black and white picture was grainy and had a tendency to roll. I missed the movie theater.

TWENTY-FIVE

Summer fought back Sunday with a warm south breeze to remind Glendale of the fine sunny days it'd soon be missing. I skipped my ice cream bar to hear what Mr. Horlacher learned at the pool hall. I stuck close to Luke thinking they'd meet after church.

"Aren't you going to Tony's?" Luke said.

I shook my head. "I want to know what happened at the pool hall."

Luke studied my face as he rubbed his chin. "I've trusted you so far, and to my knowledge, you haven't let me down. Come on."

I followed Luke to the back of the church where Ed Horlacher waited.

Mr. Horlacher smiled and winked at me. "Got to be in the know, do you?"

"I didn't tell anybody," I said. "Not even Bruce."

"Well, I had to tell Thelma," Mr. Horlacher said. "She raised a ruckus about my going to the pool hall."

"Hope you didn't get into too much trouble," Luke said. "Did you learn anything?"

"Not much. There was a lot of loud talk and drinking. I think the biggest attraction was that Rogers was buying. People drifted in and out. They'd come over, get a beer, listen for a bit and leave."

"Any plans?"

Mr. Horlacher shook his head. "Nothing specific. A few suggestions like painting communist on the side of the plant. Some for it. Others said it's vandalism, and they didn't want to get in trouble with the law."

"That's good," Luke said. "Glad to hear some people have good sense."

"Rogers kept insisting Hrabosky is a communist, and patriotic people shouldn't allow him in town. He mentioned McCarthy and how communists are anti-American. A couple of guys made fun of him. Said he's just mad about the lawsuit. Only a few agreed with Rogers."

"Got some names for me?"

"Tom Shepherd, the big guy who lives out west by Brazilton."

"I know him. He's a big blowhard who thinks he knows everything," Luke said. "I've never had any trouble with him."

"Dave County from down around Beulah."

"I'm surprised at that. He's always seemed a reasonable man."

"That sleazy lawyer from Radley."

"Ed Frownfelter. He was Rogers's lawyer for the lawsuit against Emile. Anybody from here in town?"

"Rogers's boy and Alex Buckner is all."

"Everett Smithton runs with them," Luke said. "Was he there?"

"Didn't see him," Mr. Horlacher said. "From what I witnessed, I'd say it's all talk. I doubt they'll ever do more than get together, drink and shoot off their mouths."

"I appreciate the information, Ed," Luke said. "Say, I understand your boy had a great game Friday night."

"Couldn't have done better. A reporter from the *Pattonburg Sun* will be in town tomorrow. Going to write an article on Rob."

"Bruce told me about that," I said.

"Thanks again, Ed." Luke offered his hand.

Mr. Horlacher took it. "Anytime, Luke."

Dan got a letter from the school with an explanation and his new class schedule. The courses were the same but room numbers were different. The *Glendale Courier* carried a long article about the beginning of the high school year. As students would make up the hours missed, the school day would be extended by ninety minutes each day for the first twelve weeks. The day would begin at seven in the morning and end at ten until three.

All students were required to bring sack lunches. To evenly extend classes, an additional thirty minutes would be added to first, third and fifth periods on A day and to second, fourth and sixth periods on B day creating a rotating schedule. After twelve weeks, the usual schedule of beginning at eight o'clock and ending at two-fifty with an hour for lunch would be reinstated. The superintendent apologized for the inconvenience and encouraged all to do their best. He invited all students and parents to an open house on Saturday. Dan wanted school to begin but dreaded the long days.

Pete and I rode our bikes to the high school Wednesday after school to snoop around.

"It's Mrs. Murran." I pointed to my piano teacher's car, an old red Dodge.

Pete laughed. "Watch people pull over."

Sure enough, oncoming traffic got out of her way as she wandered over the center line and back. She passed us and we turned around to watch her progress. A white Pontiac roared up behind her and honked. The driver revved his engine, decided to pass her and clipped the Dodge's fender. Mrs. Murran's car jumped the curb and straddled the sidewalk. The white Pontiac sped away.

"Did you see who was in that car?" Pete said.

"Yeah. Glen Smithton and Dan was with him. Let's see if she's hurt."

We dropped our bikes and ran to the damaged car. Several other people were talking to Mrs. Murran who had a cut on her forehead.

"I have a tissue," a lady said.

Mrs. Murran pressed it to her forehead. "I'm all right, really. It's just a bump. What about my car?"

"Got a crumpled fender is all," a man said. "Easy to fix."

Luke pulled to a stop behind Mrs. Murran's Dodge. "What happened here?"

Several people talked at once, but Luke got the gist of it.

"Glen Smithton, you say."

"And your boy in the passenger's seat," the man said.

"Mrs. Murran, how are you feeling?" Luke said.

"I'm fine." Mrs. Murran glanced at the blood-stained tissue. "Need to get a bandage on my head."

"I'll drive you to Dr. Hader's," Luke said. "Orville, would you get this car off the sidewalk and park it?"

"I can drive it to her house, if that's okay," Orville said.

"That would be a big help," Luke said. He helped Mrs. Murran to his car.

We watched Orville back the car down over the curb and drive away.

"Wonder what happens now," Pete said.

"Luke will arrest Glen," I said, "and Dan . . . well, I wouldn't want to be in his shoes."

"You got poison ivy? You keep scratching."

"My scabs itch," I said. "They're coming off."

"Still want to go to the high school?"

"No. I want to get home and see the fireworks."

We retrieved our bikes, pedaled through the square and headed south past the fire station. Two men washed a firetruck on the driveway and we stopped to watch.

"Hello, boys," one of the firemen said.

Pete and I said, "Hi."

"Are you a real fireman?" Pete put down his kickstand.

"Real as real can be." He turned off the hose and walked toward us. "I'm Mike and that's Alan."

"I'm Mike, too," I said. "He's Pete."

"Glad to meet you," Mike said. "You live close?"

"Couple of blocks down Pawnee," Pete said. "You sleep here?"

"Sure do. Eat here, too, when they get the kitchen in. Alan's a good cook."

"But you don't live here, do you?" I put down my kickstand.

"No. There are three crews that overlap and we work in forty-eight hour shift. Then we have a day off," Mike said.

"We really need a fourth crew," Alan said, "but the mayor tells us that'll have to wait."

"Always have six men here ready to go," Mike said.

"I hope you don't have to go anywhere," I said.

"I hear you," Mike said. "We've been learning our way around town. Ate at Esther's Café for lunch."

"My mom works there," Pete said.

"Is that Bernice?" Alan said.

"Yeah. How'd you know?" Pete said.

"You got the same reddish hair."

"My dad's the police chief," I said.

"You're Luke's boy?" Mike said. "He drops by most every day. Brought us an apple pie your mom made. That went down real nice."

"I've got to get home," I said.

"You boys drop by anytime," Mike said. "We can always use company."

The house was silent when I got home. Mom hemmed a skirt with needle and thread, and I could smell something delicious cooking in the oven.

"Is Dan home?" I said.

Mom nodded. "In his room. He told me what happened. Said you were there."

"Yeah." I shifted around on my feet.

"Your dad called. Neither of you is to leave the house."

"I didn't do anything." I scuffed the carpet with the toe of my shoe.

"I'm only relaying the message."

"It's not fair."

"Nevertheless, that's the order." Mom returned to hemming the skirt. "Sit down and do your homework."

I stomped to the kitchen table and slammed down my books. I wanted to see the fireworks but never expected any of them to be aimed at me. My mind was in such a turmoil that I couldn't concentrate. A train going thirty miles per hour leaves the station at 6:45. At what time will it arrive in Chicago forty-five miles away? This should be easy. I shouldn't be punished. I'm a witness. I did nothing wrong. This isn't right. A train going . . . oh, I read this already. It'd take an hour and a half arriving at . . . let's see . . . 8:15. Finally a car crunched up the drive and a door slammed.

Luke strode through the kitchen and stood at the bottom of the stairs. “Daniel Jonathan Martin,” he bellowed, “get down here right now.”

I closed my math book.

“And you stay there, Mike,” Luke said.

“I didn’t do anything,” I said.

“I know, but I want you to hear this so you won’t have the same problem Dan does.”

Dan entered the kitchen warily.

“Sit down.” Luke pointed to a chair at the table.

Dan sat in a chair across from me.

Luke paced. “I don’t know where to begin.”

“I didn’t do anything, Dad,” Dan said.

“You were riding around town with Glen Smithton.”

“You’ve never said I couldn’t.”

“I shouldn’t have to.” Luke’s face reddened as he faced Dan. “I thought we raised you right. Raised you to make wise decisions. Your mother was right all along. We never should have allowed you to go near the Smithton Garage.”

“We had to check on the rod at the body shop.”

“You had to go?”

“I wanted to see it. He’s having it painted a bright yellow.”

“You can’t always do what you want. You made a bad decision. Several people witnessed the accident and now your name is linked with Glen’s.”

Dan shrugged. “Nothing wrong with that. You said yourself he wasn’t a bad kid.”

“That was before I saw him this summer with Alex Buckner and his buddies. I’ll not have a son of mine getting a reputation as a hooligan.”

“Glen isn’t a hooligan.”

“Maybe not yet but he’s headed that way.” Luke resumed his pacing.

“What did you do to Glen?”

“I gave him a ticket for careless driving and leaving the scene of an accident.”

Dan’s face fell. “He’ll never speak to me again.”

“I hope he doesn’t.”

"I begged him to go back. He said it'd be okay because I was with him."

Luke snorted. "I don't operate that way. If you had been driving, I would've ticketed you the same way."

"So now you're telling me not to ride with Glen?"

"No." Luke pointed his finger at Dan. "I'm telling you not to go to the Smithton Garage ever again."

"That's not fair!"

"School starts Monday. Your mother will pick you up after football practice and you will not leave the house."

"Is that all?"

"For now."

Dan stomped up the stairs to our room and slammed the bedroom door.

TWENTY-SIX

The article in the *Pattonburg Sun* about Rob took up a whole page. One picture showed him in his football uniform with Coach Meadow. Another pictured him in the air catching a pass. Teachers praised him as a student, and the coach at Pattonburg College said he was keeping an eye on Rob as an excellent recruit. Rob's parents commended him as a hard worker around the farm and a model son with Christian values. I didn't read the article until after school Friday as it was so long. I cut it out and saved it along with the article about Luke's nabbing the burglars.

The game Friday night should have been a home game, but it would now be played in Pattonburg at College High. As freshmen didn't suit up for the game, Dan gained permission to go with Rev. Norris and Dean. I crowded into the back seat with Bruce and Madge while Mr. and Mrs. Horlacher occupied the front. Madge kept standing up to see over the front seat, and Bruce and I punched her in the back of the knee to knock her down amid protests and giggles.

"Settle down, boys," Mr. Horlacher said. "We're coming into Pattonburg, and I need to concentrate on my driving."

We drove through the business district to reach the college in the south of town. Though the stores were closed, I pointed out the Singer shop where Grandma Ada worked and the store where we bought Dan's suit.

"I'd forgotten Luke grew up here," Mrs. Horlacher said. "Seems like he's always been in Glendale."

"He went to college here, too," I said.

"I guess he started dating Joan about twenty years ago," Mr. Horlacher said.

"That's right. Same time we were dating." Mrs. Horlacher patted her husband's arm.

We drove by a row of fraternity and sorority houses and a couple of dorms before finding the parking lot for the stadium.

"This is the college stadium," I said.

"College High plays their games here, too," Bruce said.

I had enough money in my pocket for admittance and a drink. The stadium must've had thirty rows of seats and not the metal planks of Glendale's stadium but actual seats. Bright lights gleamed overhead as we made our way to the visitor's side. Lush grass covered the field rather than the scraggly clumps our field had. When the College High team played in Glendale, they probably ridiculed our pathetic facilities. The Glendale supporters at the game would've filled the seats at home but were diminished in the sea of empty seats. The College High fans across the field fared no better.

Glendale won the coin toss and elected to kick so they'd receive the ball to begin the second half. The College High Buccaneers slammed into the line, threw an incomplete pass and ran the ball to the fifty before Rob sacked the quarterback and they had to punt. Glendale ran the punt back to their opponent's forty-five. Rob went out for a pass which was broken up.

"They're double teaming him," Bruce said.

"Must've read that article in the newspaper," I said.

Rob caught the next pass between two defenders but was immediately tackled. A roughing-the-passer penalty was tacked on to give the Glendale Trojans a first down. They ran the ball for a short gain but were held on third down. The attempted field goal failed, and the Bucs took over on the twenty-two yard line.

I recognized many of the Glendale fans who yelled and screamed encouragement while the cheerleaders shook their pom-poms, turned cartwheels and led the Pep Club in cheers. I located Dan sitting with the Johnson girl. A different crowd attended the high school football games—mostly students and their parents—while the Bombers ball games drew a wide spectrum of the townspeople. To my relief, Alex Buckner and his two henchmen were not at the football game.

Coach Meadow ran up and down the sidelines substituting players from the bench directly below us. Rob came out for a breather and got a cup of water. He poured it over his head and took another to drink. After consulting with Coach Meadow, he ran back onto the field. The Bucs scored on their next series of downs, but the point after hit the upright and went wide. The Trojans received the kickoff and returned it to their own forty-six. After a twelve-yard running play, Rob went out for a pass followed by two defenders. He zigged to the left, eluded the defenders, caught the pass and ran for a touchdown.

Bruce pounded my back, screaming with joy. "Boy, wasn't that great?"

"Sure was."

"He left those guys in the dust."

The extra point went through and the Trojans led seven to six at halftime. Bruce and I took Madge to the concession stand which sold everything from hotdogs to ice cream bars. At Glendale's games, choices were limited to soft drinks, candy bars and popcorn. We made it back to our seats through a crush of excited fans for the second half.

The Trojans received and ran the ball to their forty-yard line. Rob went out for another pass tailed by his two tormentors. The pass sailed high. Rob leaped and caught the ball. The two Buc defenders slammed him to the ground. The crowd rose to their feet, so I stood on my seat to see.

The referee signaled a catch, and a roar arose from the crowd. Rob got to his feet, shook his head, staggered a few feet and collapsed. The crowd's roar became a moan, and I clutched the back of the seat in front of me to keep from falling.

Coach Meadow ran onto the field, knelt beside Rob and motioned to Dr. Hader who joined him. Mr. Horlacher left the stands, went through a gate at the end of the stadium and ran onto the field.

"Come with me." Mrs. Horlacher followed her husband to the gate and we trailed her.

"What happened?" Madge said.

"Wait and see."

Dr. Hader signaled to the ambulance at the end of the field, and two men took a gurney from it. They wheeled it across the grass to Rob, lowered it, and eased him onto its surface.

Mr. Horlacher came to the gate. "He's in and out of consciousness. You go with the ambulance. I'll follow with the kids."

Mrs. Horlacher ran to catch up with the gurney bearing her son.

"He's dead!" Madge began to sob.

"No, he's not dead, sweetheart." Mr. Horlacher picked up his daughter. "Let's go."

Mr. Horlacher trotted out of the stadium to the parking lot. Bruce and I hustled to keep up with him. I heard the ambulance howl away as we jumped into the back seat and Mr. Horlacher started the car. Madge cried in the front seat.

"What happened, Poppa?" Bruce said.

"The doctor thinks he hit his head on the ground hard." Mr. Horlacher turned the car north and sped down the street.

"Those guys had him targeted," Bruce said.

"I'm sure they didn't mean to hurt him."

"That one time they tackled him, they kept piling on," Bruce said.

"And they were penalized for it." Mr. Horlacher stopped at a light.

"It was that newspaper article," Bruce said. "They shouldn't have printed it."

"Rob wanted them to." When the light turned, Mr. Horlacher stomped on the accelerator.

"Where are we going?" Bruce said.

"St. Mary's Hospital." Mr. Horlacher glanced at Madge. "Dry your eyes, sweetheart. Rob will be fine. Instead of crying, say a little prayer for him."

Mr. Horlacher turned in at the entrance for the emergency room and parked. "Remember there are sick people here. Don't go making a racket."

We followed him into the hospital. A nurse manned the counter at the entrance, and Mr. Horlacher asked for directions. We walked down the hallway to a waiting room where we found Mrs. Horlacher.

She clutched her husband's arm. "They took him through that doorway a few minutes ago and told me to wait here."

Mr. Horlacher put his arm around his wife. "Has he regained consciousness?"

"He's still in and out, but he's breathing fine on his own." Mrs. Horlacher's voice broke and she held back a sob. "Sometimes he lay there in the ambulance looking like he was sleeping. I held his hand and talked to him, but there was no response. When his eyes opened, I'm not sure he even recognized me."

"They'll tell us something in a few minutes." Mr. Horlacher turned to us. "Have a seat everyone. Thelma, if you could watch the kids for a few minutes, I'd appreciate it."

Bruce and I sat side by side across from Mrs. Horlacher who held Madge.

"It's okay, honey." Mrs. Horlacher dried Madge's face with a tissue. "God will take care of Rob. You know God watches over us, and He knows about Rob."

"Will He come to the hospital?"

"He's already here, honey. You can't see Him, but He's in with Rob."

Mr. Horlacher returned. "I've called Luke and Joan. They'll be here shortly."

We waited and waited. Mrs. Horlacher paced and asked what was taking so long every few minutes. Bruce clenched and unclenched his fists as though he wanted to hit somebody. Mr. Horlacher consoled Madge who alternated between tears and quiet resignation. I didn't know what to do or say. My muscles ached from the tension. Luke and Mom came but still we had no information. Rev. Norris, Dean and Dan joined the group. Rev. Norris led us in prayer and we waited. The game over, Coach Meadow and Dr. Hader rushed in. We waited some more. Finally a white-coated man opened the door and asked for the boy's parents. The Horlachers disappeared behind the door with him, and we waited again. Time inched by. Mr. Horlacher reappeared, his face ashen, and sat beside Madge.

"He's being admitted," he said. "The doctor says there's a lot they don't know about brain injury. Normal treatment is rest, but if it's more serious than a mild concussion, other treatments are called for."

"How serious is it?" Luke said.

"They don't know. They can't see into the skull. Maybe someday but not now."

"Has he regained consciousness?" Coach Meadow said.

"He's in and out."

"You mentioned other treatments," Mom said.

Mr. Horlacher hesitated. "The brain swells, you see. They'd have to relieve the pressure against the skull."

"You mean they'd . . ." Rev. Norris glanced at Madge.

"They've called in a neurosurgeon to evaluate Rob," Mr. Horlacher said, "and there was mention of transferring him to KU Med."

"You bought the sports policy offered through the school?" Coach Meadow said.

"Yes. That'll help some." Mr. Horlacher hugged Madge. "Joan, could Bruce and Madge spend the night with you? Thelma and I want to stay here."

"Of course. We'll help in any way we can."

Almost no one spoke on the ride home. Madge sat between Luke and Mom, her head on Mom's arm. In the back seat between Dan and Bruce, I felt drained of energy as though I had run a long distance. A weight pressed on my chest making it hard to breathe. I wondered if Rob would be able to play again this season and why Rev. Norris didn't finish his sentence.

"Who won the game?" I asked Dan.

"We did, by one point."

At home, Duke seemed to know something was wrong. He greeted us with wagging tail but didn't bark and jump around like he usually did. Mom ordered us to brush our teeth and wash up and assigned beds. Madge would sleep with her, Luke got my bed, Bruce took the couch, and I slept on the living room floor using cushions from the deck chairs as a makeshift mattress.

A steady, cold rain fell Saturday morning. Mom jumped at every outdoor sound and glanced at the phone every few minutes, but it didn't ring. Bruce and I played checkers at the kitchen table while Madge helped Mom make a cake.

After lunch, Mom drove Dan to the high school open house. Bruce and I entertained Madge with Old Maid, Slap Jack and Go Fish. Mom and Dan returned and still no phone call. The dark afternoon deepened before I heard a car door slam, and Mr. Horlacher appeared at the door.

Madge ran to her father. "Poppa. Poppa. You're here."

Mr. Horlacher tossed her in the air. "I sure am, sweetheart."

"How is he, Poppa?" Bruce said.

Mr. Horlacher sat heavily in a living room chair with Madge on his lap. "They've taken him to Kansas City for surgery. Thelma went with them."

"Oh, Ed. It's quite serious then," Mom said.

"I'm afraid so."

"You look beat," Mom said. "The kids can stay here and let you get a good night's rest."

"I appreciate the offer, but I thought I'd take them home," Mr. Horlacher said. "They need to clean up, change clothes. I want to drive to Kansas City in the morning."

"You could drop Bruce and Madge at church. We could keep them tomorrow and tomorrow night. They have school Monday."

"Andy Brackett's been doing my milking. I want Bruce to help him with that. I'll talk to Andy. Maybe the Bracketts can keep the kids. I'll call and let you know."

I sat at the kitchen table playing solitaire while Mom fixed dinner. I could hear Dan upstairs playing a record.

"Quiet on the square today," Luke said as he hung up his hat. "Have you heard from Ed?"

"He picked up the kids." Mom stirred the chili on the stove. "They've taken Rob to Kansas City for surgery."

Luke rubbed his chin. "It's bad, huh."

"I don't want Dan playing football," Mom said.

Luke sat down at the table across from me. "I've been thinking about that myself. I had a chat with Hader. He says a serious brain trauma can do most anything. Affect your ability to speak or to learn."

"You mean Rob could be disabled like Malcolm?" I said.

"Hader says it's possible, but that kind of injury is hard to predict. It depends on what part of the brain is injured."

"I don't want it happening to Dan," Mom said.

Luke sighed. "He's not going to like this."

"Let's get it over with and have dinner."

Luke looked at me. "When Dan comes down, you go upstairs."

"He can't hear you with the music so loud," I said. "I'll go up and get him."

I picked up my cards and trotted up the stairs. Dan lay on his bed, hands behind his head.

"Luke's home," I said. "He wants to talk to you."

"What about?"

I shrugged. "He said to come get you."

Dan sat up. "Don't touch my record player while I'm gone."

I heard him thunder down the stairs and tiptoed after him to sit on a step and listen.

"Have a seat," Luke said. "I'm sure you know how seriously Rob's been injured."

"Mr. Horlacher said he'd have surgery," Dan said.

"Yes. They'll remove part of the skull to allow for swelling," Luke said. "But he may never be the same."

Dan said, "What do you mean?"

"Some of his senses may be affected. Speech, for instance. The ability to walk. They just don't know until the swelling goes down."

"He may never play football again?"

"He shouldn't," Luke said. "Another hard hit to the head could kill him."

"That's awful," Dan said. "He was the best player on the team."

"Your mother and I have decided we can't let you play football," Luke said.

"What?" Dan's voice rose. "Not play? Just because of a freak accident?"

"Football's a tough game," Luke said. "We don't want anything happening to you."

I heard a chair scrape back. "This is ridiculous. I can't go to Smithton's Garage. I can't play football. What do you want me to do? Hibernate in my room?"

"You can play basketball and baseball," Mom said. "Run track."

"This is all your fault," Dan yelled. "Football's a man's game, and you just don't understand it."

"It's a risky game," Mom said, "but it is only a game and not worth the risk."

"You don't care about what I want," Dan said. "You only care about yourself."

"You won't talk to your mother that way," Luke said.

"And you. You don't have the backbone to stand up to her."

"I happen to agree with her," Luke said. "I've thought about it all day."

"You can't make me quit."

"I'll call Coach Meadow tomorrow and tell him your permission to play has been revoked," Luke said.

"I'm leaving."

I heard the back door slam.

"It's raining," Mom said. "He doesn't even have a jacket."

"He needs to cool off. Smithton's Garage is closed. He'll probably go to the Norris house to let off steam with Dean."

"Maybe Rev. Norris can reason with him."

"I'll give him a call."

I tiptoed back to my room.

TWENTY-SEVEN

After the emotional turmoil surrounding Rob's injury, the following week seemed calm and peaceful, but it didn't last. Rev. Norris brought Dan home and he apologized. Luke called Coach Meadow who said three others had dropped from the team. Luke put up forms for a concrete pad in front of the basketball goal, and Dan helped him pour the cement. The church took up a special collection and merchants set out donation jars and cans to help offset Rob's medical expenses. Mr. Horlacher returned home Thursday evening bringing good news. Rob's swelling subsided and he was fully conscious and talking. Soon, they'd transfer him to the Glendale hospital.

High school classes began. The school board cancelled homecoming originally scheduled for the Friday night home game against Franklin, but the carnival set up on the square for the weekend as planned. Pete and I enjoyed the carnival Friday night when the rides and booths lit up in bright colors, and I went back Saturday afternoon with Bruce when farm families crowded the square. Crispness in the air required a jacket and a bright sun threw shadows onto the pavement. The octopus rose, fell and spun eliciting screams. The merry-go-round's calliope accompanied the squeals of its riders. A ride on the Ferris wheel gave us a view of the entire carnival. We watched Dan throw a baseball, knock over a triangle of stacked bottles and win a small teddy bear for the Johnson girl. After the summer's series of disasters, Glendale's residents felt they deserved a weekend of fun, and all went home tired and satisfied.

About midnight, the town whistle blew, the phone shrilled and disaster came again. Fire struck Write Publishing, Mr. Hrabosky's printing enterprise. By the time we reached the scene, flames shot from windows on all three floors, and the firemen arched water onto the roof.

"Guess George Buckner wasn't the firebug," Mrs. Parkinson said.

"Look. Leroy Beach and the volunteers have brought the pumper truck," Mr. Parkinson said.

"The other crew's fighting it from the back," a man said.

"It has to be arson," Mr. Gladding said. "That's the only way the building would be fully engulfed like this."

Pete stood beside me. "Hope nobody's in there."

"If they are, they're a goner," I said.

"Malcolm works here," Pete said.

"It's after midnight," I said. "He wouldn't be here now."

"Will Pattonburg and Harrington show up for this one?" Mrs. Parkinson said.

Her husband shook his head. "Don't think so. We've got three crews on it."

"Wouldn't make a difference anyway," Mr. Gladding said. "It's a total loss."

"Lot of paper to burn," Mom said.

The inferno roared and popped. The building moaned as part of the roof gave way and new flames shot into the sky. I remembered hearing the presses run on the third floor the day Pete and I followed Mr. Hrabosky at the beginning of the summer. I glanced behind me. We stood in front of Kelvin Rogers's house just as Pete and I had that day. Mr. Rogers, his wife and Junior stood on the stoop watching the conflagration.

The Norrises joined us.

"Sure glad there's no wind," Mr. Gladding said.

"This is just awful," Rev. Norris said. "I pray no one gets hurt."

"I'm sure you're thinking of Vinny Valetti," Mom said, "but this hurts us all."

"Emile Hrabosky, mostly," Mrs. Parkinson said.

Mom nodded her head. "Yes, but now his employees don't have a job which means no money to spend. That hurts the businesses in town."

"I never thought of it before," Mr. Parkinson said," but all this loss of property hurts the city and the school district."

"How's that?" Mrs. Parkinson said.

"They get less from the property tax," Mr. Parkinson said. "Say the newspaper reports a loss of fifty-thousand dollars. That's fifty-thousand less on the tax rolls."

"I never thought of it either," Rev. Norris said.

"I'm glad we have these firefighters," Mr. Gladding said.

A side wall next to the parking lot bulged out and the firemen moved back. It gave way. Bricks from the lower floor crashed onto the parking lot while those above them plunged straight down.

"Wow!" Pete said. "That was great."

We could now see into the building, and the firemen aimed directly at the flames.

"It has a steel frame," Mr. Parkinson said.

"I guess the bricks weren't loadbearing," Mr. Gladding said.

"Whoever's doing this is ruining our town," Mrs. Norris said.

"At least he's not burning homes," Mrs. Parkinson said.

"I've seen enough," Mrs. Gladding said. "Gene. Joy. Let's go home."

"She's right, George," Mrs. Parkinson said. "If there's another fire, I'm not coming. Not even if the entire square burns. I've seen too many fires as it is."

Mr. Parkinson frowned at his wife. "You want to go home?"

"I have to open the café. I need a few hours' sleep."

"I'll come by after lunch," Pete said.

"We'd better get home, too," Mom said. "We have church in a few hours."

Rev. Norris chuckled. "Seems I do, too."

"Where's Dad?" Dan picked up the Cheerios box and poured a bowlful.

I cut a banana over my cereal. "He hasn't come home."

"And I don't understand it," Mom said. "He ought to at least call."

The phone rang.

"That'll be him now." Mom grabbed the phone. "Hello . . . Why . . . Who . . . Oh, no . . . She might not know. With her Parkinsons, they don't sleep together . . . They have live-in help. Maria. She usually answers the phone . . . Okay. The boys and I will go on to church . . . Have you eaten . . . Good . . . Okay . . . I wish you didn't have to." She hung up the phone.

"What happened?" Dan said.

Mom stood staring at the phone. "They found a body."

"Who?" Dan said.

"They aren't sure. It's too badly burned to identify." Mom turned to us. "Your dad thinks it may be Emile."

"Malcolm works there," I said. "He cleans the presses after they close."

"They're waiting for the coroner," Mom said. "He said he may be all day, so finish your breakfast and get ready for church."

By noon, the news spread through the congregation and probably across Glendale and beyond. After church, Mom drove down Hamilton to where a barricade blocked the street. Two cars marked Kansas Bureau of Investigation sat beside the barricade along with a coroner's van.

The afternoon passed slowly. Pete and I played Horse with Dan and Dean, losing every game as we weren't very good at basketball. We switched to Dan and me against Dean and Pete then Dean and me versus Dan and Pete which made the scoring a tossup and more fun. We walked up to the square and watched the carnival pack up, ready to move on to their next engagement.

Luke showed up for dinner with the news that the KBI out of Pattonburg would lead the investigation, supervise the autopsy, establish the identification of the victim and determine the cause of death. No one had seen Emile Hrabosky since Saturday evening when he told Maria and his wife he had to return to the office.

I'd almost drifted off to sleep when someone knocked on the front door. I sat up in bed. Duke raised his head and looked at me. Dan continued to snore. Ever curious, I quietly opened the bedroom door and tiptoed down the stairs to hear voices in the living room.

"Would you like some iced tea or coffee?" Mom said.

"No, thank you, Mrs. Martin. It's late. We won't stay long."

"Well, sit down, Ralph. Malcolm," Luke said. "How can I help you?"

Malcolm Carroll and his dad. I knew his dad was the butcher at Roman's Market, and that made me remember Blackie, Bruce's steer.

"My boy has something to tell you," Mr. Carroll said.

I heard Luke say softly, "What is it, Malcolm?"

"Mr. H." Malcolm sounded scared.

"That's what he calls Emile," Mr. Carroll said. "He has trouble saying Hrabosky."

I heard the rocking chair creak, so I knew someone was sitting in it. It was Mom's favorite chair.

"What about Mr. H, Malcolm?" Luke used his most reassuring voice.

"I hurt him." Malcolm spoke so softly I wasn't sure I heard him correctly.

"Let's start at the beginning," Luke said. "Were you at the printing shop Saturday night? That's last night."

Malcolm cleared his throat. "Yes."

"Why?"

"My job. Clean the presses."

"I thought you did that Friday night," Luke said.

"Yes." Malcolm paused. "This was special, Mr. H said."

"Special? How?"

"Something to print. In a hurry, see? Didn't finish Friday."

"So the presses ran Saturday," Luke said, "and Mr. H asked you to clean Saturday night rather than Friday night."

"Yes." Malcolm's voice lightened. "I went to the carnival."

I remembered seeing him there riding the merry-go-round with Alex Buckner and his buddies.

"Did you clean the presses Saturday night?" Luke said.

"Yes."

The rocking chair creaked again and someone coughed.

"And then what did you do?"

"Go to the office. Get paid."

"Did you get paid?" Luke said.

The furnace came on making it hard to hear, so I moved down closer to the bottom of the stairs.

"Yes. Mr. H paid me."

"Then what happened?"

"Mr. H said to sit down."

"Why?"

"He would read something." Malcolm's voice rose. "No, I said. So I didn't sit."

"Why did you say no?"

"Lies," Malcolm said. "About Merica."

"You think Mr. H prints lies about America?" Luke said. "Why do you think that?"

"They tell me,"

"Who tells you?"

"My friends. Alex and Ev and Junior."

"I've tried to keep him away from those three," Mr. Carroll said. "Seems they always find him."

"What did Mr. H do when you said he prints lies?" Luke said.

I heard someone shift around on the sofa. "He said no. Not lies. Truth."

"Did you argue with Mr. H?"

"Some. Not good."

"What do you mean when you say not good?"

"He's not good at arguing," Mr. Carroll said.

"Malcolm." Luke paused. "What caused you to hurt Mr. H?"

"He put his arms around me."

"He hugged you?"

I didn't hear an answer.

"What was wrong with that?" Luke said.

"Sex. He wants it."

I heard Mom gasp and the rocking chair creaked several times.

"Mr. H said he wanted sex with you?"

"No. They told me about him."

"They told you that Mr. H wanted sex with men? With you?"

"Yes. They tell me many times. He's a very bad man."

"What did you do when he hugged you?" Luke said.

"Shove him away."

"Okay. What happened then?"

"He tripped. Fell. Hit his head on the desk. Lay on the floor."

"Oh, dear," Mom said.

"Was he unconscious?"

"Don't know." Malcolm sounded panicky. "Went to sleep, maybe."

"His eyes were closed?"

"Yes. Asleep."

"Was he breathing?"

"Don't know. Wouldn't wake up. Moaned."

"What did you do?"

"Went for help. Mr. Rogers across the street."

"What did Mr. Rogers do?"

"Said to go home. Mr. H would be okay. He would help him."

"You went home?"

"Yes."

A long pause followed.

"Malcolm," Luke said. "Show me how Mr. H lay on the floor. Can you do that? Lay on the floor in the same position as Mr. H."

I heard shuffling as though Duke turned around several times before lying down.

"Is that it?" Luke said.

"Yes," Malcolm said.

"Mr. H lay on his right side, his cheek on the floor?"

"Yes."

"Okay. You can get up, Malcolm."

"What do you think, Luke?" Mr. Carroll said.

"I can't discuss an ongoing investigation," Luke said. "I'm not even in charge. The KBI has yet to identify the victim or establish a cause of death. When they do, Malcolm may need to speak to them, that is, if the victim is Emile Hrabosky and foul play is involved."

"So we wait?" Mr. Carroll said.

"Yes. I'll keep in touch with you, Ralph."

"I'm not sure I can stand the tension," Mr. Carroll said.

"I'm sorry," Luke said. "That's all I can advise."

"Let's go home, son," Mr. Carroll said.

"Malcolm's an honest man, Ralph. I believe everything will be okay."

"Thanks, Luke."

I heard the front door shut.

"Will everything be okay?" Mom said.

"The body did not lie in that position," Luke said, "and it wasn't near the desk."

I tiptoed back to my bed. *I knew they'd get Malcolm into trouble. They lied to him. Got him believing Mr. Hrabosky was bad. Got him thinking he was a communist. Got him afraid. Luke's got to stand up for Malcolm. He didn't know Mr. Rogers hated Mr. Hrabosky. He went to the wrong person for help. I bet Rogers killed him and he'll let Malcolm take the blame.* I lay awake for a long time.

TWENTY-EIGHT

At breakfast, I glanced through the article about the fire in the Pattonburg newspaper. I hung around the house so long that Mom questioned me. I didn't want to go to school. I might miss some action. I lunched with Grandma Jenkins who knew none of the town gossip about the fire and dashed home after school to find Mom just as uninformed. Pete and I circled the square visiting the music shop, the hardware store and Rexall Drug hoping to overhear news of the investigation. Nothing. Luke said he'd heard no word from the KBI. Mom visited Rob in the Glendale hospital. She said bandages covered his head and balance caused him problems.

Luke knew more Tuesday. "The autopsy results are back," he said at dinner.

"It's Emile?" Mom said.

"Yes." Luke took another piece of chicken fried steak. "They used dental records for identification."

"How did he die?" Mom said.

His mouth full, Luke waved his fork for time. I feared asking questions would reveal my unauthorized eavesdropping and hoped Mom's curiosity paralleled mine.

"They don't know," Luke said. "No smoke in the lungs, so he was dead when the fire started."

"Maybe he was shot," I said.

"No sign of that," Luke said. "No stab wounds. Some debris had fallen on him, so some bones were broken. All seemed to be post mortem."

"What's that mean?" I said.

"After death," Mom said. "I'm surprised they couldn't find out what killed him."

"Forensic science is still imprecise," Luke said. "Maybe someday."

"Surely they didn't call it accidental," Mom said.

"It's officially suspicious," Luke said, "but they didn't have enough evidence to label it homicide."

Mom hesitated. "Will he need to talk to the KBI?"

"I believe so. It's arson, after all," Luke said. "He'll need a lawyer. I've recommended Crosby Kennedy. He's the best we have in town."

"When will he do that?" Mom said.

"Tomorrow. I'll go with them."

I wanted to scream out that Rogers killed Mr. Hrabosky, but I wasn't supposed to know what Malcolm told Luke.

Mom turned her attention on me. "How was your piano lesson?"

"Fine. Mrs. Murran gave me a new piece called 'The Maple Leaf Rag.' She said it'll help me when we get to jazz."

The conversation veered away from the fire and Mr. Hrabosky's death.

After school the next day, I stayed close to home waiting for Luke. He arrived in time for dinner but never mentioned Malcolm. Instead, the conversation centered on Rob and on Dan's performing with the band during halftime at Friday's game with Pawnee. I lingered at the dining room table working on my Egyptian project and listening to any exchange between Mom and Luke in the living room. Mom crocheted a baby afghan for Mrs. Beach, and Luke read a book on crime scene investigation. I heard no mention of Malcolm. Having reached a level of extreme frustration, I folded up my project, screwed up my courage and marched into the living room.

"What happened with Malcolm?"

Luke's eyes widened as he looked up at me.

"Yes," Mom said. "I've been dying to know."

"How do you know about Malcolm?" Luke said.

I expected this question. "I listened on the stairs the other night. I haven't told anyone."

Luke closed his book. "Your curiosity will get you into real trouble someday, young man."

"I know how to keep my mouth shut," I said, "and I haven't let you down."

Luke rubbed his chin. "That's true. I suppose tomorrow's newspaper will print something about Malcolm's volunteering information."

"Were you in on the questioning?" Mom said.

"No, but I listened with Jim Nance, the county attorney."

"Why was he there?" I said.

"He's the one who decides whether to bring charges or not," Luke said.

"Did Malcolm tell the same story?" Mom said.

"Mostly." Luke sighed. "They didn't handle it well. Crosby and I warned them that Malcolm was easily confused and needed to be handled carefully, but they shouted at him, threatened him and got him upset and mixed up. Crosby kept interrupting to get the questioning back on track. He threatened to leave if they didn't quit yelling at Malcolm."

"Why did they bully him like that?" Mom said.

"It was obvious they wanted a confession," Luke said. "After he finally told about going for help, they went back and asked why Malcolm's friends told him to kill Emile. That totally stumped Malcolm as he hadn't said anything like that."

"I hope Crosby stepped in," Mom said.

"He did." Luke reached for his nightly cigar. "Then they asked what he used to hit Mr. Hrabosky. Malcolm seemed stunned. Crosby told the interrogators to check the tape as Malcolm had said he pushed Emile not hit him."

Mom put her crochet away. "How did it end?"

"Crosby said to have the statement typed and he'd read it through before Malcolm signed," Luke said. "I talked to Jim Nance afterward who said they have no evidence against Malcolm, and he won't file any charges."

"What about Rogers?" I said. "I bet he killed Mr. Hrabosky."

"They'll question him tomorrow. Probably have him in for a statement." Luke rose to his feet. "Now I'll have my cigar and off to bed with you."

"Jim Nance called," Luke said at dinner the following evening. "They questioned Rogers who said he went into the plant to help Emile and found him a bit groggy but otherwise fine, so he left."

"Well, that verifies Malcolm's story," Mom said, "but what did happen to Emile?"

"Let me finish," Luke said. "They knew gasoline was used as an accelerant, so they questioned employees of service stations in town. Arnold Wells at the Conoco station said Rogers was in late Saturday night. Had him gas up the truck and fill a five-gallon can in the truck's bed."

"They've got him for arson?" I said.

"Yeah. They got a warrant and searched Rogers's property. Found an empty five-gallon gas can in his shed. They've arrested Rogers for arson."

"What about Emile's death?" Mom said.

"They'll question Rogers tomorrow to see if his story holds up," Luke said. "Nance asked me to sit in."

"I heard him say the plant should burn down with Mr. Hrabosky in it," I said. "He said Mr. Hrabosky was a communist."

"That doesn't prove he killed Emile," Luke said. "It might show premeditation for setting fire to the plant."

"Speaking of communists," Mom said. "I heard Senator McCarthy on the radio today."

"What's he up to now?" Luke said.

"He says communists have infiltrated the Army Signal Corps, and there's a dangerous spy ring among Army researchers. He'll begin another investigation. He also claims to have a list of one-hundred-thirty subversives in defense plants."

"That Senator killed Mr. Hrabosky," I said.

"You're a dope, Squirt," Dan said.

"If it wasn't for him, Rogers wouldn't have gone around claiming Mr. Hrabosky was a communist."

"McCarthy may have contributed to that," Luke said, "but if either Malcolm or Rogers killed Emile, it wasn't only because of McCarthy. Mike, you know it's more complicated than that."

Dan frowned. "How would Mike know anything?"

Luke chucked. "Well, son, while you were helping Glen Smithton with his hotrod, Mike had what I'd call an unusually enlightening summer."

Luke came home early Friday afternoon so we could go to the football game and see the band perform at halftime in Pawnee, a forty-five minute drive away. Dan left with the band on the school bus, but Mom and I anxiously awaited information about Rogers's interrogation.

"He had his lawyer with him," Luke said. "The same one he used for the lawsuit against Emile."

"What did Rogers say?" Mom said.

"At first he stuck to his story," Luke said. "He went to the plant, Emile was okay so he left. Then they presented the evidence about the gas can and said they knew he set the fire, and they had evidence to prove it."

"Did they?" I said.

"Not really. The gas can evidence was circumstantial, and the fire destroyed whatever evidence might have been in the building."

"They lied?" Mom said.

"Law enforcement is allowed to do that."

Mom frowned. "Seems unethical to me."

"Rogers changed his story," Luke said. "He said he went into the office and found Emile's body. He knew Malcolm was in trouble, so he went back home, got the gas can and filled up at Conoco."

Mom sighed. "So Malcolm accidently killed Emile."

"Rogers set the fire to protect Malcolm?" I said. "I don't believe it. Malcolm didn't kill Mr. Hrabosky. Rogers did."

"Rogers claims he found Emile dead," Luke said. "But the stories don't add up."

"Why not?" Mom said.

"You remember Malcolm said he shoved Emile who fell hitting his head on the desk."

"And Emile lay on his side with his cheek on the floor," Mom said.

"Rogers claims Emile was on his back next to the bookcase on the right hand side of the room, and that's exactly where we found his body."

"I tell you Malcolm didn't kill him," I said. "Rogers did."

"I think he did," Luke said, "but there's no evidence to prove it. Rogers stuck to that story through very intense questioning."

"Nance won't file charges?" Mom said.

Luke shook his head. "Not for murder unless further evidence shows up. Rogers is charged with arson and unlawful disposal of a body."

"It's not right," I said. "Mr. Hrabosky's dead. Rogers should be charged with murder."

"Our justice system depends upon evidence," Luke said. "Suspicion isn't evidence. Even the autopsy was inconclusive."

"What about the last note Mr. Hrabosky got?" I said. "He didn't open it. He said the only fingerprints on it would be whoever wrote it."

Luke rubbed his chin. "I forgot about that. I'll talk to Nance about it. Be interesting to learn what's in it. Now that a crime's been committed, I think we should find out if Rogers wrote it. It still wouldn't prove he killed Emile."

"Rogers admits to arson," Mom said. "He'll go to prison?"

"Yes. I think he'll try to make a deal with Nance to avoid a trial," Luke said. "We discussed it and I told him what I think happened. I also told him what you overheard at Tony's Market and about Rogers harassing Emile and trying to form a group against him. I explained about the lawsuit, too. Nance won't let Rogers get off easily. He even said he might charge him with manslaughter where the burden of proof is lower."

"Did Rogers set the other fires?" Mom said.

"He was questioned about that," Luke said, "and he maintains he had nothing to do with them."

"I still say it's not right. He went around calling Mr. Hrabosky names," I said. "He's as bad as that loudmouth senator who's always talking about communists."

"Guys like McCarthy and Rogers inflame people's fears and prejudices," Luke said. "They teach others to hate."

"Just like Alex Buckner and his gang taught Malcolm to fear and hate," Mom said.

"So that's what killed Mr. Hrabosky?" I said.

"It's a complicated issue," Luke said. "Kelvin Rogers is a bigot, probably close to a white supremacist. He'd probably belong to the Klu Klux Klan if there was a chapter around here. He just used the label communist to justify his hatred of Emile. I'm afraid I'll never understand guys like that."

I was just a kid when the summer of fires ended—a kid who thought the world should be a perfect place. Looking back, what happened seems almost inevitable as though the events were swept forward on an unrelenting tide. Glendale's residents moved on but the town was never the same. Or maybe I wasn't the same.

The school district consolidated with two smaller ones and built a new modern high school.

Turnbow's car dealership survived and rebuilt as did Valetti's Mill. Windy Markmann and Leroy Beach moved to Pattonburg, so Glendale lost the movie theater and the farm implement dealership. Mrs. Hrabosky relocated to Chicago to be near her son, and the Hrabosky house fell into disrepair.

Kelvin Rogers was convicted of first degree arson and sentenced to twenty-fire years to life. He went to prison and never returned to Glendale. The New York Yankees won the World Series besting the Brooklyn Dodgers in six games.

The following year, Senator Joseph McCarthy was discredited and censured by the Senate, but his years of investigating America's institutions left a swath of ruined lives and reputations.

Made in the USA
Lexington, KY
23 October 2016